PRAISE FOR
THE SUBMISSIVE SERIES

The Training

"Very passionate. . . . The characters are very easy to relate to and there is a depth to their feelings that is intriguing and engaging . . . intense and very, VERY H-O-T. Definitely worth reading!"   —Harlequin Junkie

"Written with a good sense of literary flow, keeping the story moving forward, keeping the characters balanced. . . . There is great emotion here . . . quite compelling."   —Book Binge

"Hot and intense. . . . [I] look forward to Tara Sue Me's future endeavors."   —The Good, the Bad, and the Unread

"The story of Nathaniel and Abby continues, but with an interesting twist . . . fascinating."   —Bookish Temptations

The Dominant

"I was blown away."   —The Good, the Bad, and the Unread

"This was truly an amazing read, and I found myself staying up until three a.m. just to finish it."   —Louisa's Reviews

"Steamy . . . I was shocked at the depth of it!"
                         —Under the Covers

"I love it when an author writes from the male POV . . . completely worth it."   —Bookish Temptations

continued . . .

The Submissive

"For those *Fifty Shades* fans pining for a little more spice on their e-reader . . . the *Guardian* recommends Tara Sue Me's Submissive Trilogy, starring handsome CEO Nathaniel West, a man on the prowl for a new Submissive, and the librarian Abby, who is yearning for something more." —*Los Angeles Times*

"This book is going to make you say 'Fifty What of What?' . . . [Me] is so talented and captivating."—Southern Fiction Review

"Very spicy . . . quite well written, and certainly entertaining." —Dear Author

"An interesting read." —The Book Cellar

"Wonderfully done, full of emotion and intensity . . . different from so many others out there." —The Good, the Bad, and the Unread

"I really enjoyed the *heck* out of it." —Under the Covers

PRAISE FOR
THE PARTNERS IN PLAY NOVELS

Seduced by Fire

"Titillates and captivates from the very beginning." —*Romantic Times* (top pick)

The
Enticement

The Submissive Series

TARA SUE ME

 NEW AMERICAN LIBRARY

New American Library
Published by the Penguin Group
Penguin Group (USA) LLC, 375 Hudson Street,
New York, New York 10014

USA | Canada | UK | Ireland |Australia | New Zealand |India | South Africa | China
penguin.com
A Penguin Random House Company

First published by New American Library,
a division of Penguin Group (USA) LLC

First Printing, April 2015

LIBRARY OF CONGRESS CATALOGING-IN-PUBLICATION DATA:

Me, Tara Sue.
The enticement / Tara Sue Me.
p. cm.—(The submissive series; [4])
ISBN 978-0-451-47451-3 (softcover)
1. Sexual dominance and submission—Fiction. 2. Man-woman relationships—Fiction. I. Title.
PS3613.E123E58 2015
813'.6—dc23   2014039100

Printed in the United States of America
1   3   5   7   9   10   8   6   4   2

Set in Perpetua
Designed by Sabrina Bowers

To my children:
I joke that by growing up, you make me feel old,
but the truth is, you keep me young.

Acknowledgments

They say writing a book is like giving birth. They lie. I've had two children via C-section, and all I did was lie on a table. Writing a book is much harder. And they don't give you drugs.

With that said, there are several awesome people without whom you either wouldn't be holding this, or else what follows would be so horrific, you'd wish you weren't.

Adam Simpson and the entire team at Simpsons Solicitors, I don't care what anyone says about lawyers. Your calm professionalism is a balm in this crazy world. I'd say, "Let's do it again," but I never lie to anyone in the legal field.

Steve Axelrod, my agent and guide in this crazy, wonderful, terrible, frustrating, magnificent industry. I've heard it said writing is an art and publication is a business. Thank you for helping me balance both. I promise to never again bring up dino porn at lunch.

Rebecca Grace Allen, girl, I love you like no one's business. Thank you for telling me you hated Nathaniel and DNF'd draft #3 so that by draft #5287, I could finally say, "Yes, this is it." I'll always save a seat for you at table #69.

Cyndy Aleo, without you, this book would have no plot, and I would have no hair. Thank you for always shooting straight, telling it like it is, and saving room for me on your lap. I hope to one day have *just a touch* of your attitude, spunk, determination, and zero fucks to give.

Elle Mason, you make me smile. Your enthusiasm keeps me going, and though I hope no one ever reads our chats, I'd be hard-pressed to make it through the day without them. You're my pixie-dust-covered twin pervert, and I wouldn't have it any other way. P.S. DG called. He said he loved me more.

Fiona, you are a dear, sweet, beautiful soul. I truly hope our paths cross one day so we can meet.

Claire Zion, my editor beyond compare, you treat my words with kindness when needed and viciously cut them when they're not. In short, you make my story beautiful and let it sing.

Eden Barber, your last-minute thoughts were just what I needed. I'll forever be grateful you didn't NANO.

Mr. Sue Me, only you have seen me at my most worst, but likewise, only you have seen me at my very best. I hope when it's all said and done, there have been more of the latter. Thank you for saying, "You know, if you wanted to . . ."

And, you, if you've ever stood in line to see me or stopped by my table because no one else would, if you've ever sent me an e-mail telling me how much my story touched you or e-mailed me wanting your money back, if you've ever read my book, reviewed my book, hated my book, or loved my book, if you ever walked by my book and said, "Hello!" or saw it and whispered, "I can't believe. . . ." THANK YOU from the bottom of my heart.

The
Enticement

Chapter One

There were times I felt I came alive only at night. When the world was quiet around me and the kids were asleep and for a few precious hours there was nothing but me and Nathaniel. Those sacred nights had become more and more infrequent lately, as there always seemed to be something else to do, but I often thought I could survive on the anticipation alone.

I checked in the bathroom mirror to make sure my face didn't reflect the day's stress. Satisfied, I pulled my hair out of the ponytail it'd been in all day and brushed it until it fell soft and loose around my shoulders. I threw the yoga pants and T-shirt I'd been wearing into the hamper. Before heading into the bedroom, I took the body lotion Nathaniel once said smelled like sin wrapped in silk and ran it over my arms and legs. I rummaged through my lingerie drawer and finally settled on a long opaque satin nightgown. Silver, of course, since that was his favorite color on me.

Most nights I didn't take so long getting ready for bed, but tonight was different. When he'd gotten home, we'd chatted briefly before our two kids interrupted us. I'd swallowed a laugh as four-year-old Elizabeth expressed her grief at not finding the purple crayon she insisted she had to have for the castle she was coloring. Not to be outdone, our eighteen-month-old son, Henry, kept his arms uplifted and repeated, "Dada! Dada! Dada!" until Nathaniel swept him into the air.

After that, the room was filled with Henry's delighted shrieks. At least it was until Nathaniel caught a whiff of something.

"Again?" I asked. "I just changed him less than an hour ago."

"Has to be the antibiotics," Nathaniel said, which was proba-bly true. Henry was desperately trying to get rid of recurrent ear infections, but the medication upset his stomach. "Come on, big guy, let's get you changed." As they walked away, he looked over his shoulder. "We need to talk later, Abigail."

Abigail.

Hearing my name from him like that stopped me in my tracks, lit my body with desire, and echoed in my brain throughout din-ner, baths, and bedtime. As he, no doubt, knew it would. When he called me Abigail, it didn't matter that I wore his collar only once a month or that sex was otherwise often hurried and infre-quent. With just one word, my husband became my Master. And my body didn't only respond; it begged for his dominance. Just thinking about the way he said it, in a tone of voice that managed to sound so matter-of-fact and commanding at the same time, sent shivers up and down my spine.

I walked down the stairs and found Nathaniel in the living room, reading. He looked up as I entered, his green eyes travel-ing over every inch of me. I took a seat beside him and my heart rate increased as he slipped a hand into my hair and pulled me close for a kiss.

"You smell incredible and you look sexy as hell," he said against my lips.

"You're not bad yourself," I replied, running my fingers through his black hair. He'd changed out of his suit when he'd gotten home and throughout the evening had worn the old jeans that hugged his ass and a T-shirt that similarly hugged his abs—my favorite outfit for him.

He pulled away and settled his back against the couch. "I had a call today from Simon."

"Oh?" Simon had moved into the area years ago and was part of our BDSM group. He, like Nathaniel, was a Dominant.

"He's met someone online and she's relatively inexperienced. He was wondering if they could come over on Saturday."

Before getting pregnant with Henry, we'd started mentoring couples. Years ago, my weekend with Nathaniel's old mentor and his wife, Paul and Christine, had helped me so much. I wanted to do the same for new submissives. But after getting pregnant and, in particular, after giving birth, there hadn't been much mentoring going on.

Without thinking, I stroked my bare neck, missing the long, intense playroom sessions that lasted all weekend. These days they were just about as likely to happen as me getting forty-five uninterrupted minutes to make dinner.

"I'm probably the one in need of a mentor session," I joked. "It's so long between our scheduled dates."

Nathaniel didn't laugh. "I miss the way we used to be, Abby."

"I know . . . me, too."

He leaned forward and studied me silently for a few seconds. "Is everything all right?"

"Yes, everything's fine. Just life happening."

"I wonder when we decided 'fine' was an acceptable way to live?" He took my right hand and twisted the ring there. The one he'd given me on our wedding day that symbolized his dominance over me. "I wonder if once a month is enough? I miss seeing you kneel before me, wearing only my collar, waiting for me to decide how I'll use you."

"Oh, Nathaniel."

"Shhh." His finger traced my lips and brushed the hollow of my throat. "You miss it, too. You know you do. The way you yield your body to me, longing for the release you know I'll give."

I didn't even attempt to argue. I knew for a fact how many times I'd nearly begged him to take me over his knees and spank me during the week. The release I found with him was so soothing. Held tightly on my stomach across his lap. His free hand striking my ass over and over.

Other times I'd watch him move around the house and I'd remember how years ago, he'd be the one watching me. I recalled how his eyes would follow me until finally he'd get up and either force me to my knees or push me against a wall. His barely controlled lust kept me constantly ready for him.

"Show me I'm right. Show me how much you miss it." He slipped his thumb inside my mouth. "Suck it like a good girl."

My belly tightened as I drew his thumb into my mouth. I could deny him nothing when he touched me.

"That's it," he said. "Do it good enough and I'll let you taste my dick. Do it really good and I'll take you over my knees and bring out the strap."

I opened my mouth in shock.

"Suck it, Abigail. I didn't say to stop." When I continued, he started talking once again. "You think I don't know what you want? What you need? You're due for a sound thrashing and a long, hard fuck."

I moaned around his thumb and he slid his other hand to cup my breast, gently rubbing my nipple.

"That's it, my lovely. Suck it. Think about how turned on

you'll be when I drag you across my knee. Imagine me spanking your ass and fucking you with my fingers."

I bucked my hips up, trying to get some pressure on my clit, but he tightened the hand at my face. "Be still. You haven't earned my cock yet, much less an orgasm."

I kept up my work on his thumb, sucking and licking, just as I would have if his cock was in my mouth. All the while, his fingertips fondled my breasts. It drove me mad that he wasn't paying any attention to anything below my waist.

Finally, he slipped his thumb from my mouth. "I hope you don't have anything else planned for tonight because I'm going to *fucking wear you out*."

"Please," I moaned.

A wicked look came over his expression. "But not just yet. First, I'm going to fuck that mouth and throat of yours. Then maybe I'll take that sweet pussy. Or beat your ass. I haven't decided yet."

"Yes, Sir. Please. All of them."

"Greedy girl." He nodded to the floor.

I slowly rose to my feet and slipped the gown over my head.

"Very nice," he said as I lowered myself before him in the middle of the room. "Spread your legs. Let me see how wet that greedy pussy is."

It had been over three weeks since I'd knelt and I struggled a bit getting into position. The entire time he watched, sitting relaxed on the couch. The only sign he was affected was the growing bulge of his erection.

"Something to work on," he said. "Your knees are still out of habit. Though I do see you've waxed."

I held back a snort. Like I'd ever forget THAT again. "Yes, Sir."

"Come get my cock out."

I crawled over to him. Years ago I hated crawling. It still didn't rank very high on my list of things I loved to do, but I knew how much he enjoyed watching and that alone made me hot when I did it.

I made my way over to him and knelt up between his legs. He leaned back into the couch, giving me room to move. I palmed him several times through the material of his pants, enjoying the way he grew harder.

"Take it out," he said through clenched teeth. "Now."

I worked my hands up to the button of his pants and undid it, then slowly took his zipper down. He lifted his hips, allowing me to slide his pants and boxer briefs off. I sat back on my heels once I had him naked from the waist down.

"All this for me, Sir?"

He stroked himself. "Every fucking inch. Be a good girl and give it a kiss. Just lightly on the tip and then hold still."

I licked my lips. I loved taking him orally. Loved everything about it. The way he felt. The way he tasted. The way he would moan, deep in his throat. Needless to say, I wasn't thrilled about just giving him a little kiss.

With a sly smile I came up to my knees and bent my head, my dark hair falling around my face. Very slowly I lowered myself and kissed him the way he asked, remaining in place after.

"Now hold your hair back with both hands and keep your mouth open."

My heart pounded. It'd been months since we'd had any sort of power play during the week. This felt so good in every way I realized we had to schedule more time.

"Now, Abigail. I don't want your hair in the way of my view as I fuck that sassy mouth."

"Sorry, Sir."

I spread my knees wider for balance and, holding my hair behind my head, I opened my mouth, offering it for his use. I thought he'd thrust himself up and into my mouth, but he surprised me by grasping my hands and pushing my head down.

I had only enough time to relax my throat before he filled it with his cock.

"Fuck, yes." He pulled my head up and brought it back down. "Fuck."

He started a punishing rhythm, working my head and eventually his hips, powerfully, as he used my mouth for his pleasure. He wasn't soft and he wasn't gentle, somehow knowing, as he usually did, that I didn't need his tenderness. I needed my Master. And I needed him to take control away from me.

My eyes started to water as he hit the back of my throat. But even so, my own arousal grew and I shifted my hips trying to find a small measure of relief. Surely there was something. The edge of the couch. Part of his leg. Something.

"Fuck." He yanked out of my mouth. "Got to stop."

I halfheartedly got back into position on my knees. I really wanted to finish him off, to take him to the edge of his own control, and feel him lose himself in me. But, if he pulled back now, that could only mean he had more in store for us.

Which was why I didn't understand when he pulled his clothes back on and tucked his still erect cock inside.

"I've changed my mind," he said. "Neither one of us is coming tonight."

"What? What happened to your hoping I didn't have plans? To wearing me out? To—"

He stopped me by putting a finger to my lips. "Stop right there or I'll make good on my threat to beat your ass."

I almost decided to say something. The small touch of dominance he'd given me wasn't enough. Maybe goading him into a spanking would be worth it.

"You better wipe that thought out of your mind," he said, as if reading my thoughts. "There are better ways to get what you want."

I knelt patiently and waited for him to explain.

"I'm going to ask Linda to keep the kids overnight Friday and bring them back Saturday evening."

Linda was Nathaniel's aunt. She and her husband had raised him after his parents died in a car accident when he was ten. I'd never met his uncle, who had passed away several years before we met. He also had a cousin, Jackson, who was like a brother to him. Jackson had fallen in love with my best friend, Felicia, when I introduced them, and they had married too.

"And," he continued, "if you're okay with it, I'll call Simon and tell him we're on for Saturday?"

"I think I'd like that," I said. With the kids spending the night with Linda, Nathaniel and I could play a bit on Friday night, even before Simon came over with his girlfriend.

The smile on his face told me he knew how I'd answer. "I'll call her in the morning and let you know. If she agrees, once she picks the kids up on Friday, you are to prepare yourself and wait in the playroom for me to get home. Understood?"

"Yes, Sir."

"Then on Saturday, Simon and his submissive will come over." He pulled me to him and whispered coarsely in my ear. "After, I'll make good on my threat to wear you out. You won't be able to move for three days without remembering the wicked things I did to your body. You'll lose count of the number of times and ways I fucked you."

I whimpered and tried to rub my legs together, desperate to ease the longing that pulsed between them.

"Not going to happen, so you better stop. Or else Simon and his submissive will watch as you're punished." He put a hand on my knee and squeezed. "Now, since you brought me to the edge,

I think it's only fair that I reciprocate. Get on your hands and knees, presenting that needy pussy to me."

I knew better than to argue. If I complained about not coming tonight, he might not let me come during the weekend, just to prove a point. I crawled back to the middle of the room to better position myself.

"Don't look so put out," he said with a smile.

"You're evil. Did you know that?" I asked, while moving into position.

His laughter sent chills of anticipation down my spine. "Oh, Abby, you've yet to see just how truly evil I can be."

I shivered the next day, remembering that laugh and those words as I sat at my computer. Years ago, when I was a new submissive, Nathaniel had given me a journal to document my journey of sexual submission. I'd quickly filled that notebook with my thoughts and questions, and even my fantasies. When I filled a second, I'd suggested to Nathaniel that I keep the journal online as a blog.

I'd expected him to say no, but instead he agreed with me. His only request had been that I never wrote anything that could lead back to either one of us or our family. In the beginning he'd simply read my posts, but now it had grown to the point where he commented on them as well. My readers always liked it when he did.

I started out with Nathaniel as my only follower, but we were both amazed at how rapidly my readership grew. What began as a way for me to document my thoughts and experiences for myself and my Master had grown into a blog visited daily by thousands of people. The Secret Life of a Submissive Wife was growing into a real phenomenon.

Even so, I had never imagined getting an e-mail like the one currently sitting in my in-box. I read it again for the fifth time, just to be sure I wasn't making it up.

> Dear Submissive Wife,
>   I work at Women's News Now. As you may be aware, we are part of the National News Network, the second-largest media corporation in America. I have been an avid reader of your blog, almost from day one. I love the way you discuss BDSM. You make it real, approachable, and sexy.
>   We are planning to increase our coverage of intimate relationships. As part of that expansion, I'd like to know if you'd be interested in talking with me about potential opportunities for you at WNN.
>   My contact information is below. I look forward to hearing from you soon.
>
>   Meagan Bishop

My hands trembled and I sat dumbfounded. I had actually been contacted by someone who worked for National News Network. Not only that, they read my blog and wanted to talk to me about "opportunities." What kind of opportunities?

They owned several leading magazines as well as a handful of television networks. I didn't know enough about them to know what else they had their hands in. Either Meagan would tell me or I could do some Internet research.

I glanced at the clock. I couldn't call Meagan back immediately because it was time to pick Elizabeth up from preschool.

Probably for the best, anyway; I didn't want to appear overly eager. I would pick Elizabeth up, we'd have lunch, I'd cross my fingers that both she and Henry would take a nap at the same time, and then I'd call this Meagan Bishop back.

I found it difficult to think about anything other than the e-mail. I tried calling Nathaniel, but I got only his voice mail. I hung up with a sigh. I was busting to tell *someone* but it'd probably be more fun to tell him in person. And by the time he got home, I'd have spoken to Meagan, so I'd have more information.

Lunch took forever. While Elizabeth ate, I threw dinner together in the slow cooker. Henry refused to let anyone help him eat, so of course, when he finished, he had to be cleaned up. Fortunately, he went down for his nap quickly, but Elizabeth loved being read to and would try as hard as possible to stay awake so I could read multiple stories. She usually fell asleep halfway through the second and today was no different.

The house was blissfully quiet when I made it down the stairs to the library. I opened the e-mail again and, with my heart thumping so hard I could take my pulse by watching my shirt, I called the number Meagan listed in the e-mail.

"Meagan Bishop," she answered brisk and businesslike.

I was surprised she answered her phone herself but I realized it meant she must be a pretty direct person. I liked that. "Meagan, hello. My name's Abby. I run the Submissive Wife blog. I got your e-mail."

"Oh, hey. Did you say your name's Abby? I'm so glad you called. I've been dying to talk to you." Her tone changed. It became friendly and less brash. "I love your blog. The writing, the content, all of it."

"Thank you."

"I feel like I halfway know you already, just from reading you. Crazy, isn't it?"

"Not too much," I said. "I try to be realistic and everything I write about actually happened. I don't make anything up. What you read is the real me."

"I thought so but it's so good to have you confirm it."

"I'll be happy to answer any questions you have."

"There will be plenty of time for that. Right now, you're probably wanting to know more about our interest in you and your blog," she said.

"I'll admit I'm very curious about what opportunities you have in mind."

A hint of her businesswoman persona slipped back into her voice. "Ultimately, that will depend on you and what you feel comfortable with. And we're willing to break it up into baby steps. You can start out slow and if you want to do more and the need is there, we'll look into you doing more."

I smiled. "Baby steps. I like that."

Meagan laughed and then continued. "We're wanting to start a roundtable talk show about love and sex. As a tie-in, we need someone to write content for the Web site and we want that person to know what they're talking about. You could still keep and post to your personal blog."

My head spun. Me? Write? For a job?

"Meagan, I'll admit my first thought is that surely you can find someone with more experience to write for you," I managed to sputter out.

"Of course we could," she said. "But we don't want them. We've seen your work and we want you. Like I said before, your voice, your use of language is delicately sensual and that appeals to a lot of people."

"Thank you," I said, but my head was absolutely spinning. "Listen, I'll have to give it some thought and get back to you."

"Yes, please, take some time to think about it. For now, I'll forward you some information. Also, if you think you're interested, there's a meeting in April in New York City. We'd love to have you come talk with us."

I took the dates down and we said good-bye. I didn't realize how long we'd been chatting until we hung up and Elizabeth came down the stairs.

I held out my arms and she gave me a not-quite-awake-yet hug. "Sleep well, Princess?" I asked her.

She nodded. "Can I cook with you tonight?"

"I've already started dinner, but you can help me make biscuits."

That woke her up. Henry would probably sleep for another thirty minutes, so I gave Elizabeth another quick hug, said, "Come on," and we headed to the kitchen.

I waited until the kids were in bed for the night before bringing anything up with Nathaniel. I found him in the living room watching a college basketball game while on the phone with his cousin Jackson. Technically speaking, they weren't really talking; they were arguing about a call one of the referees just made. I sat down beside him and waited for them to finish. Nathaniel ended the call when the game went to commercial break.

He smiled. "Tell me."

I didn't even ask how he knew I had been waiting to give him some news. After so many years together, it had become second nature for him to read me so well.

"I got offered a job today," I said. "A writing job."

"You applied for a job?" There wasn't any judgment in his voice, just surprise.

"No, nothing like that. They found me through the blog." I summarized the call with Meagan while he listened intently.

"Wow," he said when I finished. "What an incredible opportunity for you. You are going to meet with them, right?"

"I really want to." I realized exactly how much when I said it out loud.

"Then do it. Chances like this don't often fall in our laps."

"To think something that started as a journal could possibly lead to writing for NNN's Women's channel."

"I expect all the credit," he teased. "Since I'm the one who made you start the journal in the first place."

I punched his arm. "Going online was all my idea."

"I know." His expression grew serious. "I always said you were a wonderful writer. It's about time someone else noticed. I'm proud of you, Abby."

"Thank you."

He brushed my cheek softly. "I had a phone call today, too. Though not nearly as exciting as yours."

"Simon?" I guessed.

"Yes. His girlfriend's name is Lynne. He said they'd be over at nine on Saturday."

"Tell me about her. I don't remember her from our last meeting with the group."

He shook his head. "She wasn't at it. Simon met her online a few months ago. They only met in person about three weeks ago. She's really new."

Without coming out and saying it in so many words, he was letting me know not to expect anything too intense in the playroom Saturday. Knowing Nathaniel the way I did, he wouldn't want to do anything that could potentially turn someone off to the lifestyle.

"Simon's really smitten, huh?" I asked. Though I didn't know him too well, he'd been in the group for a good number of years and played with a variety of women. I couldn't recall him being in a long-term relationship.

"Well, he wouldn't be the first Dom in history to become *smitten* with an inexperienced submissive." His hand moved to my knee and danced along my inner thigh. "I've never regretted collaring a certain untrained newcomer to the scene."

"That certain untrained newcomer is thankful you took a chance on her."

"The difference, I think, is that you were a natural, and apparently Lynne is very skittish." He frowned. "I wouldn't have had you over for the weekend if you were skittish."

"Are you worried about Lynne? Do you think she's jumping into this simply to be around Simon?"

"I thought about that, but Simon said it was just her personality. To be honest, I'm going to set aside some time for the two of you to talk. I'd like your view on her."

I raised an eyebrow at him.

He laughed. "Don't look at me like that. You're an excellent judge of character and you've been in the lifestyle long enough to have an honest opinion about things."

"I guess that makes sense." What would it have been like if a more experienced submissive had talked to me before Nathaniel collared me all those years ago? Would they have found it odd I wanted to submit only to him and not any other Doms?

I set my hand over his and entwined our fingers. "I'll talk with her, but keep in mind, the heart isn't the most rational organ."

His smile was soft and warm. "I know that all too well, Abby. All too well."

Chapter Two

Friday afternoon I waved good-bye to Elizabeth and Henry as they drove off with Linda. The silence of the house greeted me when I stepped back inside and I stood in the foyer to let the stillness wash over me. I took a few deep breaths as if I could inhale quiet and make it a part of my body. I'd enjoy the quiet while I could; it wouldn't be too long before I'd miss the messes and giggles.

As it had every other free moment I'd had this week, my mind immediately drifted to Meagan and her e-mail and phone call. I had answered her the night before and was waiting for her to confirm our meeting dates and times.

Thrilled to finally have some private time to be at the computer, I went into the library and checked to see if Meagan had replied. I tapped my foot as I waited for my e-mails to load and my heart jumped up to my throat when I saw she had. I read over the information she sent, marking on my calendar the meeting details. She'd also sent more information about the television show.

I finished reading everything and looked at the time. Four thirty. *Shit.* I shut the laptop down and hurried up to the bedroom. I'd have to rush if I was going to have time to prepare for Nathaniel. He worked in the city, so it'd take him a while to make it home to our Hampton estate.

He expected me to be in the playroom, waiting, by five o'clock. I barely made it.

Normally, a feeling of peace and contentment washed over me as soon as I knelt in place. But as I dropped to my knees the only thing on my mind was Meagan's e-mail and the upcoming meeting. I thought about who I'd have watch the kids and what I'd wear to the meeting. My brain spun around in multiple directions before I realized how much time had passed. I couldn't be entirely positive because he didn't have a clock in the playroom, but I was fairly certain it was about a quarter after five. *Where was he?*

My knees ached. He wouldn't mind if I stood up and stretched, would he? He'd never know and I'd hear him when he entered the house and could quickly get back into position. I wouldn't even have to do it that long, just a quick stretch and roll of my shoulders.

Should I or shouldn't I?

Another minute passed.

I should.

I lifted my head—and screamed.

Nathaniel was standing in front of me.

"Abigail."

"Fuck, you scared me," I said, my body shaking. How did he get into the house, much less the playroom, without me knowing?

"Obviously," he said.

I straightened my posture and took a deep breath.

He walked with careful steps over to me. He simply stood

quietly for several long seconds before saying, "Put your forehead
to the floor with your ass in the air and remain like that so I can
enjoy the sight of you."

I was comfortable for about zero seconds. The position was
humiliating; I knew how exposed I was. Behind me, he saw everything. I could hide nothing. To keep my mind off what he was
looking at, I thought once more about the blog and the upcoming
meeting.

Based on how the weekend went, I would have plenty of material to post. I wouldn't have to resort to our past like I'd been
known to do. The last three posts had been recycled from years
ago. The downside to recycling posts was that he didn't comment on them.

"You're not with me, Abigail," he said in warning.

He was right, so I cleared my mind of everything except him.
I focused on what he needed and how to give it to him. At the
moment, that was obedience. But thoughts of what he needed
made me think of topics I could write about and it hit me that
I'd have to find a way to fit blogging into my daily routine. It
could no longer be something I did haphazardly.

I'd been a bit scattered since first receiving the e-mail. What
I needed to do was create a schedule. Check e-mails only during
specific times. I should probably set a schedule for writing, too.
If the position proved to be what I hoped it might be, I needed to
make sure everything was organized and balanced.

Behind me, Nathaniel sighed. "Move to the table. On your back."

I stood up slowly, afraid if I moved too quickly I'd get dizzy
from having my head down for so long. I didn't look at Nathaniel
as I crossed the room to the padded table. I knew I'd probably
see disappointment in his eyes and I hated that more than anything.

I climbed onto the table, my body nearly sighing as it sank

slightly into the supple leather. I closed my eyes and gave a tiny gasp as he blindfolded me.

"To help you concentrate."

So it was that noticeable? I cringed inwardly that the weekend had gotten off to such a bad start and took a few deep breaths to clear my head. His hands swept over my shoulders and down my side. One of his fingers brushed a ticklish spot and I stifled a giggle. There were times he would tickle me during play, but I didn't think this was one of them.

He made a noise deep in his throat and I stiffened. Maybe he'd wanted me to laugh. I wasn't sure, and with the blindfold I couldn't read his expression. I focused on his touch. He stroked over my hips, but didn't go below my waist. He wasn't gentle, so I didn't think he was trying to be ticklish, but he wasn't as rough as he sometimes got.

I jerked when his lips pressed against my hip bone and again when he gave it a light nip. Usually, it would have turned me on, but at the moment, I was too concerned I was doing something wrong.

Which was stupid, I told myself. He wanted me on the table ready for his use and that was what I was doing. The only wrong thing was being so worried and scattered. I tried to force myself to relax into his touch.

There are times your mind can come up with crazy stuff. On the table, trying to feel nothing but his touch, my brain came up with the most ludicrous thoughts:

Maybe you're not submissive anymore.

You're doing everything wrong.

This probably means you shouldn't take the job.

I wasn't sure how long I stayed on the table, lost in my own mind, imagining nonexistent mess-ups. But I knew the minute something was horribly, horribly off.

His hands started at my ankles and moved up the inner portion of my leg. Moving slowly and intently, he circled my thighs
and then slid a finger into me. I couldn't hold back the yelp that
followed because it fucking hurt.

"You're not the slightest bit aroused," he said, sounding just
as surprised as I was.

"I'm sorry, Master," I choked out. "I don't know what my
problem is."

He slid the blindfold from my eyes and I blinked in the soft light,
finally focusing on his worried expression. "You think you should
apologize?" he asked. "Why is it your fault I'm not turning you on?"

"The way you say it makes it sound like you're doing something wrong."

"Sit up," he said, helping me get upright. "One of us doesn't
have to be doing something wrong. It could be any number of
things and is probably a combination of several."

"But—"

He placed a finger against my lips. "Stop. You shouldn't need
a reminder that it *is* wrong for you to argue with me in the playroom."

"Sorry, Master."

His lips brushed mine. "Let's go for a jog together, clear our
heads. Do you have something you can put together quickly for
dinner?"

I ran through what I had in the refrigerator. "I have some tuna
that won't take long to cook. I'll do that with a salad."

"That sounds delicious." His smile was easy now and my heart
lightened. While I knew not to look for something or someone
to place blame on for my lack of arousal, I couldn't help but think
that if I hadn't been so distracted, the evening might have been
different. But Nathaniel was aware I'd been distracted and he
wasn't placing blame.

Our jog together reminded me of how we used to be when I wore his collar every weekend. We knew each other so well now, our bodies automatically adjusted to the other's speed. Granted, he could run a lot faster and farther than I could, so in reality he was probably the one adjusting his speed. I felt touched by his love when I thought about how he was doing that. It was a beautiful evening and we headed out at an easy pace. Apollo whined when we didn't take him with us, but he was getting older and would hurt himself trying to keep up with us.

We jogged around the perimeter of our estate. I'd forgotten how much I enjoyed running with Nathaniel. Every so often, I'd peek out of the corner of my eyes to watch him. There was such grace in the way he moved. Such strength in his legs.

He caught me one time and smiled. "I think I'll have you jog naked next time." I almost tripped over my feet and he reached out to steady me. "Careful."

"What?"

"Have you jog naked. I've never had you do it. It might be fun."

I snorted. "For you."

"Exactly."

We turned slightly and headed toward the flower garden. It was spring and we'd recently had some landscaping done, so many of the plants were small and new.

"Like little babies," I said.

"The cleomes?"

"Yes, it's like we have a little plant nursery."

He didn't say anything for several strides and then he surprised me with, "Are you pregnant?"

"Because I mentioned babies?" Honestly? Where had that come from?

"It just seemed strange bringing up babies in the middle of the garden."

"It was just a metaphor." I still didn't make the connection. Unless he meant something more with his question. "Do you want a third child?"

We'd talked about it when I was pregnant with Henry and at the time, we'd decided to have only two. I really hadn't given much thought to another child. It hadn't even registered in my mind that it would be something that could happen.

He slowed to a brisk walk and I followed. Good. The slower pace would give me time to think.

"I hadn't thought about another child until right now," he said. "I'm content with two. A third? I don't know. That would give us odd numbers. We'd have to have four to even it all out."

I laughed. "That's seriously part of your thought process? Not which room we'll put them in or if we'd have time for everyone or even if we would need a bigger car to fit five or anything like that, just that the number is odd?"

"My mind likes even numbers." He spoke so matter-of-factly, I couldn't tell if he was being serious. Sometimes his dry sense of humor threw me. But then he gave a little grin to show he was joking. At least a little bit.

"Then I'm going to say *I don't think so* to child three, because I don't think I could do four." My mind still couldn't wrap itself around three. Four? There were plenty of women who could do it. I didn't think Felicia would have a problem, for instance, but I couldn't get there. "The doctor visits alone would do me in. Can you imagine two more children with ear infections like Henry has had?"

"No. I honestly can't." His nose wrinkled up. "And the diapers."

"Right? I'm looking forward to when Henry's out of them and the entire house is potty trained."

He laughed softly and reached for my hand. "That will be a wonderful day."

We walked back to the house and it wasn't until we stepped

inside that I realized I hadn't thought of the blog the entire time we were outside or jogging. Instead, I'd been caught up in spending time with Nathaniel, simply enjoying the evening with my Master. It wasn't just the sex I missed when I didn't wear his collar; it was everything about our D/s relationship.

Once inside, he stroked my cheek, told me he'd eat at seven, and went to take a shower. Since it was a bit late, I took mine in the bathroom attached to the old submissive bedroom I used so long ago. That way I could start dinner without being sweaty and having to wait for Nathaniel to finish.

While I prepared our supper, I tried to remember how long it'd been since I'd served him a meal while wearing his collar. I couldn't recall. I pulled out my favorite china, a set I'd found in the attic right after our engagement. It was Japanese inspired and decorated with vibrant reds and blues. I assumed he would have me serve him in the dining room, so I prepared the table for one.

He entered the dining room at seven and his lips curved up slightly when he saw the china. "Very nice, Abigail."

"Thank you, Master."

I remained standing to his side while he ate and a feeling of peace and contentment washed over me. I needed this. It was part of who I was, of who we were. We had to make room in our schedules for it.

He suddenly pushed back from the table. "Come here, Abigail."

I looked at his plate in shock. Was something wrong? Was the tuna raw or overcooked? It had looked good when I took it out of the oven.

"Here." He patted his thigh. "Sit in my lap."

Oh. Well, that was much better than burned or undercooked fish. I threw my shoulders back and climbed into his lap in as sultry a manner as I could. *This would be more fun if I was naked. Or if he was. Or if we both were.*

"Open." He held a forkful of tuna to my mouth. I parted my lips and he slipped it inside. "Good, isn't it?" he asked.

"Not bad," I said, licking my lips. "Maybe a little heavy on the pepper."

"Mmm." He focused on my eyes. "I think it's just right."

"Thank you, Master."

He fed me a bite of salad and a drop of Italian dressing landed on the corner of my mouth. I shifted to get his napkin, but he shook his head. He leaned forward and wiped it away with his thumb.

"May I, Master?" I asked, stilling his wrist with my hand.

"Yes."

I kissed his thumb and then sucked it into my mouth, all the while keeping my eyes on his. His eyes had grown dark and his breath was ragged. I wanted him to kiss me, to touch me, something. But he inhaled deeply and pulled away.

"You need to eat," he said.

I didn't feel hungry at all, but lunch had been hurried. If I didn't eat now, I'd be wide-awake at two in the morning with a growling stomach. He took his time feeding me and after a few bites, he put the fork down and held his wineglass to my lips.

Usually when he fed me while I wore his collar, we'd be in the playroom. Sitting at the dining room table felt slightly wanton. He shifted his hips and his erection pushed against my thigh. He ignored it, focusing his attention on ensuring that I ate. Bite after bite he fed me, giving me sips of wine in between. Being so close to him, sitting in his lap, I was acutely aware of every inch of him. The firmness of his thigh, the strength of chest, his warmth.

"I should fuck you on the table," he said.

It was so easy to picture. He'd stand up and lay me down on top of the table. Maybe even pushing the dishes aside like they always did in the movies. I'd put on a dress for dinner and all he'd have to do is lift the hem to my waist. I didn't have any underwear on. He could take me so easily. It would require hardly any effort for him to climb up along with me, or roughly grab my legs and pull me to the edge.

Please.

"Abigail." His fingers danced along my upper thigh, dipping a bit lower to tease the hem of my skirt. He stroked my knee and ran his hand almost, but not quite, up my leg entirely. "Tell me. If I fingered you now, would you be wet?"

"Yes, Master." I squirmed just a little, letting him know he should feel free to check.

"It would take nothing for me to lift you onto the table and have my way with you." He whispered in my ear, "I've never had you on the dining room table."

"That's a travesty, Master. We should fix it."

He ran his tongue along my earlobe and I shivered at the sensation. "That we should, my lovely. And we will. But not tonight."

I gave a half whine. *Why? Why when I wanted him so badly?*

"I know what you're thinking," he said.

Of course he did; at times it was as if I'd married a fucking mind reader.

"Your poker face is nonexistent," he continued. "And trust me, I want it as badly as you do. But I'm going to make us both wait for it. It'll make it so much better." He cocked an eyebrow. "Or, at least, that's what I recall you saying about why we shouldn't have sex the month before our wedding."

Damn his perfect memory. "Yes, Master. I remember. I also remember we both decided that going that long without sex wasn't the best idea I ever had."

"Then we'll both sleep easy tonight knowing we won't have to wait an entire month this time."

Much to my surprise, I did sleep well that night. It was difficult to explain, but I often felt closer to him when I wore his
collar. True to his word, we didn't have sex at all. When I
climbed into bed after him and he pulled me to him, I almost
begged. Instead, I gave a sigh of contentment and focused on the
feeling of his arms around me.

Protected.

Secure.

If I felt closer to him at times while in his collar, I also felt
more protected. Not to say I didn't feel that way during the
week, but there was something about being in his collar. Branded
as his and his alone, I knew he would go through hell and back
to keep me safe.

He turned his head and kissed my hair.

I lifted my face. "Kiss me, Master."

I knew from experience he would never deny me at least that
much. He didn't disappoint, pulling me close and pressing his
lips to mine in a slow and sensual kiss that curled my toes.

I couldn't wait for the next day.

Chapter Three

The doorbell rang the following morning while I was in the bedroom getting ready. I'd served Nathaniel breakfast in the dining room, but unlike the previous night, he asked me to join him. With one last look in the mirror, I made my way into the hallway.

I ran into Nathaniel as he was heading down the stairs. When he saw me, he stopped.

"Lift the sweater."

I dropped my eyes and lifted the hem of the sweater, allowing him just a glimpse of the lacy black corset underneath.

"Very nice," he said, dragging a finger along the material over my belly. His voice and touch nearly left me in a puddle of desire. "Though I can't wait to see you completely naked."

"I feel the same, Master."

He cupped the back of my neck, drawing me closer and running his fingers along the hair at the nape of my neck. "Feeling better today, my lovely?"

I lifted my head and met his eyes. They were dark with a desire that I felt all the way to my toes. "Yes, Master. Much."

"Good." He brushed his lips gently to mine and then took my hand as we made our way to the door.

Simon and Lynne stood on our porch. His left arm was around her shoulders and it took only a quick glance at her to see why. She looked like she'd jump out of her skin if anyone looked at her wrong.

"Simon," Nathaniel said. "Welcome to our home."

"Thank you," the lanky man with sandy-colored hair said. "This is Lynne."

"Nice to meet you," he said and her eyes grew big, almost as if she expected him to whip out a flogger and handcuffs right there on the front porch. He lowered his voice and nudged me forward. "This is my wife, Abby."

Being introduced to me seemed to relax her only a tiny bit. Her eyes were still wary and her muscles tense. Though in fairness, I no longer thought she'd take off running back to the car.

"Abby," Nathaniel said, still using the voice he'd use to talk to a wild animal. "Why don't you take Lynne into the kitchen while Simon and I talk in my office?"

I waved for Lynne to follow me and she gave Simon a quick peck on the cheek before stepping over the threshold. As we walked down the hall, I pointed to the room on our right. "That's Nathaniel's office where the men will be. I was going to put some sandwiches together for lunch. Come keep me company?"

I wasn't surprised when she didn't say anything, but simply followed me into the kitchen. I took out the bread and raised an eyebrow at the petite blonde, who still looked like she was seconds away from dashing out of the house.

"You know, if you don't want to watch, if it makes you too

uncomfortable, or if you want to wait and reschedule, I don't have a problem telling the guys."

She straightened her shoulders and I swore I caught a glimpse of a backbone. Good thing, too. It took a strong woman to submit.

"I'm fine," she said and there was a steel edge to her voice that surprised me. She took a deep breath. "I'll admit I'm just a bit intimidated by you and Nath—Mr. West. And the idea of watching. But I have to do this. For me."

There was a truth to her words that her expression reflected. And the once timid woman now looked like the brave mouse attempting to remove the splinter from the lion's paw. I felt more at ease seeing the transformation.

"Hearing you say that makes me so happy," I said, working on the sandwiches. "But you can call him Nathaniel. Hardly anyone calls him Mr. West. And it's completely understandable to be intimidated watching someone for the first time. I know I was."

She walked to stand beside me at the counter and reached for the bread to help me. "Is it weird for you? Playing in front of people?"

"It was the first time. Hand me the mayo, if you don't mind." I put a light layer on one side of the bread. "But it got easier and easier each time. To be honest, it's now a turn-on for me. One, because I know he likes it, and two, because I enjoy serving him and knowing someone's watching me."

"Do you know what he's doing today?"

I left her to finish up the sandwiches and started cutting fruit for a salad. "Oh, no. What would be the fun in that?"

She laughed. "It's hard for me to go into something not knowing what's going to happen."

"But that's the beautiful thing about submission. Letting go of the need to know everything, to do everything, and think everything. When you know, love, and trust your Dom, there's a thrill in letting him take control because you know he knows, loves, and trusts you, too."

"And that's what safe words are for."

"Right."

"Have you ever said your safe word?"

"Yes." I grinned. "Before me, Master had never had a sub use her safe word. It's only happened a few times, but I've used mine. I like to say it's because I'm a challenge, but truthfully, I was new to the scene when he collared me. How would I know what my limits were if he didn't help show me?"

"Simon had me complete a checklist."

"That's a good start. With a checklist he knows where to draw the lines. By actually playing, he'll know how close he can get to them or if he needs to adjust them."

She'd finished with the sandwiches, so I pulled out a tray and we piled them on it. I'd put them in the refrigerator along with the fruit salad. We'd eat after we played.

"There's so much to learn," she said.

"And you'll never know it all. But Simon is well respected and highly regarded. You're in good hands."

She blushed. "Not yet, I'm not. We haven't *done* anything."

I chuckled and we went back to finishing up lunch preparations. That's how the men found us a short time later. Simon walked over to Lynne and gave her a quick kiss. Nathaniel took note of her calmer demeanor and mouthed *Thank you* to me. I simply smiled and nodded.

He looked down at his watch. "Ten minutes, Abigail. The three of us will follow later."

I made it to the playroom in five minutes since I wanted plenty of time to kneel and get in the right frame of mind. Almost immediately after going to my knees I could sense a difference in myself. Nathaniel's plan from last night had worked. I should never have doubted him. I closed my eyes and focused on the air moving in and out of my lungs.

"Very nice, Abigail."

I started slightly. I hadn't heard Nathaniel come in. Matter of fact, I hadn't heard Simon or Lynne either.

Nathaniel walked around me. "I think we're both in a much better place mentally today than we were yesterday. Wouldn't you agree?"

I kept my head lowered. "Yes, Master. Thank you."

"You're welcome." He placed the end of a riding crop under my chin and forced my head up. His eyes were dark with desire and wicked intent, yet somehow completely serious. "I take responsibility for last night and you can be assured it won't happen again."

His voice washed over me, taking with it the lingering stress and guilt I had about the previous night. I felt so much lighter. It was obvious he noticed the change in me, because he smiled before saying, "I want you on the whipping bench."

He didn't tell me to crawl, so I rose to my feet and walked toward the bench, swaying my hips the way I knew he liked. I settled my body over the bench, noting he had attached restraints to the wooden frame. That usually meant he'd planned something intense and excitement rushed through my veins.

He spoke something so softly to Simon and Lynne I couldn't hear, then walked to me. Just as I thought, he picked up the restraints and bound me to the bench.

"I want to hear all your noises today, but I need you to be still. Since it's been so long, I thought it for the best I bind you."

"Thank you, Master." I appreciated his reasoning for binding me.

"Look at this ass," he said, running his hands over my flesh. "Practically begging for me to punish it."

I took a deep breath and let the air out of my lungs with a

moan. His hands felt so good. He kneaded my backside for a few minutes and then smacked it hard.

"Oh, fuck, *yes*," I nearly panted. I tried to lift my ass up for more, but he'd bound me too tightly. Instead I closed my eyes and gave myself over to the sharp pain that diffused into pleasure with his hands.

I noticed he'd stopped only when the silence of the room struck me. "Green, Master," I almost whined, wanting more.

There was no verbal reply. In fact, there was nothing for about thirty seconds. Then I heard it—the unmistakable metallic clinking of a belt being unbuckled. I sucked in a breath. How had it escaped my attention he had a belt on?

My body tensed in anticipation. There was something about his use of a belt in the playroom. He could wield one *just so*, making me feel pain or pleasure depending on his desires. Whenever he'd use one, he would wear it for the next day or two and the sight of it around his waist never failed to remind me of how it felt against my skin, guaranteeing instant arousal.

He yanked the belt from his pants in one quick motion and I heard myself beg, "Oh, please. Oh, please. Oh, please," as I fought against the restraints to rub my legs together.

"Be still."

I whimpered, but obeyed. He slapped the belt against the palm of his hand and walked to the front of the bench to stand before me. With each step he took, he repeated the slap against the palm of his hand. The sound echoed in the otherwise quiet room.

His feet came into view and he dropped the end of the belt so it dangled to his side, the tail end swaying ever so slightly. "Earn it," he commanded. "Earn me marking that delicious ass and pussy."

Still holding the belt with one hand, he unzipped his pants and pushed them over his hips. His magnificent erection was inches from my face. I licked my lips at the sight of its hard, straining length.

"Yes, Abigail, I'm going to fuck your mouth and you're going to swallow everything I give you." He tapped my chin. "Open and take me."

It was awkward, but I was just able to engulf his cock in the position I was in. He pushed his hips forward and hit the back of my throat.

"All the way," he said.

Normally, I'd lift my head up, but tied as I was, I couldn't get him all the way in my mouth. Keeping the belt in one hand, he grabbed both sides of my head by my hair. He bent his knees and with that angle, I was able to take him completely.

"Fuck, you feel good." He gave a few preliminary thrusts before he started using my mouth in earnest. In binding me to the bench, he'd put me in a position to take whatever he gave me. The thought of him using me for his pleasure spurred me on and I relaxed my throat even more to allow him better access.

"So good," he said in between thrusts.

There had been times I'd served him orally when he held off his climax as long as possible. He didn't seem to be inclined to do so at the moment, though. His use of me was hard and fast and it wasn't too long before I felt his impending release. He pulled my hair harder, thrusting deep inside my mouth, and then held still.

"Going to come so hard," he said in a near growl. "And you're going to swallow it all."

He came with a grunt and I worked frantically to ensure nothing escaped. He dropped the belt and held my head, his fingers now stroking my hair. My body nearly hummed with the pleasure I found in his touch.

"So good, my lovely," he whispered. "I love the way you serve me. Holding nothing back. Giving me everything."

He withdrew from my mouth and pulled his pants up. Serving him turned me on and while he might have had some relief with his climax, I still ached for mine. He would know this and I wasn't surprised when he kept his hands running across my body, teasing here and there, as he moved to position himself behind me.

He slid a finger into me. "Perhaps you'll earn my belt by this evening. But for now, we'll start with something else I know you've been craving."

Even though I expected it, when he placed the leather strap beside my head, my heart skipped a beat. I had wanted him to spank me, but it wasn't until I saw what he had planned that I realized I needed it so badly.

"Do you wish to say anything?" he asked, dipping another finger into me and smiling with satisfaction at the wetness he found.

"Please, please, please, Master. I need—"

My words were cut short by a hard slap against my ass.

"Need what?"

I groaned. "That, Master. I need you to spank me."

He didn't say anything, but answered me with soft smacks that gradually grew harder. I tried to shift my hips—my clit was desperate for friction—but as soon as I moved a muscle he stopped.

"I bound you to the table for a reason, Abigail. Move again and I'll stop completely."

"I'm sorry, Master."

"Prove it by remaining still."

He started once more and I forced myself to remain still. As the temptation to squirm grew stronger and stronger, I closed my eyes and breathed in and out with slow, measured breaths. I cleared my mind and set my focus solely on him.

"Very nice, my lovely."

He continued, using only his hands, taking time to prepare my skin, and every so often, teasing my swollen flesh by slipping a finger or two inside me and then circling my clit. The smacks to my ass got harder and faster, yet somehow he was still pumping his fingers in and out of me.

My breathing grew choppy as his fingers went deeper and deeper, tormenting me by almost brushing my G-spot. And all the while, his other hand still rained delicious swats.

"Oh, fuck, Master," I said as he pressed a third finger inside me.

"Such language, tsk-tsk-tsk." He hooked his fingers, pressing against the spot I needed right as he brought the leather strap down across my ass.

I squeezed my inner muscles tight to hold off my orgasm. "Fuck!"

"I wouldn't come without permission if I were you. I'd hate to turn this into a chastisement." He pushed his fingers in and out again. "I'm going to give you nine more and you're not allowed to come. I'm enjoying fucking you like this, so I'm going to keep doing it."

I wasn't going to be able to do it. I couldn't hold out while he repeated his actions nine more times. I thought about using my *yellow* safe word. I opened and closed my fist.

"You can do this," he whispered in my ear. "You will do it. For me."

His words strengthened my resolve. With his vote of confidence, I knew I could do it. And his subtle reminder that I would be doing it for him spoke to that part within me that longed and needed to scrve him.

"Nine more, Master," I said. "For you."

The strap landed again in time with his fingers. "Thank you, Abigail."

The next three landed quickly and I held my breath until he stopped and rubbed my skin, pushing the sharp ache to an ever-growing pleasure.

"How many more?" he asked.

"Five, Master. Please."

The strap connected with my backside again and I gasped as his fingers pushed back inside me.

"Count down," he commanded.

"Four."

I found that focusing on the count made it easier to get through the last three. Though by the time he'd finished ten it took all my self-control not to allow my body to give in to the release he'd artfully built me up to.

He put the strap back beside my head and shifted the fingers still inside me. "You're so wet. So ready for my cock to slide inside and fuck you. Is that what you want, my lovely?"

"Yes, Master," I whined.

He chuckled. "No, 'If it pleases you, Master'?"

"I'm being honest." I squeezed my eyes tightly. His fingers were still moving inside my achy body.

The chuckle escalated into full-blown laughter. "So you are. Thank you." His fingers left and I came close to whining again, but then he said, "Come when you want."

The warmth of his mouth engulfed me right where I needed him the most. I anticipated soft nibbles, but he was rough, licking and sucking my clit. I tensed, wanting to hang on to the overwhelming pleasure he brought my body for just a bit longer. It possibly would have worked, but he brought his fingers back into the mix and that, along with his wicked tongue, quickly made holding off impossible.

"Oh, God. *Yes,*" I moaned.

He made one more swipe of his tongue, pressed his fingers to that spot he knew so well, and I came with a helpless cry. He didn't move, but kept going with his movements.

"Again," he said, rubbing my clit.

My second climax followed, and I barely had time to capture my breath before I heard his pants unzip and he thrust into me.

"You're going to come a third time, but with my cock inside you."

I wondered idly if anyone had ever died from orgasm overdose. It didn't seem possible I could come again, but my body was now completely under his control and if he asked me to fly, I'd probably sprout wings and take off. And just like that he worked me into a frenzy for a third time.

His thrusts were powerful, each one hitting deep within me and pushing my body against the bench. Bound as I was, there was nothing for me to do but to let him use me as he wanted. I closed my eyes and let myself enjoy the freedom and release he gave me. The sharp ache of my backside made the pleasure he brought all that much more intense and before long I was back on the cusp of another orgasm.

He was close, too. I could tell by his jerky movements and the harshness of his breathing. "Damn, Abigail. You feel so good. I want to feel that pussy squeeze my cock as you come again."

His fingers swept along my clit and my body responded. I whimpered as my release followed the commands of his touch and then again when he came as well.

He left me trembling, my flesh hypersensitive, and every nerve ending standing at attention waiting to see what he would require next.

He rained kisses along my spine and I shivered. "So good, my lovely."

It was as if that was the signal my body needed. I relaxed into the aftereffects as he unbound me. I felt heavy and it took a lot of energy to keep my eyes open, so I kept them closed. He massaged my back and tenderly rubbed lotion onto my backside. Somewhere around me there were voices, but it sounded more like a gentle hum of bees and I couldn't make out the words.

He tucked a blanket around me and then lifted me in his arms. I sighed. It felt so good to be wrapped in his embrace. I buried my head into his chest and took a deep breath.

He chuckled. "I probably smell like sweat and sex. But then again, so do you."

"I like the way you smell. You should bottle it up and sell it." I inhaled again. "Nah, on second thought, I think I'll keep you all to myself."

We'd made it into the bedroom. He put me in the middle of the bed and then climbed up to pull my back to his chest. He kissed the back of my neck. "I'm keeping you to myself, too. Forever."

I let myself drift for a few seconds, easing my way to sleep, when it hit me. "Simon and Lynne."

His arms tightened around me "They're fine. I've got everything under control. What I need you to do is rest."

With the reminder I could leave the world in his capable hands, I allowed sleep to overtake me.

I dozed off and on for what seemed like hours, never falling into a deep sleep. Nathaniel stayed beside me while I rested. Every time I roused enough to be aware of my surroundings, I felt his warmth. As the fatigue I normally felt after a scene slowly lifted, I twisted around to face him.

"Awake?" he asked with a kiss.

I yawned. "Almost."

"Take your time." His thumb trailed across my bottom lip. "There's no rush."

"Simon and Lynne still here?"

"Mmm, either downstairs or outside. I sent him a text letting him know I was staying with you and they could either go for a walk or hang out inside."

"I hope Lynne's still calm and the scene didn't freak her out too much."

"Simon said she really enjoyed talking with you."

"She has a good head on her shoulders and is stronger than she looks."

"I'm glad you got a chance to ease her mind before we did anything; I think it helped a lot."

"Are you hungry? Lynne and I got most of lunch ready, and all I need to do is put everything out."

He sat up, bringing me with him. "It's a little after noon. I'll go find them while you get dressed. We'll eat on the sunporch."

He gave me a quick kiss and then left to find our guests. I stayed in bed for a few minutes, stretching, before heading to the bathroom. My body was filled with delicious aches and pains that would stay with me for days.

Nathaniel had laid out an outfit for me to wear, as well as two pain relievers and a bottle of water. I took the two pills and drank half the water. I smiled at my reflection in the mirror, seeing a woman who'd just been consummately fucked. My hair was tousled, and my lips full. The marks of our play were on my backside, I noted, turning around and looking over my shoulder.

The outfit he laid out was a short skirt, no panties, and a soft cotton T-shirt. Casual, but still subtly sexy. I quickly brushed my hair, washed my face, and got dressed.

Lynne was in the kitchen, pulling sandwiches out of the refrigerator when I made it downstairs. She smiled at me shyly. I simply smiled back, remembering the odd feeling I experienced the first time I interacted with someone after watching them play.

"Did you and Simon go for a walk?" I asked, grabbing the glasses from the cabinet and filling them with ice.

"Just for a bit," she said. "We dipped our feet in your pool, too."

"Next time you'll have to bring your bathing suits." I watched as she got out the fruit salad. "Is there anything you'd like to talk about or ask without the men around?"

She shook her head. "Simon and I talked after. It was nothing like I thought it'd be and yet exactly what I expected at the same time. I know that doesn't make sense."

I laughed. "I think I know what you're trying to say. Did anything surprise you?"

"I thought it'd be awkward, but it was really like we were watching something on TV. The two of you didn't even seem to know we were there. I think that made it easier."

"I can guarantee Master never forgot you were there, but you're right about me. My entire focus was on him."

"It was captivating, watching him. How he can be so hard and demanding and yet look at you with such love and devotion."

He didn't often have me meet his eyes while we were in the playroom, but I knew what she was talking about based on the few times he had allowed it. It was a look I never got tired of seeing and as I thought about it, an idea popped into my head.

Maybe if I could get him to video our play and we watched it?

The idea turned me on. The only thing hotter would be if there were other people watching as we played and I could see their faces as well. I fell into a fantasy of what that would be like.

"Spread your legs wide for our guests, Abigail. Let them see how wet your pussy gets in preparation for my cock."

I'm blindfolded, so I can't see anything, but I know the men are there. Watching. I'm sitting on the couch and I move my knees apart.

"Wider," one of the men says. "I can't see her clit."

Nathaniel is behind me. He pinches one of my nipples so hard, tears fill my eyes. "Spread. Now."

I part my knees as wide as I can and he lets go of my nipple.

"Better. You see now, gentlemen, how desperate she is for my cock? How her pussy gets all nice and wet, anticipating the fucking heading its way."

"Nice and tight," another man says. "Bet it fits like a glove."

"It does," Nathaniel answers, then leans down to whisper so only I can hear. "They're going crazy with lust just looking at you spread out for their viewing pleasure. I can only imagine what they'll be feeling when I'm pounding into that sweet pussy." He stands up. "Show the gentlemen how you play with your clit, Abigail."

"Abigail?"

I jumped. What?

Nathaniel had made it into the kitchen and was looking at me with a slightly bemused expression. He raised an eyebrow in an *I know what you were thinking* way. "You were somewhere else for a moment. Can Simon and I help carry things?"

"Oh, right. I wasn't. I was," I stammered. "Yes, yes, you can."

By the time we made it to the sunporch, even Lynne was laughing.

Everyone sat down and took a sandwich, and we fell into a comfortable chatter. It was the first time I'd really had a chance to talk with Simon and I found him to be friendly and intelligent. The men were discussing an issue Nathaniel was having with his security team. Jonah, his longtime security lead, had turned in his resignation and was moving to California with his fiancée and Domme, Eve. Apparently, Simon had the name of someone who could help.

As the men chatted on, I turned to Lynne. She worked as an admin for a well-known law firm that was right down the street from the public library where I used to work. Her eyes grew big as she gushed about her favorite authors.

During a break in our conversation, I realized the men had stopped talking and were looking at us. I kicked myself for not paying closer attention to Nathaniel's needs.

"Can I get something for you, Master?" I asked.

An evil smile played on his lips. "Yes, as a matter of fact, you can."

I pushed my chair back.

"Sit down."

Oh, hell.

He nodded toward his left. "When you were in the kitchen a little bit ago, you were daydreaming about something. What was it?"

He wasn't seriously asking me that, was he? But the look on his face told me he was completely serious. "It was on the personal side, Master."

"Yes."

But of course he knew that and his face held no reprieve. Apparently, playtime hadn't ended in the playroom. I didn't look at Simon or Lynne.

I took a deep breath. "It was a fantasy. I was blindfolded and naked, sitting on a couch. You were standing behind me."

He raised an eyebrow. *Keep going.*

"There were"—*fuck, this was embarrassing*—"there were men in the room. Wa-watching." While I spoke, he kept his attention on me. Never glancing away. "You were letting them look at me and whispering to me about how much they wanted me and how it'd drive them crazy when you fucked me. And we were being taped."

"Exhibitionist all the way, aren't you?" he asked, talking about the time we had sex under a blanket at the Super Bowl.

"Yes, Master."

"Would you like to one day play in front of a group of men? Have them watch while I fuck you?"

Damn. I shifted in my chair, feeling my arousal grow. "Yes, Master."

"Does it turn you on knowing that they'll look at you and want to fuck you?"

"Uh," I stammered. "Yes, Master, but I know you won't let them touch me."

"No, they won't touch you, but they'll most likely be jerking off while they picture themselves fucking you."

"I know I'm safe with you, Master."

He tucked a stray piece of hair behind my ear. "Whatever we do, you are completely safe in my care. I value you more than my own life."

I kissed his palm. It'd been a long time since he'd pushed me out of my comfort zone. Describing my fantasy in front of Simon and Lynne had been more of a challenge than having them in the playroom. But I knew as the conversation around the table started up again, Lynne wasn't the only one who'd learned something today.

Chapter Four

Simon and Lynne left shortly after lunch and Nathaniel and I lounged in the library. For a while we spoke about nothing in particular, just simple chitchat. He talked about the man Simon mentioned hiring as a consultant for security. Since Jonah was leaving in a few weeks, he thought he'd call the other guy in a few days.

We had another five hours or so before Linda brought the kids back. It wasn't a given we'd go back to the bedroom or playroom, but I hoped we did. We'd had only the one session. And our next date wasn't scheduled for another month.

I really didn't want to wait another month. But before I could say anything, he put a hand on my knee.

"Abigail."

I hoped that meant what I thought it meant. "Yes, Sir?"

"I want you on our bed, hands and knees."

My heart thumped in anticipation.

While it would have been nice to go back to the playroom,

the bedroom had its advantages. Every time I stepped into the bedroom, I'd remember the time we spent there this weekend.

He'd be following me in about ten minutes, so I undressed and went straight to the bedroom and got on my hands and knees facing the headboard. I naturally fell into my yoga breathing, glad we had this time to come together once more.

As expected, I heard him enter the bedroom before ten minutes had passed.

"Very nice, Abigail. You can relax. Stretch a bit."

Feeling slightly stiff, and glad to be moving, I dropped to my butt and rolled my shoulders.

"Are you okay?" he asked.

I turned to face him. Faint worry lines creased his forehead.

"Yes, Master. Just a bit unused to waiting."

"Is that so?" he asked and the worry lines disappeared. "Then it's going to be a long night for you. No orgasm without permission and I feel like being stingy with my permission. And while I let you be vocal this morning, this afternoon you're not to speak unless you need to safeword or I ask you a direct question. Understood?"

"Yes, Master." It was so hard sometimes to keep quiet. Took all my concentration.

"Have you stretched enough? Are you ready?"

"Yes, Master."

He walked to the bed, captured my face between his hands and kissed me. Unlike most of his kisses today, this one was urgent. He dug his fingers into my hair and I groaned at the sharp pain his actions brought. *Fuck, I've missed this.* I sank into his embrace.

His kiss made my arousal grow more intense and I wrapped my arms around him, wanting him to engulf me completely. After a few minutes he pulled back to whisper in my ear.

"I want you on your knees, facing the headboard. You may hold on to it."

I slid out of his embrace and climbed back on the bed the way he asked.

"Knees wider. You'll need the support." When I was in position, the leather tip of a crop ran down my left leg, up along the inside and back down my right.

Oh, yes, yes, yes.

He started with gentle taps all along my legs and the crop landed harder on my backside. Ever so gradually, he increased the intensity of the swats. I pushed my ass back, needing more.

"Enjoying yourself?" he asked.

I hummed in blissed-out pleasure. "Mmm, yes, Master."

"Good." He ran a hand down my backside and slipped two fingers inside. "That's all I want for you tonight and I can tell someone is definitely enjoying herself at the moment."

I pushed back, wanting his fingers deeper. I couldn't talk, but I could show him with my body how his touch affected me.

He gave my ass a slap. "And someone's greedy." More swats from the crop rained across my backside. "But I'm having too much fun teasing you to fuck you yet."

He shifted and pressed his weight along my back and his breath was hot in my ear. "That's what you want, isn't it? You want me to fuck you?"

I shivered. "Yes, please, Master."

"No." He smacked the crop so it landed between my legs. "Release the headboard, Abigail."

I let go and dropped to my butt, carefully, though, because of the ache left behind by the crop. He stood by the bed and I couldn't take my eyes off him as he undressed. He still worked out daily and his body made my knees wobble. My eyes dropped to his erection, which was so long and thick, my pussy clenched with need.

"See something you like?" he asked, a hint of teasing noticeable in his voice.

"Yes, Master."

"Tell me."

"I want your cock."

"I'm not sure you're ready." He sat down on the side of the bed and patted the spot beside him. "Put your right foot here."

I slid off the bed and stood before him, placing my foot the way he asked. The position left me a bit unsteady.

"Hands on my shoulders." When I'd regained my balance, he trailed a finger up my inner thigh, circled my clit, and teased my entrance. "Let's see if you're ready."

The feel of his finger, dipping just the tiniest bit into me, had me squeezing his shoulders.

"Is this where you want it?" he asked and his voice was all husky.

"Yes, please."

He lifted his finger to his mouth and tasted me. "So sweet."

His hands drifted to my waist and I swayed against him. "I want you in my lap. Your legs wrapped around me and my cock buried inside you." I started to move, but he didn't let go. "Lower yourself on me slowly and be still once I'm all the way in."

I kept hold of his shoulders while I moved into position. Pressing myself at the tip of his cock, he whispered, "Feel how hard I am for you?"

Slowly, I lowered myself down on him and he entered me inch by inch.

"That's it, Abigail. Take every bit of your Master's dick. Feel it push deep inside you. Claiming your body."

His jaw tightened as I continued my descent. I closed my eyes so I could concentrate on the feel of him stretching me, hard and thick inside me.

"Don't move," he said, when he was all the way inside, but I wasn't sure if he was talking to me or himself. The urge to move, to rock up and down on his cock, was so strong and tempting. I dug my fingers into his shoulder, knowing I was leaving marks.

I forced myself to breathe slower and as I calmed down, he ran his hands down my arms.

"That's it. Do you feel our connection?"

I buried my face against his neck, wanting more. "Yes, Master."

"I don't want to just be inside your body. I want to be inside your mind. I want my mark on your very soul."

Since I couldn't talk, I held on to him even tighter. *You are. It is.*

"But for right now, I'll settle for just being inside your body." He held me firmly, and with one swift move, changed our positions so I was on my back and he towered over me. He took my hands and placed them above my head. I grabbed a handful of sheet, knowing I wasn't to move.

"When I'm inside you, the only thing on my mind is getting deeper inside you." He thrust his hips forward. "And deeper." He withdrew and thrust again. "So deep, I'm the only thing you can feel." He repeated his motions. "The only thing you feel for days."

He circled my breasts and played with my nipples. *Fuck, he feels so good.* I sucked in a breath and arched my back. He started a steady rhythm, taking what he wanted and giving me what I needed in the process. Each inward thrust pushed me deeper into the mattress and I felt my control slip.

"I'm not going to push you tonight," he said, slowing down, but still moving hard and long inside me. "Come when you want."

With the permission to come, I tried to hold my release off a little longer and started reciting the German alphabet backward under my breath.

But he picked up on what I was doing. "German isn't going to help you tonight. I've got you where I want and I'm going to fuck you for as long as I can."

I fisted more of the sheets.

"My dick feels so good right now, I may stay buried in you for hours."

He could do it, too. He pressed even deeper inside and gave me a wicked smile.

"Hang on, Abigail." Taking a tight grip on my hips, he drove into me over and over. I left German behind, muttering nonsense in my desire to hold out just a little bit longer.

He was hard and rough and took me with long, slow strokes. Finally, it was too much and I bit my lower lip so hard when I came, I tasted blood.

"Yes," he said and pushed his body toward his own release until he came inside me with a primal groan.

He dropped on me and I reveled in the feel of his sated body covering mine. But he didn't stay there long. Seconds later, still breathing heavily, he pulled back and kissed me with an intensity I hadn't felt in years.

Chapter Five

I had thought something might have changed that weekend we played in front of Simon and Lynne, but things returned to the way they had always been. I didn't have time to think a lot about it, though. My meeting with Meagan was coming up and she had e-mailed me a few ideas for articles she wanted me to write. What free time I had was spent writing.

The day of the meeting, three weeks after the Saturday with Simon and Lynne, Elaina came over with her son, Maddox, to watch Elizabeth and Henry. Elaina was married to Nathaniel's childhood friend Todd. Though to be honest, she'd been Nathaniel's friend for just about as long.

We'd grown close over the years and I loved her like the sister I never had. I was riding into the city with Nathaniel and before we left, she pulled me into a hug and told me she couldn't wait to hear how everything went. I promised to call her when the meeting ended.

"Kick ass," she whispered in my ear.

"I plan on it."

Nathaniel was quiet as we pulled out of the driveway. Which was fine. The silence allowed me time to go over the questions I wanted to ask and the information they'd requested from me.

"I was thinking about this weekend," Nathaniel said about twenty minutes into the drive.

"Oh, do we have plans?" I didn't think we did. It was actually one of the few free weekends we had on our calendar. The annual black-tie fund-raiser for Nathaniel's nonprofit was coming up in a few months and he had a lot of things to oversee between now and then.

"No. Which is why I was thinking what I was."

I waited for him to continue, noting his hands tightened on the steering wheel.

"I know we don't have anything scheduled for another week or so, but I want you in my collar this weekend."

That was unexpected. Since we'd started playing every month, he'd never asked to increase frequency. Even after Elizabeth was born, we'd never progressed to anything other than once a month. We'd talked about it, but I'd gotten pregnant with Henry and that had put a stop to the discussions. We still played a bit while I was pregnant, but with a dramatically decreased intensity.

"You're awfully quiet," he said. "Are you not interested?"

"It's not that. I just wasn't expecting *that* to be what you were thinking about."

"Maybe that's why it would be a good idea."

His statement hung in the air between us while I thought about what he said. He had a point. It probably would be a good idea and I had anticipated something of the sort after our last weekend.

"Will you ask Linda to take the kids?" I asked.

His grip on the steering wheel grew even tighter, his knuckles turning white before he loosened his hands. "I think you need a reminder about what you're to be concerned about when you're in my collar."

"What does that mean?"

He looked straight ahead, but I saw his lips draw together in a thin line before he answered. "It means you're to leave the plans for the weekend up to me. I'll take care of everything. Your job is to be in the right frame of mind."

"So that means I can't ask about our kids?"

"Instead of answering, I'm going to give you an assignment. I want you to write a five-hundred-word blog post on the possible ways I might take the question you asked me. Due Friday at six."

Was he serious? I didn't know what I was going to have to work on after the meeting and here he was adding to it?

"What if I don't have time?"

"Then I will handle the situation Friday at six."

I didn't even have to ask what that meant. "Hell."

Of course, I could tell him I didn't want to wear his collar this weekend. It might actually be a good idea since I didn't know what I'd have on my plate by then. But I really wanted to.

Which meant I had to do the assignment.

"Is that a *yes?*" he asked.

I sighed. "That's a yes."

"You don't have to act like it's a fate worse than death." He glanced at me and flashed a smile. "You could look at it as another way to sharpen your writing skills."

"My writing skills are fine, thank you very much."

Even as the words came out of my mouth, I knew I was being a brat. It was just, ugh. He truly had ways to get under my skin. Deciding to make use of the time left in the car, I pulled a notebook from my purse and started jotting down ideas for the assignment he gave me.

"What is that?" he asked.

"Ideas for what I'm going to put in the blog post you just told me to write."

"Put it down."

"What?"

"Put. It. Down."

"Did you wake up on the wrong side of the bed this morning or does driving into the city always make you this grumpy?"

"I am not grumpy."

"Could have fooled me."

"I asked you if you wanted to wear my collar this weekend and I gave you a writing assignment. That does not make me grumpy. That I don't want you working on it in the car does not make me grumpy." He stared straight ahead. "You should know me well enough by now to know I don't say or do anything without reasons."

Of course I knew that. He could very well have all the reasons in the world, but that didn't mean they were right. Though, most of the time, his were.

"Let me further expand on the writing assignment," he said. "I want you to take time to think about your question to me and how I took it. I don't want you to jot down what you think the answer is or what you've discovered in your research. I want a well thought-out, contemplative post."

I shoved the notebook back into my bag.

"To help you, I want you to spend thirty minutes meditating on it tonight. You're not to write anything about it until your meditation is completed."

Thirty minutes?

I almost asked again if he was serious, but the somber expression he wore made me change my mind. Then I decided what I really wanted to ask him was where the hell did he think I was going to find thirty minutes?

"What you can do now," he said, "is to write your top three fantasies. Just a line or two."

"That sounds like more fun." I retrieved the notebook and pen.

"Good. Let me know when you finish."

Since he wanted only a line or two and since they were my fantasies, it didn't take me long. I put the pen down with a sigh when I finished, feeling just a little carsick from the writing.

"Are you okay?"

"Writing in the car doesn't sit so well with my stomach, especially with the butterflies already there." I leaned back in the seat and closed my eyes.

"No more writing then. Instead, tell me your first fantasy."

I cracked one eye open. He didn't look like he was joking. But talking about my fantasies might take my mind off my queasy belly.

"The first one I wrote down was the one we talked about when Simon and Lynne were over. The men."

"Ahh, yes. No way I'd forget that one."

Me either. I hoped he set it up one day. That would be the most outlandish scene we'd ever talked about. Men watching as I pleased my Master. His strict look-but-don't-touch rule.

"Second one?" he asked.

"That one's easy, too. More of the consensual nonconsent."

"Capture fantasy."

"Yes. I didn't write any details down, though."

"I wouldn't think you would. Rather takes away the surprise factor if you know when and how you're going to be captured."

"We haven't done a lot of that type of play, but I always like it when we do. It's a huge turn-on."

I liked role play where it was like he'd kidnapped me. Maybe he'd make me his sex slave and I had to do anything and everything he wanted. Before I could explore that particular fantasy in my head, he asked, "Third?"

"I liked this one," I said.

"Interesting. I would have thought you liked all of them," he teased.

I swatted his arm. "You know what I mean."

"Yes. Sorry to interrupt. You were saying?"

"Three was an interrogation."

"That does sound like fun," he said. "I could do a lot with that."

"In my mind, I'm bound in a dark room. All my clothes are on, but as I give you answers to your questions, every time I give the wrong answer or one you don't like, you cut away an article of clothing."

"I think all three of these are tied for best fantasy in my head."

"Mine, too. In three, you finally have me naked and I'm still all tied up and you give me another question. I refuse to answer it, so you make me take you orally. You're rough, but it's turning me on and I'm almost choking on your cock." I glanced out of the corner of my eye. "It's not exactly like breath play." That was a hard limit for him. "But close enough, don't you think?"

"Yes, pretty close. I'd have to think about it, though." He squeezed my knee with his right hand. "I won't do anything that could potentially harm you or cause serious health issues."

"But a little cock gagging?"

"Would probably turn me on immensely."

We pulled into the parking deck across from his office. I

hadn't realized the time had gone by so quickly. Because he liked getting to work rather early, we were one of the few cars in the deck.

I looked at my watch. Still three hours until my meeting. I decided I'd either stay in Nathaniel's office or go shopping or something.

"Are you coming up with me?" he asked.

"For a few minutes," I said. "I was thinking I'd head down to the coffee shop in a little bit. Not sure I'll get any coffee, though. My stomach is all queasy again."

He walked around to my side of the car and helped me out. "Abby," he said, taking my hand. "You're an intelligent, hard-working woman. Don't let nerves get the best of you—you're too good for that."

"Thank you," I said. "It's just hard sometimes. I haven't done this in a long time."

He kissed my hand. "You're going to do great."

I spent about an hour in his office, talking. He had a few ideas for the fund-raiser he wanted to run past me and I gave him my thoughts. The location we'd used in previous years wasn't available this year and he had to find a new one.

"I have got to find someone to take over running this," he said, meaning the entire nonprofit, not just the fund-raiser.

"You've been saying that for years."

"I know," he said, rubbing his forehead. "But I really mean it this time."

I just laughed. It was his pet project and he'd have a hard time passing the reins over to someone else. "I'll believe it when I see it."

"Watch me," he said, and I had a feeling he might be serious this time.

He stood up. "I have a meeting I need to attend. Are you going to stay here or go out?"

"I think I'll go out. Maybe grab a cup of coffee?"

"Let me know how it goes." He kissed me softly on the lips. "You're going to blow them away."

"I hope so."

After he left, I told his admin good-bye and I walked to a local coffee shop to pass the time. The place held quite a bit of history for me. Years ago, Nathaniel had met me here after I walked out on him. It was in this shop, in a back corner booth, that he confessed everything to me and I decided to take him back.

I took out a paperback I'd brought, but after reading the same page over and over, I gave up and put it away. One of the waitresses stopped by my table and asked if I'd like a refill. I drank half the cup before picking up my pen to write.

Nathaniel had told me I couldn't start on his assignment until I'd meditated, so I couldn't work on that. The suggested pieces Meagan asked for were complete. I tapped my pen against the table before I took my third fantasy and wrote about it in more detail.

The scene was so vivid, it was as if the bustling shop around me disappeared while I wrote the interrogation. Interestingly enough, I found I wasn't able to write the part I'd described to him about gagging on his cock.

Why? I wrote.

I thought about the question. Why could I write the entire scene, but not that part? It couldn't be because we hadn't done it. I'd written and fantasized about a lot of things we hadn't done. That was one of the points of a fantasy, wasn't it?

I wrote a few paragraphs about fantasies. The freedom they gave us. The flexibility. But none of that helped me answer my question, so I stopped and made a note that I could add more information and use it for a blog post.

Maybe, I thought, my inability to picture that part of my fantasy had little to do with me and more to do with him. I jotted down why that could be: his hard limit on breath play, fear that he would hurt me, and my uncertainty about what he would do. Nathaniel was too real and I knew him too well to even fantasize about him doing something he considered a hard limit.

Spurred on by my possible revelation, I starting writing down things I knew about him. A few things I noted were just words: strength, passion, and caring. Others were sentences: he doesn't complain when I buy cheap artwork from antique stores simply because I like the shade of blue the artist used, and he knows how to make the best hot chocolate. By the time I lifted up my head to glance at the time, I had completed three pages. I giggled, picturing him rolling his eyes if he came across my list. I folded the pages together and closed the notebook. I needed to leave in a few minutes.

My phone vibrated with an incoming text and I smiled when I saw it was from Nathaniel.

> **So proud of you. Love you and can't wait to hear how the meeting goes.**

I sent him one back. **Thank you! You make me feel strong.** His reply was fast. **If you really want to thank me . . .** **You're insatiable,** I wrote back. **Talk soon.**

I unfolded the pages in my notebook and wrote one more sentence: He always knows the perfect thing to say to make me feel better.

I walked to the headquarters for WNN, housed in the larger NNN complex and, I'll admit, it felt a bit like I was in an alternate universe when I stepped inside and looked around. Never had I thought to be interviewing for anything having to do with such a large corporation. Even though Nathaniel and I had been married for over six years, there were times I still felt awed when surrounded by wealth and power.

I gave my name and showed my ID to the security guard and stood to the side while I waited for Meagan to come escort me up. I didn't have long to wait.

"Abby," a tall woman with platinum blond hair said, minutes later. "So happy you're here. I'm Meagan."

I shook the hand she offered me and then she led me to a bank of elevators. She chatted as we went up, asking about my family, and we discovered we both had a love of golden retrievers.

She led me to her office. It was a modern-looking space, done in sleek wood and shiny chrome. Not my preference, but it seemed to match her.

"Have a seat," she said with a wave to a chair that looked more like a piece of art than a place to sit.

She sat in a chair beside me instead of taking her place behind her desk, and a huge smile covered her face. Her hair was super straight and it swung back and forth as she talked. "I am so thrilled you're here. I've been looking forward to meeting you."

"Thank you," I said.

"This is going to be wonderful. I just know it!" She held up a hand. "But I'm getting ahead of myself. Let me tell you what I'm thinking. We'd initially like for you to write a series of blog posts for our Web site that'll match our latest television episode. We're thinking the post should go up the day before the episode airs. But I think you should do something different for the first post. Really grab everyone's attention."

I had gathered as much from her earlier communications. She talked a bit about content and timeline expectations. It all sounded reasonable.

"I have a question about privacy," I said. "Will you be able to keep my name from the public?"

"Of course, I totally understand the privacy concern. You can keep on being known as the Submissive Wife."

That was my biggest concern. In a perfect world, it wouldn't matter that I was a submissive and that I wore my husband's collar. Unfortunately, the world wasn't perfect and people didn't always treat my sexual preferences with respect.

And I didn't even want to think about the kids hearing something.

"Thank you," I said.

She picked up some papers from her desk. "I wrote down a few of the themes of our upcoming episodes: taking charge of your sexuality, sexually mismatched partners, and sex toys. You can take a look and see if you have any questions."

"How many posts a week were you thinking?" I took the papers and looked through them. Nothing surprising. Written on each week's theme were suggested questions: Where do you find reputable information? How do you find like-minded people? That sort of thing.

"I know the questions look a bit on the boring and tame side." Mischief danced in her eyes. I was willing to bet she could be trouble if the situation presented itself. "Those were questions the production team thought up. I'm giving you permission to do something else. Besides, I want the first post to pack a real punch. Knock the world on its feet."

I looked over the list of topics, and they did look to be on the boring side. "What's your production team going to say if I don't take their suggestions about what to write?"

"Trust me. If the post gets enough hits, they won't care what it's about."

"I like you," I said with a tiny laugh.

"Seriously." She took the top paper from my hand and started to read. "List of Web sites you recommend for those looking for more information. Really? Or this one, BDSM defined. Not too bad, you could probably work with that and do something." She flipped to the second page. "Spicing up your sex life. Like that hasn't been done to death. The horse is dead—leave it alone."

She went to the third page and shook her head, not even bothering to read. "What I'm saying, Abby, is make this section of the Web site *yours*. Don't feel like you're limited by these suggestions. We approached you because people love your site and they love it because it's you. Not a corporation telling you what to do."

I liked where she was going with her advice. I didn't think I could take her up on the offer if the company wasn't going to give me control of my own content.

"I'd much rather be able to decide on what to write myself. I don't know if I can be forced to write something."

She handed the papers back to me. "Now, I will say, there are probably a few topics we won't publish. But in looking over your blog, I haven't seen you write on any of them, so I think we're good. If you're unsure, you can always run the idea by me first."

"Thanks. If I decide to write for you, I'll keep that in mind. I'll have to think about what I could do for the first post. I don't particularly like any of these suggestions." I raised an eyebrow to make sure she was in agreement with me, and at her nod, I continued. "I'd like to do something completely different for the first post. Something, like you said, not necessarily new, but for certain something most people wouldn't have seen or read."

"Yes, keep going."

"Something that appeals to the population at large. It has to have a hook to draw them in. And after they finish reading it, they want to come back and read the next post." I paused, trying to think of something that met that criteria.

"Sort of like an author who ends a chapter with a cliff-hanger and you can't put it down, but have to keep going," she said.

"Right. Or like when they end the entire book on a cliff-hanger."

"Exactly like that. I have a love/hate relationship with those types of books."

"You know, I was a librarian before I had my second child and stayed at home."

She leaned forward, all curious like. "No, I had no idea."

"That's what I was doing when I first became a submissive for the man who would be my husband."

"Interesting. There might be something there. The librarian with a kinky side. Or something about the quiet type. Maybe how you can't judge people."

"I feel like I need to write these down. These are great suggestions." I especially liked the one about judging people. I often found myself doing that, even with those in the lifestyle. Not as much now as I had years ago, though. And though I tried not to assume anything about people's sex lives, something about Meagan made me think she had experience in the BDSM lifestyle. "One thing I have to remind myself is that even if you know someone's kinky, you can't automatically tell which role they fall into."

"Abby, I have a feeling you are the *perfect* person for this position. I sincerely hope you give serious thought to accepting it."

I sent Nathaniel a text as soon as the meeting was over and I was in a cab headed back to the penthouse we owned in the city.

Meeting went great. Will tell you all about it when you get home.

His reply was immediate.

So glad to hear. Have been thinking about you all day. Can't wait to hear the details.

I smiled and typed back a quick "Love you" before calling Elaina to see how the kids were doing. Nathaniel wouldn't be off work for another three hours, so to help pass time until we left for the estate, I got out a notebook and pen and began to brainstorm on possible topics for the first post.

I'd jotted down only a page of notes when the sound of the door opening caught me by surprise. I stood up. Housekeeping wasn't due until the next day and the building manager would have sent either Nathaniel or me a note before using his master key to enter.

I broke into a silly grin when Nathaniel walked into the room.

"Hey," he said, wearing his own silly grin.

"You're early," I said, walking over to him. "I wasn't expecting you for another few hours."

"Like I could work without knowing how your meeting went." He dropped his briefcase and the corner of his mouth quirked up. "So, tell me the details."

"Mmm." I reached up and slipped my hands under the lapels of his suit jacket. I pushed it up and off his shoulders. He shrugged out of it and when it fell to the floor, I said, "You're looking at the latest employee of WNN."

A huge grin covered his face and he pulled me into a tight embrace. "Of course they love you. They'd be crazy not to."

"It wasn't just me. They really liked my writing."

"It's a package deal. They go together."

"Come here," I said, taking his hand and leading him to the couch. "I'll tell you all about it."

We sat on the couch for hours, he on one side and I on the other with my feet in his lap, and just talked. I told him all about the meeting and how I was brainstorming ideas for the first post. He was always a good person to bounce things off of.

He started a sensual massage of my feet while I explained the details of the position and how things would work. When I'd finally told him everything, he grew serious.

"I'm proud of you, Abby. I think this is going to be a wonderful opportunity for you."

"Thank you. I'm really excited about it."

"As you should be."

I took my feet from his lap and shifted so I was beside him. "How long do we have until we have to leave?"

He slipped an arm around my shoulders. "Todd was going by the estate when he got off work, so another hour or two."

"I have an idea on how we could spend that time," I murmured, drawing close to him.

His hands entwined in my hair and his breath was warm against my skin. "Come here and tell me all about it."

"There's a phrase writers use." I traced the button on the top of his shirt, circled it a few times before unbuttoning it. " 'It's better to show, not tell.' "

His breath caught as I continued undoing his shirt. "I think I'm going to like your new job."

Hours later, we were at home and the kids were in bed. Nathaniel asked me if I wanted to go for a swim since I didn't head for bed like I typically did, but I told him I needed to get my thoughts together for my first post and do his required meditation. I didn't plan to write it yet, but all evening my fingers had been itching to get something down on paper.

I took a blank journal and curled up in the library on a couch with Apollo at my feet. I wrote down a few things, planning to later look over all the ideas and decide which one I wanted to do first.

My phone buzzed and I looked down in surprise to see it was Christine, the wife and submissive of the man who had mentored Nathaniel.

"Hey, Christine."

"Abby! It's been ages! How are you?"

In the early part of my relationship with Nathaniel, he'd taken me to Paul and Christine's house in New Hampshire for a weekend. Though we had been in a power exchange relationship for months, that weekend had been the first time I'd ever seen anyone else play. It had been an eye-opening experience for me in many ways.

One of the things I'd taken away from the weekend was the knowledge that I wanted to mentor new submissives. Now, as I chatted with her on the phone and we caught up with each other, I realized that the blog would be another way for me to mentor.

I told her as much.

"It sounds like a wonderful opportunity," she said. "I think it's important to show the public what BDSM is and what it's not."

"I hope I can do that."

"There was a case here recently where a submissive was stalked and later assaulted as she left a club one evening." There was a rustling of papers. "I printed out the newspaper article on it because she came to one of our meetings about a year ago."

I vaguely remembered Nathaniel mentioning the incident. But I never heard what happened.

"Here it is," Christine said. "They didn't find the man who did it. The sad thing is the way the media painted the woman. They twisted it so much, it came out sounding like the woman had asked for it."

Nathaniel hadn't told me that part. "That's horrible. That poor woman."

"Assault is never justified, but to hear some people, it wasn't that bad because she was kinky."

"What the hell does that have to do with anything?"

"Right? That's what Paul and I said. We had a group discussion about it."

"Let me get my hands on the person who said that."

She laughed, but with a touch of sadness. "How about instead you get your hands on a keyboard and work on fighting the battle that way."

"Kind of like the mighty keyboard instead of the pen?"

"Exactly. If you can educate just one person, then maybe that person will tell someone else and they'll tell another person and before you know it there won't be any more stories like that one in the newspaper."

"The sad thing is, some of the public might see the assailant as what a Dom is like," I said. "When I worked at the library, I once overheard a group of women talking about BDSM. Two of the ladies were trying to explain the difference between BDSM and abuse. It was so hard not to jump in and give my opinion. After all, that was the first time I'd ever come across a group talking about BDSM in my library."

"Yeah, that must have been strange. But now look at the great opportunity you have to educate so many people." Her voice dropped a notch. "And I can't wait to brag to my friends about the famous writer I knew back when she was a novice submissive."

"Blogger," I corrected. "I wouldn't say I'm a writer yet. I'm a blogger."

"Semantics, Abby." I pictured her rolling her eyes at me. "It doesn't matter what you call it."

We talked a few more minutes before saying our good-byes. By that time, Nathaniel had made it back in the house, having decided to swim by himself. He came into the library and shook his head at me, showering me with water droplets from his hair.

I shrieked and held my hands up. "What are you doing?"

"Getting your clothes wet so you have to take them off."

I brushed the water drops off my arm. "There are better ways to go about getting me naked."

"But this was more fun."

I loved seeing him so lighthearted and playful. Almost made up for him getting me wet.

"I'm going to get you back," I threatened, trying to think up something evil and mean I could do to him in return.

"I look forward to it," he said with a wicked grin.

"Well," I said, standing up. "You'll have to wait. I still have the thirty-minute meditation you assigned me."

His grin fell. "Damn. I didn't expect that to bite me in the ass."

It wasn't the first time I wanted him to bend a rule or tell me I didn't have to do something he'd commanded. And just like all the other times, I knew he wouldn't change his mind about my assignment. So I gave him a quick kiss and headed upstairs.

Chapter Six

Three weeks later, Meagan called the Friday morning after my first piece went up.

"Abby!" she nearly yelled and I held the phone away from my ear. "You won't believe it! It's fabulous!"

"The post generated a lot of hits?" I guessed.

"It's beyond that. It *is* a hit. It's beat the next-highest story on WNN by nearly double the number of hits in its first twenty-four hours."

I was stunned. *My piece?*

"You're speechless. It's okay. I was, too. Your idea to play up your husband's wealth was brilliant. People are all about rich, good-looking Dominants." She took a hasty breath. "If you keep generating this much interest, we're going to have to rethink your role. But, hell, we'll talk about that later. Let's celebrate! Free tonight?"

I could hardly keep up with her, the way she bounced from one topic to the next. "What?"

"Let's go to a club. Me and you. Tonight!"

"Tonight?" My mind calculated all the things I'd need to do. "Let me call Nathaniel and arrange for someone to watch the kids. What time and where?"

We made arrangements for her to come by the penthouse and then I called Nathaniel.

"I think it's a great idea for you to go out and celebrate," he said. "We'll spend the weekend in the city?"

I thought that would be perfect and we arranged a time to meet at the apartment so he could watch the kids. I buzzed around the house, packing a few things and walking around in a general daze. I still couldn't believe my piece had generated so much attention.

"You're the real deal, Abby," Meagan had said before we hung up. "You're the wife and submissive of one of the wealthiest men in the city. Who just happens to be one of the best-looking, too. Of course, your readers don't know what he looks like, but still."

"And you can write," Nathaniel had added when we talked. "Don't sell yourself short or think it's just because you married me. It's what you're writing that people are responding to."

Once Elizabeth made it home from preschool, I loaded everyone into the SUV and we took off to our penthouse. After arriving, I sent Nathaniel a text letting him know where we were and he sent one back saying he'd be getting home early.

I tried to keep my mind occupied. Elizabeth and I baked cookies, and after Henry's nap, we all went for a walk in Central Park. We would pass people and I'd wonder if they'd read my article. Surely the odds were good at least some of them had. I hid a smile as we left the park; it was like I had a secret.

Nathaniel was home when we made it back. I gave him a quick kiss before heading to the bathroom to get ready. It'd been a long time since I'd been out to a club. I sorted through my closet, trying to decide what to wear. I finally settled on a short, black, one-sleeved lace dress. I loved the way I looked in it and it would be perfect for clubbing.

I pulled my hair into a loose knot, put on some makeup, and slipped into my heels. On my way out of the bedroom, I twisted in front of the full-length mirror.

Not bad, I thought. *Not bad at all.*

Nathaniel was in the living room with the kids and he gave a low whistle when I entered the room. "You look incredible."

"Thank you." I leaned over and kissed him. "Maybe you and I should hit the town soon."

"Mmm." He ran his hand over my ass. "It's a date."

"You're missing a sleeve, Mommy," Elizabeth said.

"Oh no, baby. It's supposed to be like that."

She wrinkled her nose. "That's silly."

"I suppose it is a little silly." I gave her a hug and kiss and told her to be good for her father.

"We'll be fine," Nathaniel said, as I told Henry good-bye. "Elizabeth is going to invite Henry and me to a tea party. She promised I could wear her purple boa and that she'd serve the cookies you two made earlier."

"Sounds like a great evening." My phone vibrated with a text. "Meagan's downstairs. I'll see you guys later."

Meagan was waiting for me in the lobby. I was a bit surprised to see her wearing a trench coat.

"Is it supposed to rain?" I asked, after she gave me a bone-crushing hug.

"No, I just didn't want to show off my outfit." She raised an eyebrow at my dress. "Ready?"

"Let's go."

She hailed a cab and once inside, I leaned back and took a deep breath while she gave the address to the driver.

"Ready to have some fun?" she asked.

"So ready."

The drive took a bit longer than I thought it would and when we pulled out of the city, I turned to Meagan.

"Where are we going?" I asked.

"A new club. Well, the club's not new, but the management is."

I looked out the window again. "And it's where?"

"Almost there." She pulled out a compact and checked her reflection and patted her hair. Satisfied, she looked up and gave me a grin. "I'm going to buy you a drink when we get there. I had a meeting this afternoon with the execs and they are over the moon with you."

I relaxed a little. "I'm so glad it was successful."

She nodded. "Here we are."

I got out of the taxi and looked around. It was nothing like I expected. There was no music, no lights, no people. What we had pulled up to looked like a warehouse and there wasn't even a name posted out front. *What the hell kind of place is this?*

As we approached the building, the door opened and a massive bald guy stepped out.

Meagan trotted up to him. "Derek."

The bald guy nodded. "I'll take the coat."

"Thank you, Sir." She slipped out of her raincoat and I couldn't stop the gasp I made. Under the coat, Meagan wore only a tiny pair of underwear and a black leather corset.

The doorman gave a grunt of approval. "I'm working the front for another half hour, but I'll reserve us a room for later if you'd like." He glanced up at me. "Your friend can join us if she loses the dress."

"We'll see," Meagan replied. "And no, she can't."

"Meagan," I said, as understanding dawned. "What kind of club is this?"

"A BDSM club," she answered without so much as blinking. "What did you think it was?"

Now that we were closer, I heard the rhythmic thump, thump, thump of a bass inside the club—and it matched the thumping of my head. I spun around to face Meagan.

"What the hell?" I asked.

"What?"

"You're a sub?"

She lifted a perfectly shaped eyebrow. "Actually, I only sub for men. I top women."

Her matter-of-fact confirmation of being in the lifestyle didn't surprise me. I couldn't say the same for her role. "You're a switch?"

"I suppose. If you have to put a name to it."

"That's awesome. I don't know many switches." I wondered if she'd let me interview her sometime. "Let's get a drink."

"I can arrange that." She snapped her fingers at a scantily dressed waitress. "Michelle, bring my friend here a cosmopolitan."

The waitress bowed. "Yes, Mistress M."

I shook my head and looked around the club for the first time. It was dingy for lack of a better word and smelled like sharp arousal mixed with sweat. Everything was gray and had a general run-down look. Paint peeled off several walls and the concrete floor was stained. Red and blue strobe lights flashed in a corner serving as a dance floor. In the opposite corner, two men were setting up a demo.

Michelle returned with my drink and I finished it in four swallows. It burned going down my throat, but I found I rather enjoyed the sensation.

"Damn, Abby," Meagan said.

I motioned for Michelle to bring me another. "I'm celebrating."

"I wasn't being critical. I'll join you."

Michelle quickly returned with our drinks and we toasted the blog.

We didn't order anything else after the second drink. Not long after our glasses were cleared, the man from the door came by and asked Meagan to dance.

He lifted his eyebrow my way before taking off with her, but I shook my head. Nathaniel would be mad as hell if I danced with someone at a BDSM club. *Nathaniel.* Shit. I didn't want to think about what he'd have to say about Meagan's idea of "clubbing." I mean, he'd thought I'd gone out for an innocent night of dancing with my new boss. This was hardly the scene he'd expected either.

Nathaniel and I had been to a few clubs in the city before. We hadn't been to any since Henry was born, though. Looking around at the crowd made me want to plan a night out with him soon. I enjoyed being out in public as my Master's submissive. And I had really enjoyed the few times we'd played publicly.

The male couple in the corner had started their scene. In another time and place, I might have drifted closer to watch, but I really didn't feel like it. For some reason it didn't seem right without Nathaniel. I thought about calling him, but there was no point. I was already here. I turned back to the dance floor, but couldn't see Meagan or the guy she was dancing with.

Michelle walked by with a tray of drinks, so I flagged her down.

"Yes, ma'am."

"Have you seen the lady I came in with?" I asked, not wanting to use her real name and not comfortable calling my boss "Mistress M."

"Yes, ma'am. She went into one of the private rooms with Master V."

Well, wasn't that fantastic? She left me alone in a BDSM club where I knew no one and had no clue as to protocol. It really wasn't like her and she probably had a good reason, but I was slightly pissed. "Can you bring me another drink?" I asked.

The drinks must have been stronger than I thought, because when I hopped down from my stool midway through the third, the room swayed a bit. Or maybe it was me. I squinted at my watch. Meagan had been gone for over an hour. The male couple had finished some time ago and had left the demo corner empty. I watched as a group of people went down a hallway, probably to a private room.

During the time Meagan had been gone, several male Dominants had approached me. I'd turned them all down, of course. When Nathaniel and I went to a club together, I had to get his permission before talking to another Dom. Under the circumstances, however, I felt it acceptable. After all, I was turning them down.

Surely Meagan and her guy were finished now or at least in the middle of some aftercare. I'd just walk down the hallways to see if I could find them. I thought about calling a cab, but I didn't want to leave my new boss alone, even though it appeared she may have done that to me.

I wobbled a bit more than I expected. Maybe two drinks would be my limit in the future. I looked down the first hallway, but found only closed doors. I might not know this particular club's protocol, but I knew it would be frowned upon to open a closed door at any club.

Not ready to give up, I walked back to the main room and down a different hallway. This one boasted closed doors as well, but at the far end, the very last room had an open door. Doubtful that would be the room Meagan was in, but I didn't have anywhere else to look. I walked down the hall and poked my head inside.

"Hello, there, pretty," the man inside said. "Why don't you step inside for a minute?"

"No, thank you." I stepped in the middle of the doorway so I could see who I was talking to. "I was looking for someone, but she's not here."

The man in the room stood up. He was heavyset and didn't appear to have shaved for a day or two. He stepped close to me and I smelled the alcohol on his breath. I tried to back away, but he somehow managed to maneuver himself in a way that made me move to the side. When he stepped into my personal space again, I shifted and found myself inside the room.

"There we go," he said blocking the doorway. "Now I have you inside by your own free will."

My mind was still fuzzy about how I wound up inside, and I blurted out the first thing I could think of. "I'm drunk."

His smile was evil. "Nah, you're just relaxed. Works better that way, I think. Your body can take more."

My heart sped up. One flick of his wrist and I'd be locked inside with him. The fuzzy edges around my mind started to hum. "I actually want to leave now," I said.

"Why would you want to go? We haven't even started yet."

"Now. Move."

He leered at me. "I don't like the way you're looking at me, little sub." His hand moved to the doorknob. "I'm going to have to remind you how you're supposed to talk to your Top."

I swayed and shouted the one thing I could think of, "Red!"

"Bitch." The leer left his face and he went to close the door, but at the last second, a booted foot kept it from shutting.

"I heard someone safeword," the owner of the boot said, opening the door and looking inside. "Everything okay?"

We both answered at once.

"No."

"Yes."

The man at the door was tall and dark, and he wore a frown. He crossed his arms and looked from me to the other man. "What's going on?"

"Just a little disagreement with my sub."

"I am not your sub," I said, but it probably would have had more impact if it wasn't slurred when it came out.

"How much have you had to drink?" asked the stranger at the door.

"Three?"

He mumbled something under his breath that didn't sound like it should be repeated in front of ladies or children and glared at the man who'd claimed I was his sub. "She safeworded and even if she hadn't, she's not sober enough to consent."

The other guy wasn't going to back down. "Who are you?"

"I'm a guest who's here for the weekend. And from what I can tell, I won't be back." He turned back to me. "Are you alone or are you with someone?"

Before I could say anything, I was interrupted.

"She's with me," the man who had trapped me in the room said.

Moving faster than I would have thought possible for a man of his size, the dark guy shot his hand out and grabbed the other man by the throat. "She safeworded. You are no longer involved in this conversation. If you continue to act otherwise, I will call the police and file assault charges."

The guy nodded, which was quite an accomplishment considering how tightly the dark man was holding him.

"Let's go somewhere we can talk," the dark man said to me.

I hesitated, suddenly uneasy. He was acting like my savior now, but who could tell? I might be trading one nightmare for another. He pressed his lips together.

"Of course," he said. "You don't know me. Let's go into the main room."

That sounded safer. I nodded and we made our way down the hall. Once back in the main room, I collapsed on a couch, suddenly exhausted. I realized all at once just how drunk I was and how close I'd come to being assaulted. I burst into tears.

"Hell," dark man said. "It's okay. You're safe."

He looked around as if he didn't know what to do. He held out a hand, but then took it back. Finally, he grabbed a napkin from a nearby table and passed it to me.

I sobbed for a few more minutes and eventually calmed down to mere hiccups. "I . . . I . . . Thank you. The lady I came with left me and I was trying to find her. I. . . . I just want to go home."

"I think that'd be for the best. I'd call you a cab, but I don't think you should go by yourself." He ran a hand through his hair. "Is there someone I can call to pick you up?"

I thought about having him call Nathaniel, but decided it'd be better to deal with this myself. I shook my head.

"My name's Jeff Parks." He pulled out his wallet and handed me a card. "I'm a security expert and work very closely with the Wilmington, Delaware, Police Department. That's the number for the switchboard. Feel free to give them a call and ask about me. I can also provide you with the number of an attorney I've played with numerous times. It's as much of a reference as I can give on short notice."

I simply had no choice but to believe him.

He sensed my hesitation. "Ma'am, if I'd wanted to take advantage of you, I wouldn't be going through all this. I insist my subs be sober and provide consent." The corner of his lip quirked up. "Call me egotistical, but if you're going to be pleasantly sore and achy in the morning, I damn well want you to remember how you got that way."

I smiled for the first time in hours. "Will you call me a cab, Mr. Parks?"

"Yes, ma'am."

Shortly after the cab arrived and I gave the driver my address, my eyelids grew heavy. I resisted sleep, but the temptation to give in grew too great. My last sight before succumbing was of Jeff, looking out his side window.

"Hey," he said, what seemed like seconds later. "We're here."

Those two words filled me with dread because I knew Nathaniel would be pissed. My dread grew even greater when Jeff insisted on walking me to the door after paying the driver.

"You don't have to," I said. "My husband, uh, Master, is going to be upset enough as it is."

"Ah, so you *are* a sub?"

"Yes."

"If it were me and my sub was drunk, alone, and in the situation like you found yourself in, I'd be ready to pound someone into the ground."

"Yes, so you see why it's best if you leave now."

"No, that's even more reason for me to stay."

He had that Dom look that told me he wasn't going to change his mind. He was actually very dour-looking. I'd probably be scared if I wasn't so drunk. Fuck, I was so drunk. Nathaniel was going to kill me.

Nope, Mr. Parks wasn't going to change his mind. I knew his type. Hell, I'd married his type. I glanced down at his left hand. No ring.

"Do you have a sub right now?" I asked.

"No."

"You're not going to expand on that, are you?"

"No."

"A man of few words."

"Yes. And you're stalling."

We walked inside and I waved at the doorman. Together, Jeff and I rode up to the penthouse and I gave silent thanks the kids would be asleep when we arrived.

At our floor, I opened the door and stepped inside. I wondered where Nathaniel was.

I heard him before I saw him.

"Abby, you're back sooner than I expected." He walked into the foyer with a smile that disappeared when he saw Jeff. "Who's this?"

I waved at Jeff. "This is Jeff Dark. Dark man. Dark Dom."

He stepped closer. "Are you drunk?"

"Slightly." I held up two fingers. "I had three."

He glared at Jeff. "What the fuck is going on and who are you?"

Jeff held Nathaniel's gaze and simply crossed his arms across his chest. "A Dom who knows better than to let his sub go to a shady BDSM dive, get drunk off her ass, and have to be rescued from a would-be rapist who doesn't know the definition of a safe word."

"Excuse me?"

"You can ask her, but if it wasn't for me . . . Well, I don't like to guess, but the man she was with didn't take too kindly to her use of the word 'red.' "

The tops of Nathaniel's ears grew red. I'd never seen that before.

"Abby," he said, so calmly I felt cold. "What the fuck happened tonight?"

My words rushed out. "Meagan's a switch but didn't tell me and took me to a BDSM club and went off with a guy and I might have had too many drinks and when I went looking for her I got trapped with a guy and this guy got me away from him." My stomach rolled. "I think I'll vomit now."

I ran to the hall bathroom and when I returned, the men were shaking hands.

"Good to meet you, Jeff," Nathaniel said. "Glad I had a chance to meet you before our meeting on Monday, though I wish the circumstances were different."

"Likewise." Jeff lifted a hand in my direction. "Good night, Mrs. West."

" 'Night."

Jeff gave Nathaniel a curt nod and left. My heart beat wildly as Nathaniel turned to me. He didn't look angry anymore, though; he looked shaken and scared, a combination I'd never seen on him before. At the sight of it, all the night's events hit me at once and I crumpled into sobs again.

"Abby," he said, hastening to gather me in his arms. "It's okay. You're okay. I have you."

"That man . . ." I started, but couldn't get out any more.

"Come here." He lifted me up and carried me to the bedroom, all the while whispering to me. I clung to his shirt like it was a life vest. In that moment, it probably was.

"I'm going to take your dress off," he said once he set me on the bed. "Are you okay with that or do you want to do it?"

"You do it." The man at the club hadn't touched me, but I needed Nathaniel's hands on me to help erase his memory.

He turned to get my cotton nightshirt out of a dresser drawer. He picked my light blue one, my favorite because the material was so soft. Ever so gently, he helped me to stand and unzipped my dress. His fingers didn't linger like they normally would have, but were quick and efficient.

In no time, he was pulling the sheets back so I could crawl into bed. It took him only seconds to step out of his own clothes and join me. I don't think I'd relaxed entirely from the minute I stepped into the club until Nathaniel pulled me to his side in bed.

"I'm sorry," I whispered. "I should have called you the minute I realized what type of club it was, or at least when Meagan left me."

"I'm going to call her tomorrow and speak with her about this. As one Dominant to another. I know she's your boss, but what she did crossed a line. You're *my* submissive."

I hiccuped and gave him a nod. I understood why he needed to talk to Meagan even though I didn't necessarily like it.

He stroked my hair. "We'll talk about it later. Right now I just want to hold you." His voice cracked at the end and I knew he needed to hold me as much as I needed him to.

I curled up into him as close as I could. "I was so scared." It was all I could say before I started crying again. He murmured soothing words I couldn't make out and simply held me until I couldn't cry anymore.

By then, we were both exhausted and fell into an uneasy sleep.

When I woke again, it was morning. Or early afternoon. And I was alone. The curtains were closed so no light came through the windows. Good for sleeping, but not useful in gauging time. I rolled to my side and checked the clock. Ten thirty! I couldn't remember the last time I'd slept so late.

On my nightstand were a bottle of water and two pain relievers. I swallowed them greedily. My head hurt like a bitch when I moved. I stretched out in bed and willed my brain to stop throbbing.

I finally gave up and decided to get up. While making the bed, I suddenly realized how quiet everything was. The penthouse was smaller than the estate house; some noise should have been present. Two young kids were bound to make some sort of ruckus. I stepped into the hallway to see if I could hear anything. That's when I overheard Nathaniel on the phone.

"I don't want to hear any excuses," I could hear him saying. "It's simply unacceptable behavior for someone claiming to be a Top." He paused. "It doesn't matter that she wasn't acting as your submissive at the time. She was in your care. How would you feel if I left one of your bottoms at an unknown club, when I knew she'd been drinking?"

He surely got that phone call out of the way early. I needed to talk to her as well, but I'd wait until evening.

"I'm glad you see my point," he said. "I'm not going to claim I've been the perfect Dominant, but I've become a better one because I was called out on behavior that was wrong."

I crept back into the bedroom to shower and change. Whatever conversation he was having with Meagan was between the two of them. Besides, my head hurt too much to think about it for too long.

I stood under the shower for a long time. The warm water felt good and washed away the last of the grime I felt from the night before. It was as if I stepped out of the shower a different person than I had been when I entered.

My stomach started rumbling while I dried off and I hurried along so I could grab something to eat and check on the kids. I knew they were fine with Nathaniel, but I needed to see them. I pulled on a robe and stepped into the bedroom to find Nathaniel peeking his head in.

"I heard the shower," he said. "How are you?"

"Better after my shower."

"Is Mommy awake?" Elizabeth squeezed past her father. "Mommy, you're up. Daddy said we had to be quiet because you were sleeping. Are you sick? Are you better now?"

I pulled her into a hug. "I wasn't feeling good, but I'm better now. Especially since I've had a hug from you."

She beamed at me. "I fixed you oatmeal. Daddy helped."

"Sounds great," I said. "Where's your brother?"

"Here he is," Nathaniel said, holding the door open for a toddling Henry.

"Mamma!" he called and then ran as quickly as his stubby legs could go, laughing as I swung him up in my arms.

"Did you help with the oatmeal, too?" I asked, smelling his hair to drink in his clean little boy scent and wrinkling my nose instead at the scent that met me.

"No," Elizabeth said. "But Daddy let him throw the trash away."

"Trash can's his new favorite toy," Nathaniel explained.

"That explains the smell." I passed him to Nathaniel. "He needs a bath."

"Linda will be here in about fifteen minutes. She's going to keep them until tomorrow night."

Had he made the arrangement with his aunt because he didn't want them around for what he had in mind? The penthouse didn't have a playroom. Before me, he'd never brought a woman to this space and we had never seen the need to add a special room. He'd always brought a toy bag with him when we stayed in the city.

I was more subdued as we all walked to the kitchen. Elizabeth chatted about the tea party she'd had last night and how Henry wanted to eat all the cookies. Of course at the word "cookie," Henry pulled on Nathaniel's leg and said, "Please."

"Not so early in the day," Nathaniel replied.

They all sat at the table with me while I ate and Nathaniel made sure I drank plenty of water. Even though he had been easygoing and lighthearted, there was an underlying tension between us. Faint, but there nonetheless. I might feel better physically after last night, but mentally there were still issues we had to deal with.

Nathaniel felt it too, I could tell. He was jovial and playful with the kids, but the tension in his jaw and the rigidity of his spine belied the front he put on. It was still noticeable when Linda came by. She didn't question anything, but gave us each a quick hug before gathering the kids and heading out.

The silence that hit me when the door closed behind them was louder than the kids had been.

Nathaniel brushed my cheek. "Come to my office in ten minutes. You can leave the robe on if you prefer."

What followed had to be the longest ten minutes of my life. After he left, I cleaned my bowl and tidied up the kitchen. With two minutes remaining, I slipped out of the robe and walked to his office wearing only my panties and a bra.

He stood leaning against his desk and nodded to the floor in the middle of the room. Everything felt so cold as I slid to my knees, bowed my head, and waited.

And waited.

And waited.

His office floor was made of wood and it didn't take long for my knees to start aching. Within minutes, they hurt as much as my head. All of which he knew, I was certain.

"Look at me," he finally said and I lifted my eyes to meet his troubled ones. "What happened last night scared the hell out of me. I can't imagine how it made you feel. You went through something I never wanted you to experience and though neither one of us probably want to, we have to discuss it." He nodded toward the chair across from his desk. "Go sit down."

He remained standing, watching as I crossed the room to do his bidding.

"Even without your collar on, are you still my submissive?" he asked when I'd sat down.

"Yes, Sir." I wasn't wearing his collar, so I didn't have to call him anything. Yet, somehow doing so seemed appropriate.

"When we go to a BDSM club together, who protects you?"

"You, Sir."

"And how am I to protect you when I'm not there?"

"You can't, Sir."

"Exactly. Outside of the fact that you are mine and any Dominant wanting to interact with you has to obtain my permission, you are truly my only treasure, my beloved, my life. I would kill to keep you safe and I can't do it if I'm not with you."

Tears stung my eyes.

"If it hadn't been for Jeff last night, you would have been assaulted. That man would have put his hands on you, hurt you, and done things I have nightmares about. And the entire time it was happening, I couldn't stop him because I wouldn't have known to."

I sniffled. "I'm sorry, Sir. I understand I should have called."

"You were wrapped up in yourself and didn't think about the consequences your actions could have had."

"Yes, Sir. I see that."

He sighed. "I'm torn on what to do. I should cane you for going to a club without my permission. You know better. I understand that you didn't know that woman was bringing you there. But let's make one thing clear to start: You are not to interact with any Dom inside a club without getting my approval. You know this."

I started trembling at the mention of a cane. I fucking hated those things when used for punishment. And he was right. I had known better.

"But you were nearly assaulted and I can't find it within me to punish you corporally after such an incident."

I waited for what seemed like hours. Based on past experiences, the tension between us wouldn't go away until my actions had been dealt with. Our lives were governed by rules that were not followed by the world at large. They were there because it was what we needed. It didn't mean they were always pleasant.

"Go stand and face the wall," he finally said.

I swallowed a groan before he heard it. I hated standing against a wall. He'd had me do it only a handful of times before. But in looking over my options, I reminded myself it was better than the cane.

I rose to my feet before he could accuse me of stalling and walked to the back wall opposite his desk. It was possible he'd want to sit and observe me while I stood. On the way, I made certain not to look his way. He'd probably be standing with arms crossed, or wearing that cool, distant look. Probably both.

I stood an inch from the wall with my hands by my side. Too late, I realized the spot I'd picked was under an air vent blowing cool air. Or maybe he'd known I'd pick that spot and that's why he chose to have me join him here instead of in the living room. Who could ever tell with him?

The cool air danced along my exposed back, instantly making my skin pebble with gooseflesh. I wouldn't get too cold, but it certainly wouldn't be comfortable.

"You are to stand as still as possible," he said. "And because you'll probably be tempted to think only about how cold you are, I want you to think about how I felt when you walked into our house with a strange man. Then I want you to imagine how scared I was when I realized the danger you'd been in."

If I knew him at all, once he allowed me to move, he'd ask me to write down the thoughts I'd had while I stood. Anytime before when I'd stood against a wall, he'd tell me how long he was going to have me stand.

"I haven't decided how long you'll be there," he said as if reading my mind. "Time begins now," he said.

At first it was difficult to think about anything other than the discomfort of the air temperature. But I focused on his warning and forced my mind to imagine his thoughts last night.

As I stood there, the image that kept coming to my mind was a picture of him arriving home with a strange woman after I knew he'd been out partying. The impact of that image gutted me. Just thinking about it, even knowing it was only make-believe, hurt. How in the world must he have felt last night not knowing what was going on?

Then I made myself explore the idea of how it would feel to know he was in danger and be unable do anything about it. The terror of knowing everything was fine would be only marginally lessened when the potential outcomes were considered. And those feelings would be only intensified with him. As a Dominant, it was part of who he was to be a protector.

Then, to add insult to injury, I'd been drunk. That was another circumstance that was completely within my control. No one forced me to drink; I'd made the choice to continue.

When I combined all those things together and looked at them objectively, I began to see outside of my perspective and understood his wrath and fear. And I hated the way my actions made him feel. One of my greatest joys was serving him: anticipating his needs and meeting them. Last night, even though it had not been my intention, I'd failed miserably. The problem was, I'd been distracted by the thrill of my new job and had let myself forget I was first and foremost his sub.

Just as I had that heart-wrenching thought, I felt the surprising touch of his warm thumb wiping away tears I didn't know were falling.

"Why the tears, my lovely?" he asked. His voice was gentler than before.

"I've realized how much pain I caused you last night." I blinked away the wetness still gathering in the corners of my eyes. "And I know what I've imagined in no way comes close to what you actually felt, because you had to live it."

He brushed the other cheek. "I would give up all I have to keep you safe."

I nodded, unable to formulate words that could convey the true depth of just how sorry I was.

"Look at me," he said, cupping my chin in the palm of his hand. When I met his eyes, he continued. "You're going to write lines."

"Yes, Sir."

"Two hundred times: 'I will not drink irresponsibly and I will not go to a club without being in the presence of my Master.'"

I hated writing lines. It was humiliating because it made me feel like a ten-year-old. And the tediousness of it, the same one line two hundred times? But the reality was it sounded reasonable and he was really letting me off rather easy. The encounter I had must have really thrown him. "Yes, Sir."

"I couldn't bear it if anything happened to you. Don't do that again."

"I won't, Sir." But I realized this didn't feel right. I had really wronged him, and I needed to feel harsher consequences to be able to feel right with him again. "But, please, will you use the cane?"

His lips parted in surprise. "What?"

"I won't feel like this is behind us if I just write lines. I *need* you to cane me. My offense was too serious for less." Part of me was thinking I was certifiable to be begging for this, but deep inside I knew only that would let me move past last night. And I thought he probably would feel the same if he could get past his fear and upset.

"You know you don't have to do this?" he asked.

I nodded. "I want to. I need it."

He studied me for a time before finally agreeing. "Three strokes of the cane."

"Thank you, Sir."

"If I'm going to cane you, you're to address me as Master."

I smiled despite the somber situation. "Yes, Master." I freely took his love and support and, at times like this, took his pain. I knew from experience when it came to pain, feeling the physical would ease the emotional.

"Underwear down to your ankles and hands against the wall."

I slid my panties down, baring myself in offering to him. Filling my lungs deeply, I put my hands on either side of my head. He'd had me stand like this the previous time he'd punished me with a cane. Sensual scenes were done lying down.

"These will be hard and fast," he warned. "Neither one of us will enjoy this."

"Thank you, Master." I was glad he would go fast; at least that way it'd be over sooner.

He didn't reply, but took a step back. I braced myself, trying not to tense up even when I heard the thin reed whistle through the air. The first one landed on the fleshy part of my butt and I gasped at the bite it left. The second landed directly under it and I hadn't caught my breath before the last and hardest fell under the second.

I choked back a sob.

"Hold position," he said and I concentrated on not moving a muscle. His words were the only thing that could persuade me to do so. Without his command, I'd have reached behind me in an attempt to ease some of the ache left by the cane. I'd learned, though, that just as his role was to enforce our rules, so it was his role to ensure we made our way back together afterward.

From behind me came the sound of movement, and within seconds he was at my side. His hands stroked leisurely, applying lotion across my skin. He didn't say anything, but I felt his emotions in his touch. If taking pain from him eased my own, then accepting his tender massage allowed me to let everything go.

"Turn around," he whispered.

Without hesitation, I turned. He put his hands on my shoulders and ran his hands down my sides. My body relaxed under his touch and he recognized the second it'd done so. His lips started at my cheek and inched their way down my neck. He cupped my breast and unclasped my bra. He bent low and eased my panties all the way down and off my legs.

"Come with me," he said, holding out his hand. I took it and we walked to our bedroom. Once there, he had me climb into bed while he undressed.

He slipped his shirt over his head. "I need you." His pants joined the shirt on the floor and he crawled up on the bed facing me. "I need to show you what you mean to me."

He took me in his arms and our joining was sensual and slow. His fingertips danced along my body, touching me everywhere, claiming every part of me. I was content to simply let my hands roam over whatever part of him was close.

His lips were soft as he tasted my skin and I sighed against him. But even though he was gentle, there was no weakness to be found. Every caress, every brush of his flesh across mine whispered one truth.

You are mine.

And my own confessed in return.

Yes. Always.

Later that afternoon, I was in the middle of writing my lines at the desk we had in the bedroom when Nathaniel popped his head in.

"Meagan's here to see you," he said.

My stomach fell to my ankles. I knew we had to talk, but did it have to be so soon?

"You spoke to her this morning," I said.

"Yes," he stated. "She's waiting in the living room."

I put my writing down and followed him. Instead of sitting on the couch, we found her pacing in front of the window. She turned when we entered, but didn't say anything. She looked horrible, her complexion paler than normal and her forehead creased with worry.

"I'm going to go for a walk," Nathaniel said. "To give you two some privacy."

She waited until the door closed behind him to speak. "Abby. I am so sorry."

The easy thing would have been to tell her it was okay and that everything was fine, but it wasn't okay and everything wasn't fine.

"That was a rotten thing to do last night," I told her. "I was in a place I didn't know, drinking, and I had no idea where you were."

"It was completely irresponsible of me and there's no excuse for it."

I crossed my arms. "At least tell me why."

She waved toward the couches and we sat down. She on one side and I on the other. "I only planned to dance, honestly. I had no intention of playing last night. After we had danced a few songs, I went to the bathroom. When I came out, Master V said he'd told you that we were going to a private room. I should have talked to you anyway. I should have. But it'd been . . ." She shook her head. "There's no excuse. There's not. And your husband was right to call me on it."

My heart softened just a bit. Her voice shook and she certainly looked distraught.

"I can't say I'm happy he called you," I said. "But I understand why he did it."

She didn't speak for long seconds. Almost as if she was weighing what she'd say next. "Abby," she finally said, "I totally understand if you don't want anything to do with me, but please don't let last night interfere with your work at the station. I'll step aside and let someone else work with you."

I sighed. I wasn't sure if she was just saying that because she didn't want to get in trouble or if she really cared. "I'll be honest. I'm not happy with what happened last night, but I won't let it affect my job. And I don't want you to step aside, but it's going to take some time for us to get back to where we were."

For the first time since I'd seen her that day, she looked somewhat hopeful. "Thank you, Abby. I'll make it up to you.".

Chapter Seven

The next few weeks were crazy. Henry's ear infection didn't get any better, so no one was sleeping and I had to spend an entire day in New York taking him to a specialist. Nathaniel was trying to find someone to take over the running and management of his melanoma nonprofit and that required late nights in the city. One weekend, he actually had meetings on Saturday, so the kids, Apollo, and I stayed at the penthouse so we could spend time with him. Fortunately, Jeff had been able to get his security issues taken care of, so at least that was one less thing he had to worry about.

Evenings after the kids went to bed weren't any better. I spent a lot of time online chatting with Meagan and working on my first few pieces. I had parts of about four potential blog postings and I stressed over them more than I should have. But the way I saw it, this was my introduction to a large number of people and I needed to write something that represented the best of me.

Three weeks after the incident, I'd just turned the computer off for the night when Nathaniel entered the library. He'd been swimming and his hair hadn't dried yet, but he'd changed out of his swim trunks into his tan drawstring pants. After his laps in the pool, he must have been down to the wine cellar, because he had two wineglasses and a bottle of my favorite red.

"Finished?" he asked. He held out a glass and lifted an eyebrow. At my nod, he handed one to me and filled the glass.

"Thanks." I took a sip. "Mmm, that's good. Not quite finished, but I'm closer than I was."

He tilted his head toward the couch and we sat down together. He twisted in his seat, facing me better. "I have a conference next month."

"I remember you mentioning it. Innovations in Finance and Banking. Delaware, right?" It didn't sound interesting to me, but they had invited Nathaniel to be one of the speakers.

"Yes, and I'd like for you to go with me." He dropped his voice. "As my submissive."

"How long did you say it was?" I asked, my brain already running through everything that would need to be taken care of: the kids, Apollo, and, now that I was working, what to do about the posts that would be due.

"A week." He placed his wineglass on the table beside the couch. "And I want you to wear my collar the entire time."

"A week?" I asked, confused. Where had that come from?

"Yes."

"But I thought . . . Wouldn't you . . . Shouldn't we?" I had so many random thoughts and questions, I couldn't focus on one long enough to voice it. Why did he want to play for a week? Why bring it up now?

"Let me reassure you, I have no interest in you being a twenty-four/seven submissive. But"—he shrugged—"the idea of you wearing my collar for a week, out of town? It holds a certain appeal."

Years ago, on our first visit to Paul and Christine's, I'd mentioned to him I'd like to wear his collar for a week. He'd said then that while he wasn't opposed to the idea, he felt our relationship was too new for that kind of extended play. Looking back, it had been the right decision. At that time, I hadn't yet reached the point where I felt I could tell him *everything*.

Now, though, I had no such problem and he was better at communication, too.

"We never have gone for a week, have we?" I asked. He'd told me when I first brought it up that we'd revisit the idea of week-long play once he believed our communication to be open enough.

"No, we haven't. I'm bringing it up now because I think time away from our normal routine is exactly what we need."

The idea of wearing his collar for a week still held an appeal for me, though it was in a general, vague sort of way. Knowing it could easily become a reality made my pulse quicken.

"I confess, I'm a little apprehensive about it." I took a sip of my wine. "I'm concerned on how I'll handle it. My knees are out of practice and I'm used to telling you exactly how I feel anytime I want."

"Look, Abby, I have to be honest and ask, how's not wearing my collar most of the time working out for you?" He traced my knee. "Because I have to confess, it's not working that great for me. I can't continue to push that side of me away."

That's what we had been doing, I realized. We'd been pushing those needs aside. Maybe not intentionally, but there was always so much to do and we both felt the children came first. But that was a dangerous path to walk, to never take care of our own needs.

And I allowed myself to admit, I missed wearing his collar. And the more I thought about it, the more and more wearing it for a week sounded good.

"I don't want to push our needs aside all the time, either," I said. "Let's do it. I'll wear your collar for a week in Delaware."

I spoke to Linda the next day and explained Nathaniel had a conference and wanted me to go with him.

"To be honest," I told her, "I can't remember the last time we went away. Just the two of us."

"I understand, Abby. I remember vividly how crazy and tiring it is with little ones."

I loved Linda. Though no one could ever replace my mother, Linda always treated me as if I was one of her own. "Do you think you can keep the kids while we're in Delaware?"

"It won't be a problem. Matter of fact, if you like, I can just stay at your estate. That way it'll be easier on them and Apollo," Linda said, proving again I had the world's best in-laws.

Note to self: Make sure Nathaniel locks the playroom and hides the key. "That would be wonderful. Thank you."

"It'll be a joy to keep them. Though I always thought your first trip away together after Henry's birth would be to your chalet. Not Delaware."

I laughed. I couldn't help but smile at the mention of the wedding present Nathaniel had given me. We hadn't been to our honeymoon chalet in Switzerland since Henry was born. I wasn't quite ready for my children to be in a country different from the one I was in.

"We do need to visit there," I said, looking out the window. Maybe in the fall we could take a long weekend and go. We hadn't traveled much since Henry had been born.

"Either way, just know I'm here if you need me."

I thanked her again and we said our good-byes and hung up. I couldn't wait to tell Nathaniel everything was taken care of. My body shook with anticipation at the thought of wearing his collar for such a long time.

Just the time we'd recently had together had been incredible; my body might not be able to physically handle the pleasure he'd have planned for a week.

"That's certainly an interesting expression on your face." Nathaniel's voice brought me back to the present and I spun around to greet him. He'd told me he'd be leaving the office and city early today, because we had a birthday party later in the afternoon for Maddox, Todd and Elaina's son.

He walked toward me with a sultry grin and kissed me softly. "Anything in particular you were thinking about?"

"I was thinking about how I was looking forward to wearing your collar for a week." My knees weakened at the lustful look in his eyes following my statement. I picked imaginary lint off his shirt. "Especially since Linda just agreed to watch the kids while we're at your conference."

"You asked her?"

"Mmm." I nodded. "The more I thought about going with you, the more I liked the sound of it, so I figured why not go ahead and do something about it?"

He groaned. "Normally, I'd tell you to leave the details like that to me, but right now I'm just excited that you're interested in it."

I rose to my toes and whispered, "That's not all I was thinking."

"Don't let me stop you from telling."

I dropped my hands to his waistband and ran my fingers along the smooth leather of his belt. "I was also thinking how I obviously never earned this the weekend Simon and Lynne came over. I hope I do better in Delaware."

He groaned and glanced around the living room. "Where are the kids?"

"Nap."

"At the same time?"

I understood his surprise; it didn't happen very often. I leaned in close and ran my tongue along his ear. "I'm that good."

His hold on my hips tightened. "Fuck, Abby. How long?"

"They should be down for another twenty minutes."

"Excellent, but twenty minutes isn't enough time for me to properly work you over with the belt." He rocked his hips against me. "Are you pouting? How about I put that pouty mouth to better use. I want to feel it around my cock. Do it and I'll reward you now and seriously consider bringing a belt to Delaware."

"What if—"

He held a finger to my lips. "Stop talking and get on your knees. Right now the only thing you need to be thinking about is my cock and how it belongs in your mouth."

I dropped to the floor and hurriedly shed him of his pants and boxers. Usually, I'd tease him by running my tongue around his length, but I wanted to keep him guessing, so I engulfed him all at once. He hit the back of my throat and I relaxed and took him all the way in.

"Fuck!" He grabbed fistfuls of my hair.

I started bobbing on him, sucking as he withdrew and then allowing him access to go as deep as he wanted. I alternated short shallow moves with long ones because I knew it'd drive him crazy. His breathing came in pants and I smiled around his cock, knowing he couldn't hold out much longer.

With a yell, he pulled out and dragged me to my feet.

He'd never done that before. Had I done something wrong? "What?"

He pushed me backward until I hit the living room wall. "What's the only thing you're to be thinking about?"

My knees wobbled and my arousal increased exponentially. Damn, I loved it when he was rough. "Your cock."

"Right." He took a step back and fisted his erection. "And right now it wants to fuck your pussy. Undress from the waist down. Quickly."

My fingers trembled as I hurried to unbutton my pants. I gave a shake of my leg to remove them completely and stumbled. Nathaniel's sure hands caught me and held me steady.

"Careful now. A trip to the ER wasn't how I saw this ending." I shook my head. "It's okay. I'm good now."

"Oh, Abby." He pushed me against the wall and hooked my right leg around his waist. "You're more than good." He slowly pressed his cock inside me. "You're fucking fantastic."

"Just wait until Delaware," I teased. "You haven't seen anything yet."

"No, my lovely." He pushed his hips and moved so deep within me I clawed at his back. "*You* haven't seen anything yet."

I decided to push him a bit. After all, I didn't want to become predictable. "Really? You have new moves or are you going to be using the same ones you always do?"

"Are you seriously questioning my moves?" He rotated his pelvis against me and I moaned at the sensation of how he felt inside me. "I think you are. You want me to show you moves?"

"I just questioned if you had any new ones, Sir. A verbal reply is fine—you don't have to show me."

"Like hell." He pulled out of me and spun me to face the wall. Grabbing my hands and pinning them above my head, he growled out, "Keep them here. Move an inch and I redden your ass and not in the way you enjoy. Understand?"

"Yes, Sir." My heart pounded wildly. *Fuck.* I loved it when he took control of me like that. He roughly kicked my feet apart, so I had to bend at the waist.

He pressed against me, his cock teasing my entrance. The clock in the hallway chimed. Nap time was almost over.

"The kids will be up soon," I warned.

"They'll be fine. I'm so hard, this won't take long."

With that, he pushed into me and thrust so deep, I had to bite the inside of my cheek so I wouldn't cry out. His hands came over mine as he withdrew and entered again.

"Love fucking you against a wall," he panted. "I get so deep. You feel so good."

He could keep it up for hours, too, while keeping me on the edge. It wasn't impossible for me to come without it, but by holding my hands against the wall, there was no way for me to touch my clit.

I wiggled my hips, but his only response was to thrust harder. He rocked against me, pushing my lower body forward. I whimpered. I was so close, but unable to reach it without my hands.

"Please," I begged.

"I know what you want," he said. "I'm just not ready to give it to you yet. Enjoying this too much."

"I need," I panted.

"You don't need. You want." He picked up his pace. "There's a difference."

"So close."

"I know." He went faster and harder. "I know."

I kept quiet then. Sometimes begging worked. This wasn't one of those times. I closed my eyes and lost myself in the feel of him, the strength, the drive, and the power. If he just touched me, I'd come so fast. But his hands remained where they were.

His hips shifted and he hit a different spot within me, making my eyes widen in surprise. "Oh my God!"

"Come," he said with a hint of smugness.

Though it happened for me so rarely I thought it nearly impossible, with one more thrust inside me he made me come simply by being inside me. I shuddered around him, my climax sending tremors through my body.

"Shit," I managed to mumble. "How'd you do that?"

He didn't say anything, but stiffened behind me as he reached his own release. He was still breathing heavy when he withdrew and pressed a kiss to my back. "Just wanted to show you my moves."

"I'm thinking about calling Linda back," I said.

"Oh?" He took my hands and I stood up.

"I may not survive a week in your collar."

"Incoming!" Jackson picked up one of his three-year-old twin sons and flew him like an airplane around the living room. The child he held airborne was either Levi or Luis. From my angle on the couch it was difficult to see the tiny birthmark above Levi's eyebrow that made it possible to differentiate the two identical twins.

Felicia sat on the couch across from me. Her feet were propped on a stool and she rubbed her pregnant belly. "I'd tell him to watch out because he'll break something, but he won't listen to me when the boys want to play airplane."

The other twin stood in the doorway, bouncing up and down. "My turn! My turn! My turn, Daddy!"

Jackson swept across the room again, making a *whoosh* sound as he turned the corner where Elizabeth and Lucy, their five-year-old daughter, sat playing with dolls.

"That's dangerous, Uncle Jack," Elizabeth said. "If you drop him, he might break his clapacal."

"Clavicle," said Maddox. He was approaching ten, in a bad position, really, being too old to play with the other children but too young to be interested in the adults' conversation. He sat in a chair by himself, reading a book.

"That's what I said," Elizabeth explained patiently before turning her attention to Lucy. "Did you bring a bathing suit? Want to go swim? Mommy?"

I shook my head. "Too late tonight. We haven't had dinner yet and you have school tomorrow." Granted it was preschool, but bedtime was bedtime and we tried to keep it consistent. "We'll have everyone over soon for a swim date."

Laughter floated down the stairs, making it to the living room before Nathaniel and Todd. The two men entered, smiling. Nathaniel walked over to me and ran his arm along my shoulder before sitting down and talking to Maddox about what he was reading.

Elaina returned from where she'd been in the bathroom and sat beside Felicia. Though they'd tried repeatedly, she and Todd hadn't been able to conceive since Maddox was born. They'd looked into adoption, but nothing had worked out.

I turned my attention to Nathaniel. Maddox was explaining something in the book. It sounded like a fantasy novel. Nathaniel must have read it or heard of it because Maddox became very animated over whatever it was he said.

A timer went off in the kitchen and since Linda was changing Henry, I motioned to Elaina and we went in together to take care of it. I took the roast out of the oven while Elaina grabbed the plates and silverware.

"This smells so good," I said, putting it down to cool. "Want me to help you set the table?"

"That would be great."

Linda's dining room had changed over the years, the biggest addition being the small kiddie table she added for guests like the ones she had tonight. Sometimes the kids ate at the table with the adults, but they seemed to enjoy their own space, so tonight we were going to let them eat by themselves. Except for Maddox, who had insisted he was too old to eat at the kiddie table.

"We heard from the adoption agency," Elaina whispered, looking over her shoulder.

"Oh?" I tried to be nonchalant, but I knew how important this was to them.

Her face broke out into a huge grin. "We're picking our son up tomorrow."

I dropped the silver and she scooped it up. "Really?" I choked out.

"Yes, but we're not telling anyone until it's a done deal. You never know. I had to tell someone though. It's eating me trying to keep it a secret."

"I thought you and Todd looked different tonight."

She nodded and placed the silver around the table at each setting. "It's been a rough time. Infertility and then nothing with the adoption for so long. I feel like everything should happen right now, when I want it, and I'm learning patience is hard."

I started putting out the napkins. "I understand. It's tough when things happen you don't have control over and can't make fit your timetable."

"Sounds like you're speaking from experience."

"The things we appreciate the most are the things we have to work for. Wait for. If it's handed to us, we don't value it as much."

She cocked her head to the side. "Are you sure you aren't a psychologist?"

We laughed while we finished setting the table and then

called everyone in to grab a plate and get their food. As everyone sat, my advice to Elaina repeated in my head. It made sense, what I'd told her. Looking across the table to where Nathaniel sat, laughing and joking with Jackson, I was reminded that our own journey hadn't been the easiest, but I liked to think we valued what we had as a result.

He looked up and caught me staring. "I love you," he mouthed to me.

"Always," I replied.

Chapter Eight

A few weeks later, we were in our private jet on our way to Wilmington, Delaware. I'd felt off the entire week before. The day we left, I knew I'd been a bit of a brat. Probably because of the week ahead of us. I wanted to try wearing Nathaniel's collar for this extended period of time, but I was apprehensive as well. Plus, we'd be leaving the kids for longer than we ever had before.

I drummed my fingers in a disjointed staccato on the armrest. My legs were crossed and I swung my foot in time with the tap-tap-tap of my nails. Nathaniel reached out and put his hand over mine.

"Stop, please," he said.

I stopped my fingers, but my leg kept swinging. "I don't know why we're taking the jet. Wilmington isn't that far away—we could have driven."

He raised an eyebrow. "We're taking the jet because I want to."

I snapped my hand out from under his and buckled my seat belt. It was a petty thing to do, but I couldn't help it.

"It's not going to be easy," he said. "We've never played this long before and that alone will stretch us. But I want you to know, I do plan to push you as well. It's okay to be anxious."

I closed my eyes and leaned my head back against the seat. "I'll be fine. It's not like I've never been anxious before. I'll work through it."

But I knew it was more than anxiety; I just didn't say that to Nathaniel. But it was also him. He was different lately and it confused me as much as it turned me on. I couldn't give specific examples, but it was there and it made me uneasy.

"Just as well you get the attitude and snark out of the way before I collar you," he said. "Because I'm not going to put up with it once I do."

I turned my head to look at him. He was leaning back in his seat and though his body was relaxed, I sensed an underlying tension in him.

"Don't even think about arguing," he spoke before I could utter any disagreement. "You've been goading me for the last few days. I've already decided you'll be on the floor the first night. Keep it up and you won't sleep in my bed all week."

My mouth fell open. "You can't punish me for what I do when I'm not wearing your collar."

"Oh, you're very mistaken. I can do anything I want. And I never said it was a punishment. I simply stated a fact."

I wanted to say more, but didn't. I couldn't remember the last time I slept on the floor; surely he had a good reason for insisting I do it tonight. Just like this week. Even though it was something I wanted, he'd specifically said it wasn't working out for him the way things were. Perhaps this was his way to show me how things could work. Or maybe he was seeing if he liked it better with me in his collar more frequently.

I glanced out the window. We'd almost reached our cruising altitude. It would be a ridiculously short trip.

Beside me, Nathaniel unbuckled his seat belt and stood up. I glanced out of the corner of my eye and saw he had my platinum and diamond collar with him. I had another one made of leather but I remembered he'd said something about a cocktail reception tonight, so it made sense he'd pick the platinum one for today.

"If you're ready, Abigail," he said just a few steps beyond my chair. "Come kneel and show your desire to wear my collar."

He'd instructed me earlier to wear a dress with no hose or panties, and when I stood up, I felt cool air brush against my skin. The hem came only to my knees, so I knelt down carefully before him. As always, when I got into position to serve him, I felt restful and at peace.

I relaxed with a deep sigh as he slipped the collar into place and fastened it with a softly spoken, "Thank you, Abigail."

I looked up at him to see if he made any sort of movement that indicated he wanted to use my mouth.

"Not right now." He ran his fingers through my hair. "The pilot said there was a possibility of running into turbulence and I'd prefer not to have my dick in your mouth if that happens."

I couldn't help it—I laughed at the visual. "Ouch."

He smiled. "Come back over this way. I have something for you to do."

He pulled a large pillow from the cabinets beside my chair and placed it on the floor. "I want you to sit and write in your journal. I'd like for you to spend twenty minutes writing down your goals for the week."

He'd told me yesterday to have my journal with me and accessible during the flight, so his assignment didn't come as a surprise. I was thrown a little off guard by the fact he wanted me to sit on the floor and write.

Looking at it as a way to prepare myself for a pallet bed that awaited me that night, I settled myself near his feet and started writing. He appeared to be reading papers. If I had to guess, he was going over his notes for the meeting he had the following day. He'd already gone over them a million times, but Nathaniel was Nathaniel.

I pulled out my tote bag to get my water bottle, but remembered I'd left it sitting on the kitchen countertop. Not a problem, the jet had a refrigerator.

"Is something wrong?" Nathaniel put a hand on my shoulder when I started to get up.

"Just wanted to get some water. I left mine at the house."

"Sit back down." He buzzed for the flight attendant and I debated hopping up into my seat. Nathaniel kept his hand firmly on my shoulder, though. He must have anticipated my thoughts again.

"Yes, sir?" Margaret, the attendant, asked, stepping into the main cabin. I couldn't look at her. I pretended to be invisible.

"Mrs. West would like some water. Please bring me a bottle."

She stepped away to get it and I straightened my shoulders and steeled my spine. Why did I want water? I should have kept writing.

Margaret returned quickly and held the bottle out to me.

Nathaniel grabbed it. "I said bring *me* a bottle."

I looked her way quickly, just to see how or if she reacted, but she appeared unruffled. "Sorry, sir."

She turned and left. Completely unreadable. I supposed that was probably a good personality trait to have with her job.

Nathaniel shifted me so I leaned against his legs and pressed the bottle to my lips. I was more thirsty than I thought and I drank almost half of the bottle. In the back of my mind, though, I kept looking for Margaret to come back in.

"Tell me what's on your mind." Nathaniel stroked my cheek. He probably had a fairly good idea what was on my mind, but might think I wouldn't tell him since I had his collar on. Which wasn't the whole truth. I just didn't feel like talking about it. Because he asked though, I'd tell him.

"I wasn't expecting you to keep me on the floor while Margaret waited on us," I said.

"Did it bother you?"

"I don't know if *bother* is the right word. It's just now she knows."

He traced the line of my collar. "She's been an employee for eight years. I imagine she knows about most of what happens on our plane."

"But we've never been so blatant and in her face."

"Technically, all she saw was you sitting near your husband with his hand on your shoulder. Now, if I'd been fucking you over the armrest? That would have been blatant and in her face." He was silent for a second and hooked a finger around my collar. "We have a cocktail party tonight, which you will attend as my submissive. How will you handle five hundred people if you have difficulties with one?"

"But I'm willing to bet you won't have me kneeling on the floor at the cocktail party."

"You're able to say that because you trust me to know how far I can push you." He cupped my chin, lifting my head so our eyes met. His were so green and clear, yet filled with an emotion I couldn't name. "You do trust me, don't you?"

"Yes, Master."

"Thank you for being honest." He leaned down and kissed me. "But I only heard one *Master* in that conversation."

I swore under my breath.

He chuckled. "If you're finished with your water, you can go back to writing."

I relaxed slightly until he added, "As punishment I want your skirt up around your hips, so you're naked from the waist down. And sit in a way so I can see how wet you are."

Our suite at the conference hotel was spacious and decorated with cool tones of ivory and mint green. A dining room table for eight occupied one corner, while a baby grand resided in another.

"It'll do," Nathaniel said, giving the area a once-over.

I snorted. Typical male. The suite was beautiful and the only comment he offered was, "It'll do"? I supposed as long as it had a bed and bathroom it would be fine for him.

"I didn't mean the room itself," he said with a mischievous grin. "Though it is lovely. I meant the dining room table looked like it'd do for what I have planned."

I answered with my own mischievous grin. Whatever he had planned certainly wasn't on the mind of the designer when they were creating this space. "I look forward to it, Master."

"You should." He gave my ass a playful swat. "We need to be dressed in two hours. Go on and shower. I'll put your outfit on the bed."

We'd stayed up late the previous Saturday night negotiating our plans for this week. One requirement we'd agreed on was he would pick out what I wore. It wasn't something he usually liked, but he'd said it'd help reinforce our roles for the week. I shook my head. I'd been a submissive for a long time and still it would occasionally slip my mind that he had a head space to stay in as well.

He'd told me his requirements for the party tonight as well: I couldn't talk to anyone without his approval, I would eat only from his hand, and whenever we sat down, I would place my hand on his knee, keeping my own slightly spread.

After my shower, I toweled off and stepped inside the bedroom to see what he'd set out for me to wear. I smiled at his selection.

One of my favorites. A short silver cocktail dress with spaghetti straps and an open back and plunging neckline. I decided to pull my hair up, knowing it'd emphasize the neckline and my collar.

I found him after I dressed. He sat on the living room couch, leaned back with his hands behind his head. When I came in, he sat up.

I walked to the middle of the room and dropped to my knees.

"Abigail?"

"I know I've been a brat the last few days, Master. I just wanted to tell you I'm sorry and I'm truly looking forward to this week."

"Thank you," he said, standing and walking to me, unbuckling his belt. "Since you're on your knees, there's something we didn't do on the jet and since I'm not going to the party with this erection, I'll give you the privilege of taking care of it."

I had an overwhelming desire to have him in my mouth, so I made quick work of his pants and had his cock freed within seconds. He was kind enough not to mess my hair up, but instead kept his hands to his side as I engulfed his length.

"Fuck, yes. You have the sweetest mouth. You make my dick feel so good." He thrust into my mouth. "But you're going to have red knees when you finish. Everyone who sees them will know you've been sucking cock."

I hadn't thought about that and I stopped momentarily. He wouldn't allow it and put his hand on the nape of my neck. "Too late now. Finish me off. Take me deep and swallow everything I give you."

I was tempted to rush through and make him come quickly. He'd know what I was up to, though, and I really wanted to show my excitement at the week before us. So I took my time and worshipped his cock properly. I glanced up at one point and his eyes were closed. I added a bit more suction and before too long he released into my mouth.

He straightened his clothes while I waited for further instructions.

"Look at you." He helped me to my feet. "Your lips are swollen and your eyes are dark with lust. Your hair's the slightest bit tousled and your chest is heaving. One look at you and all anyone is going to be thinking about is dirty fucking sex." He pulled me close and whispered, "Depending on how this evening goes, maybe I'll show you just how dirty I can be."

His words never failed to turn me on, and I was jelly in his arms. "Please, Master."

He took my arm and looped it through his, and we made our way downstairs.

We were a bit late to arrive, thanks to the impromptu blow job, and the hotel ballroom was crowded when we entered. I recognized a few of the attendees from previous conferences, but the majority of them were unknown to me.

He steered us to the middle of the room where a waiter stood nearby, offering wine.

"Red?" Nathaniel asked.

"Yes, thank you." I couldn't add *Master*, not with as many ears as there were around us, and once his collar was on me, I couldn't use his given name.

He handed me a glass and I'd just taken a sip when I heard a deep voice from beside us. "Nathaniel West, I hoped I'd run into you tonight."

I turned to find Nathaniel shaking hands with a good-looking gentleman. He had dirty blond hair and gorgeous blue eyes. His full lips were curved into a friendly smile, but there was a strength in his expression I recognized.

"Daniel Covington," the blond said. "I work at Weston Bank and I'm a good friend of Jeff Parks."

My ears perked up and my cheeks felt hot at the mention of

Jeff's name. I'd really thought never to hear from or about him again after he'd finished his consulting job with Nathaniel.

"And this is Julie Masterson," he said, indicating the beautiful brunette at his side.

Nathaniel shook her hand and turned to me. "This is my wife, Abby." He ended with a nod, signaling I was free to talk with both Daniel and Julie.

"Pleased to meet you both." My eyes fell on the choker Julie wore and I wondered for a split second if it was a collar. But then I scolded myself. Odds were, it was only a necklace. *Seriously. Just because you wear a collar doesn't mean everyone else does.*

The men started talking so Julie and I stepped to the side a bit so we could talk separately. She stood with a bold confidence and I wasn't surprised when she told me she co-owned her own business.

"What do you do?" she asked.

"I stay at home with our children, Elizabeth and Henry. But I've recently started writing for WNN."

"Really?" Her eyes grew big. "I read a blog on their site."

I was dying to know if it was mine. "Which one? I know several of the writers."

She shifted her weight from foot to foot and she glanced around the room. "Umm, one on women's relationships." She fingered her necklace and whispered, "It's written by a submissive."

I couldn't stop the smile that took over my face. "Oh, well. That one's mine."

She squealed, drawing the attention of the men. Realizing what she'd done, she slapped a hand over her mouth. "Sorry," she said when Daniel raised an eyebrow. "Just girl talk."

The men went back to their conversation and she took my hand and moved us several steps away. Nathaniel's gaze followed me, but he quickly went back to his discussion.

"I love your blog," Julie said in a whisper. "You're really the Submissive Wife?"

"Yes." I didn't have a chance to say anything further because she kept right on talking.

"Everything you write is so realistic. I *feel* what you're saying. Does that make sense?" She fingered her necklace. "This is probably too much information, but Daniel's recently collared me, and reading you, it just gives me confidence. I don't know any long-term couples. You and Nathaniel give me hope that Daniel and I can last."

In her I saw myself so many years ago, when Nathaniel and I were just starting out. "Julie," I said. "I'm going to tell you the truth like I wish someone had told me years ago. It's hard. Really hard. And if you knew everything that was going to happen, you'd wonder if you wanted to do it." I thought about the road Nathaniel and I had traveled so far. All the heartache and uncertainty of the early days of our relationship. But then I thought about the love, the joy, the completeness we brought each other. "But take it from me—it's so worth it. If your Master is like mine, you'll never be happier than you are at his feet and in his collar."

"Thank you," she said with tears in her eyes. "We had the stupidest fight last night and I hate it when we argue. It doesn't happen a lot, but we're both really hardheaded."

"I know exactly what you mean." I pointed to the necklace I now knew to be a collar. "Are you twenty-four/seven?"

"No, we're not. Daniel's only Dominant in the bedroom. I wear his collar all the time, though. I like it that way—it keeps us connected."

"Like the ring I wear." I held out my right hand so she could see the second ring Nathaniel gave me when we married. "He has one, too. I only wear his collar when we're in role."

Her gaze traveled from my ring to lock on my collar. "So, tonight . . ."

"Yes, all week actually."

"Have you done a week before?"

"No." I shot her a smile. "But I'm sure you'll soon be able to read how it goes."

She laughed. "I look forward to it."

We talked for a few more minutes. Listening to her reminded me so much of myself. She told me how she was a florist and met Daniel when he happened to stop by her store the first of the year. It was that chance meeting that finally pushed her to explore her interest in submission.

"Your story is a little similar to mine," I said. "Except for one area."

"What's that?"

"I made the first move with my Master."

That hadn't been what she was expecting to hear and I laughed at her surprised expression. She recovered quickly, though. "You should blog about how you two met and have your readers share their stories."

"That's actually a great idea." Not only that, but if WNN was truly interested in doing a new women's television show, that could be a topic for a show. I'd have to run it by Meagan.

"Thanks," Julie said. "One little question, is there a reason you aren't using Nathaniel's given name?"

"I never say his name when I'm wearing his collar," I explained. "It's just a small way to help keep me in my headspace."

She nodded. "Makes sense."

Looking over her shoulder, I saw the men heading our way. "Looks like the guys have finished their conversation."

Julie sighed as she watched the men coming toward us. "If that isn't a fine-looking sight headed our way, I don't know what is."

Daniel walked up to Julie and slid his hand to rest on her lower back. She beamed up at him. Nathaniel's fingers played with the hair at the nape of my neck.

"I told your husband I'd monopolized enough of his time," Daniel said to me. "I know there are other people he'd like to speak with. But it was so nice to meet you both. Let's try to do dinner while you're in town."

Nathaniel agreed and we said our good-byes.

"You and Julie appeared to hit it off," he said when they were out of earshot.

"She's very friendly. Her story reminds me of mine a little bit. And the best part is"—I felt all giddy again just thinking about it—"she reads my blog!"

"Does she? That *is* exciting." He spoke briefly to an older gentleman who called a greeting to him before turning back to me. "Is that the first time you've met a reader?"

"The first one who isn't a friend or relative."

He smiled and started to say something, but was interrupted by another business colleague. Though he was introverted by nature, I always enjoyed watching him in a setting like this one. There was a certain kind of pride in seeing him converse so eloquently and seeing the people who listened so intently. The feeling only grew when he'd turn my way and introduce me as his wife.

We slowly worked the room, because a lot of people ended up approaching him. I smiled and nodded for the most part because he didn't give me permission to speak. I'd grown so used to being silent, I was caught off guard when he nodded after a woman our age approached.

"Nathaniel," she said, shaking his hand. She was tall and gorgeous, with honey-colored hair and long legs most women would kill for.

"Charlene," Nathaniel said. "How nice to see you again."

"Is this your wife? You must introduce me." She spoke the last word while looking me up and down. It took me only two seconds of seeing how she acted around Nathaniel to recognize her type.

Bitch had eyes for my husband.

"Yes," Nathaniel said, slipping an arm around my waist. Obviously, he knew her type, too. "This is Abby."

"Hello, Charlene." I didn't say it was nice to meet her because it wasn't and I told myself Nathaniel wouldn't want me to lie.

"Abby, I've been dying to meet Nathaniel's wife. It's almost as if he's been hiding you." She slapped his arm with her silver clutch. "What made you decide to come this time?"

"Research. I'm a writer."

"Fascinating," she said in a tone that told me she thought it just the opposite. "I do love your necklace, though. I've been wanting one like that. Where did you get it from?"

My hand automatically drifted to my collar. I wasn't expecting the question and I didn't see any way to answer other than what I said. "Nathaniel gave it to me shortly after we met."

The hand at my waist tightened slightly. A subtle way for him to tell me he heard my use of his name. It wasn't a situation I'd been in before and I didn't know if or how he'd deal with it.

But before me, Charlene's eyes flashed with envy. "Fortunate woman."

I lifted my chin. "Very."

Her eyes darted around the room. "Excuse me, you two. I see someone I need to speak with."

"She wants you," I told him as she crossed the floor to grab Daniel. I shot Julie a look of sympathy.

"Yes. And you handled her well." He pulled me toward his chest and whispered, "Except for the part when you used my name. How unfortunate there wasn't a way to avoid it. Now you'll spend the rest of the party thinking about the consequences."

My heart pounded in anticipation or trepidation, I couldn't quite determine which. He let go of my waist and pointed toward the buffet in the corner.

"Go grab us a plate," he said. "I'll get us a seat."

I said a silent prayer that no one would speak to me while I was getting our food. Fortunately, no one did and I found Nathaniel moments after filling a plate.

He'd found us a love seat. It was secluded, but we would still be in view of the attendees. He took the plate while I sat down, and once seated, I put my hand on his knee. He fed me a few bites of stuffed mushrooms and as we ate, he pointed out a few people sharing snippets of his dealings with them.

It was refreshing to have a few minutes of alone time with him, even if those minutes were technically shared with hundreds of others. As expected, it didn't last long.

"Nathaniel," a man I didn't know said, approaching us. "There you are!"

"I'll be right back." Nathaniel handed me the plate. "We're leaving in twenty."

We were back in our suite twenty-five minutes later. In our absence, the lights had been dimmed and the bed turned down. But neither one of us was ready to sleep.

"Kneel in the living room," he said, taking off his tie and unbuttoning his shirt. He didn't take it off, even when he sat on the couch and watched me move into position.

"What happened tonight, Abigail?"

"I spoke your name, Master."

"Against the rules when you wear my collar and yet unavoidable considering the situation. I find myself in quite the quandary."

In the silence that followed his words, I tried to figure out what he'd do. He stood and walked to the bedroom. When he returned to the living room about half an hour later, he had a box in his hands. He gave it to me.

"Open it."

It was a rather nondescript black box, about eight by eleven inches with no outward indication of what could possibly be inside. I carefully lifted the lid and peeked inside. A book?

"Take out the first item and open it to where the bookmark is."

It was a book. A slim volume of Emily Dickinson poems, to be exact. I wasn't sure where he was going with this, but I flipped to the marked page.

"Read the poem."

It was one I wasn't familiar with and I read it for the first time out loud to him.

> When Katie walks, this simple pair accompany her side,
> When Katie runs unwearied they follow on the road,
> When Katie kneels, their loving hands still clasp her
> pious knee—
> Ah! Katie! Smile at Fortune, with two so knit to thee!

I closed the book.

"What's the poem about, Abigail?"

"Destiny, Master."

"Yes," he said. "Tonight we're going to let destiny decide your fate. There are five black envelopes in the box, and two red ones. Open one of the black ones and tell me what it says."

I picked one of the black envelopes at random. I couldn't fathom what I'd find inside and I tore it open with excited fingers. My excitement died as I read the word printed on the card inside.

"Cane."

Fuck. I still cringed when I remembered the time, not too long ago, when he'd given me three strokes. Damn that Charlene. I really wished he hadn't given permission for me to talk with her.

"Harsh," he said in agreement. "Open one of the red envelopes."

If I had to guess, there were numbers inside the two red ones. I studied them both intently as if in doing so I could somehow read the number inside. Of course, there was no way to tell that. With a heavy sigh, and cursing Charlene again, I slowly opened the one on the left.

I had to read it twice to convince myself my eyes weren't making up the words.

"Well?" he asked, though I was certain my grin gave away which envelope I'd selected.

"With orgasm."

His lust-filled eyes met mine and the corner of his mouth lifted slightly. "Ah, the fates have smiled upon you. Go get undressed and meet me back here in ten minutes."

My legs shook just a bit as I rose to my feet. I couldn't believe how close I'd come to being caned without an orgasm. Would he have really done it? I couldn't imagine him changing his mind after he'd gone through all the trouble of creating the box and then having me open it.

Or could it be that both envelopes had "with orgasm" inside? That seemed likely to be the case. Of course I wouldn't know because he'd probably never tell me. He had a knack for messing with my mind.

I made it back into the living room, naked, in under eight minutes. He stood by the dining room table and he'd changed as well. Or at least he'd completely taken his shirt off. He'd also placed a thick pad on top of the table and covered it with blankets.

His face was unreadable as he took my hand and helped me get into position. Though the room was warm, I felt a bit cold and my body shook a bit.

He put his hand on my shoulder blade. "You're trembling. Are you okay?"

"Yes, Master. I'm a bit chilly, but I know you'll warm me up."

"Nothing would please me more."

A spicy orange scent filled the air and his warm hands massaged my favorite lotion along my back. He spent a long time working the tension from my body. I hadn't realized how tight my back was until I relaxed under his touch.

"Yes. That's it," he murmured.

His hands moved to my backside and he switched from massage to a pleasurable percussion tapping. He eased his way slowly up along my spine, swept his fingers across the back of my neck, and worked his way back down, ending with a pass of his hand between my legs.

"How are you feeling?" he whispered.

"Green, Master."

He repeated the percussion pattern several more times. Each time, I sank deeper and deeper into my headspace. My hips jerked when he unexpectedly circled my clit. I thought he might start with the cane now; surely he knew from touching me how aroused I'd become. Instead, he increased the intensity of his taps, once more working his way up and down my back.

I couldn't stifle a moan when he started smacking my backside every so often.

"You're so damn wet." He slid a finger inside me. "Going to feel so good to push my way inside."

But he didn't stop. He kept tapping and smacking until I was desperate for something. Anything. I fought to keep from grinding against the table and bit the inside of my cheek when he slid two fingers deep inside me.

Unexpectedly, the cane lightly struck my ass four times and I groaned.

"Let me hear you, Abigail." The cane tapped softly along my upper thighs. "Don't keep anything from me tonight."

He went back to spanking me and I thought he wasn't going to use the cane anymore when it came down harder across my ass. I grunted in pleasure.

"Not any harder than that," he said.

Knowing that made the few strokes that followed even more pleasurable because I didn't have any fear of them. My need for him to take me grew and nearly exploded when he started playing with my clit.

"Damn, you're soaked." He slapped my ass. "So wicked. So ready to be fucked."

I whined. "Please, Master."

"No." The cane landed again and immediately he pumped two fingers in and out of me. My hips jerked. "Who determines when you get fucked?"

"You do, Master." I hoped he decided soon. I almost begged him, but he shifted his fingers and all I could think about was keeping myself from orgasm. *"Oh, shit."*

"Not yet," he warned. "Come without permission and I *will* turn this into a punishment session."

The evil bastard continued pumping his fingers and I panted in time with them.

"Oh, oh, oh, *fuck*, oh." I fisted the blanket.

He slowed a bit. "I love to watch you squirm. Caught between obeying my order not to come and your body's need for release."

He pulled his fingers out and ran them across one of the lines left behind by the cane. The feel of cool wetness against my heated flesh almost sent me over the edge.

"Like that, naughty girl? Because I sure as hell do. Makes me so damn hard seeing my marks on your ass."

I wasn't going to be able to hold on much longer. To help, I started whispering the German alphabet backward.

"In fact," he said, not mentioning my urgent murmurings, "I'm going to take you from behind, so I can see these pretty marks while I fuck you."

Please, oh, please, oh, please.

He chuckled and I realized I'd spoken out loud. "I'm going to carry you to the bedroom and then I want you on your hands and knees on the bed."

"Thank you. Yes, Master."

He scooped me up and carried me to bed. While I got into position, he stripped out of his remaining clothes and stood in front of me.

"See this cock?"

I licked my lips at the sight of it. "Yes, Master."

"I'm going to fuck you with it. Brace yourself on your forearms so I can do a thorough job."

I whimpered at his words, but dropped forward. He moved behind me and positioned my legs a bit wider.

"Look at this greedy pussy." He slid his thumbs inside, spreading me. "So hungry for its Master's cock. Don't worry. I won't make you wait any longer."

His thumbs left, but in their place I felt his cock inch slowly inside me. He entered with slow, small thrusts, never making it in completely.

Damn it all. Just do it already!

"So damn needy," he said, and I realized I'd been pushing my hips toward him. He gathered my hair in one hand and pulled back as he thrust hard, settling himself inside completely. "There we go. Take it."

"Yes," I answered in a half hiss, half moan. "Please. More."

"Patience." He waited a second and drove himself into me. He bottomed out and gave his hips a roll, hitting damn near every erogenous spot I had.

"Oh, God. Master. *Fuck!*"

He rolled his hips again, my hair still firmly held in his hand. "I like riding you this way. Your pussy impaled by my cock. Thrusting into you and looking at the marks my cane left. There's just one thing . . . Can I go deeper?"

He pulled out and thrust back into me. I could feel him press against my butt, but he lifted his hips and with a forward push managed to get more of his cock in. I moaned in pleasure/pain.

"Ah, yes, I can," he said, sounding quite pleased.

"Oh, shit!" I gasped, balancing on the edge.

"Need to come?"

"Yes, Master."

"Come for me." He moved his hips hard and fast.

I bit the sheets as he worked his way in and out, trying to hang on just a little longer. But he slipped a finger between our bodies to tease my clit and with his next thrust, I pushed against him and let my release take over. I think he meant to hold off his own climax, but as soon as mine started, he let out a strangled cry and followed.

Exhausted from travel, party, and the massive orgasm, I collapsed flat on the bed, breathing heavily.

"Fucking hell," he said, breathing just as hard and joining me on the bed.

I wasn't sure how much time passed as we stayed that way, entwined together in bed. He absentmindedly ran his fingers through my hair and I think I dozed for a few minutes. Always in the back of my mind I warned myself not to get too comfortable since he said I'd be sleeping on the floor. I wasn't ready to head that way yet.

"I have a question, Master."

"Mmm." His eyes were closed and his reply was that of a thoroughly satisfied man and I smiled, pleased I had made him that way.

"Who is Charlene?"

"No one you should waste time thinking about."

"I didn't like the way she looked at you."

He turned his head and opened one eye. "I don't particularly care for it either, but I know who and what she is and she's nothing to me."

He closed his eye again as if saying the conversation was over. But it still continued in my head. I didn't like the woman. There was something about her that seemed dangerous, for lack of a better word. But Nathaniel probably had it all under control.

A few minutes later, he leaned over and kissed me. "Go on and get your shower. I'll take one when you get out."

Not quite ready to leave the bed, but knowing I'd feel better after I washed, I dragged myself to the bathroom. I turned the water on as hot as I could stand and took a long shower. The bathroom was completely filled with steam when I got out.

Nathaniel had hung a long silk gown on the back of the door while I was bathing. I smiled, thinking that if I had to sleep on the floor, at least I'd look good doing so.

I dried my hair and brushed my teeth before heading back to the bedroom. As expected, he'd taken the thick pad from the dining room table and made a small but comfortable-looking pallet.

It's just a way to reinforce roles, I told myself. *I've had difficulties the last few weeks.*

He looked all sorts of sexy sitting on the edge of the bed. He hadn't put his pants or shirt back on; he'd simply tugged on his boxer briefs. His lip quirked up. "Leave me any hot water?"

I held up my thumb and forefinger so they almost touched. "Maybe a little."

He crooked his finger. "Come here."

The gown swished this way and that as I made my way toward him. I swayed my hips, making the movement more dramatic. "Yes, Master," I said when I stood between his legs.

"I forgot to do something earlier." He stood up and drew me toward him.

"Really?" I asked; it certainly felt like he'd been thorough. "I can't imagine what."

He smiled down at me, and even though my body was weak and weary, when he looked at me the way he currently was, with love and desire and passion so evident in his expression, I'd walk across oceans for him.

"I forgot this," he said and lowered his lips to mine. I sighed in complete bliss as he kissed me. His lips, his mouth—I didn't think I'd ever get tired of them or take them for granted. The kiss wasn't long, but it was enough to speed up my heart and to make me think maybe I really wasn't *that* tired.

But he broke off the kiss and whispered against my lips. "I'm going to take a shower. Good night, my lovely."

"Good night, Master."

I waited until he made it into the bathroom before settling in on the floor. I squirmed a bit. It obviously wasn't as comfortable as a bed, but it was a lot better than sleeping on the floor directly. I closed my eyes, telling myself I was just resting them and I'd wake up when he got out of the bathroom.

It was cold when I woke up. And dark, I realized, opening my eyes. I reached for the blanket and touched an arm. My heart jumped to my throat before I realized it was Nathaniel.

"Did I wake you?" He'd situated himself between my legs and hiked my gown up to my waist. No wonder I was cold. In the darkness, he was cloaked in shadow. I couldn't make out his features; it was almost as if I'd conjured him.

"Mmm," I hummed, suddenly aware I was naked from the waist down and completely spread for him. "I think you did."

"How very, very rude of me." He trailed his fingers up and down the insides of my inner thighs. Lightly, barely touching me. My body ached for more, yet I remained totally still. Totally at the mercy of my Master.

He teased me with his fingers and each brush of his fingertips awakened more and more nerve endings in my body until I was panting with need. If he could just move his fingers up, just a little bit higher, and touch me right where I needed.

"Perhaps I should make it up to you for waking you up at this ungodly hour." His fingers drifted up, slowly, and went just a little bit farther, but stopped right before he got to where I really craved him. "What do you think, Abigail?"

"I would like that very much, Master." I spoke it calmly and in a tone that in no way resembled the "Yes! Damn it, yes!" I shouted in my head.

"Or maybe I could just go back to sleep," he mused, but didn't move. "Of course, it would be such a shame to have used all that energy getting out of bed to just go back to sleep."

I snorted. "All that energy?"

"I was in the middle of the most delightful dream."

The entire encounter was feeling more and more dreamlike. The feel of him and the sensation he created inside me combined and swirled together in a way that when taken with the darkness made everything mysterious. If I closed my eyes, it could be anyone touching me. And though I didn't want anyone except Nathaniel's hands on me, I had to admit the thought aroused me.

"Tell me your dream, Master," I said.

"I was sleeping," he said, lowering his head, sweeping his lips across my knee. "And I woke to find a beautiful woman flying across the room to me."

"She was flying?" I asked. Nathaniel was always so practical, so exacting, I'd always assumed his subconscious would be the same. I had no idea his mind was even capable of thinking about flying women.

"It was a dream," he said, as if that explained everything. And it would have if anyone other than Nathaniel was having it. "Women can fly in dreams."

I wasn't in the mood to debate whether his dreams could or should follow the personality he presented to the world. I was way too interested in hearing about what happened and finding out if he'd ever move his fingers so they did more than tease me. "Of course they can. Please go on."

"She whispered to me softly and sat on the edge of my bed. She shimmered all silver and white and then she was gone. I reached out to touch her and she disappeared."

For some reason hearing him describe his dream made me sad. "It doesn't sound like a happy dream."

He lifted my leg slightly and placed a kiss on my knee's underside. "You haven't heard the best part yet."

"There's more?"

His tongue licked the skin he'd just finished kissing. "Yes, because when I couldn't find her, I looked over the side of my bed. And do you know what I saw?"

The floor? The answer danced on my lips, but I shook my head. "No, what did you see?"

"I found a woman even more beautiful. In fact, she was so beautiful, I had to climb out of bed to get a closer look." He lifted his head and ran his hands up along my waist.

My body responded immediately and I sighed.
He whispered against my skin,

> *When she rises in the morning*
> *I linger to watch her;*
> *She spreads the bath-cloth underneath the window*
> *And the sunbeams catch her*
> *Glistening white on shoulders,*

He paused to kiss my shoulders. First one and then the other.
"D. H. Lawrence?" I asked as he nuzzled my neck.
"I've been reading poetry lately."
"I'm impressed."
"There's more," he said, moving down my sides and placing
kisses along my collarbone and breasts.

> *While down her sides the mellow*
> *Golden shadow glows as*
> *She stoops to the sponge, and her swung breasts*
> *Sway like full-blown yellow*
> *Gloire de Dijon roses.*

His lips traveled even lower, brushing my hips as he continued.

> *She drips herself with water, and her shoulders*
> *Glisten as silver, they crumple up*
> *Like wet and falling roses, and I listen*
> *For the sluicing of their rain-dishevelled petals.*
> *In the window full of sunlight*
> *Concentrates her golden shadow*
> *Fold on fold, until it glows as*
> *Mellow as the glory roses.*

Nathaniel reciting poetry was enough to drive me wild. Throw in the way he was kissing his way down my body as well and I was as good as gone. I clutched his head as he made his way between my thighs and slowly inched his lips closer and closer and—

"Oh, *my, shit!*" I screamed as his tongue delved inside me.

He didn't stop, but continued licking and swirling and nipping until I was writhing on the blankets, the pleasure so intense my toes were curled.

"I can't . . . when you . . . *fuck* . . . please . . ."

He stopped long enough to say, "Come," and I jerked against him, panting as I climaxed. He placed a soft kiss on my belly.

"Don't you think that was the best part?" he asked.

I had no idea what he was talking about. "The best part of what?"

He laughed softly. "Go back to sleep, my lovely." And with a press of his lips to my cheek, he climbed back on the bed.

I fell into that strange dream state where you think you're awake, but you're really asleep. I woke several times during the night, but Nathaniel remained where he was and in the morning, I'd convinced myself our entire encounter had been a dream.

Chapter Nine

I glared at the clock and went back to writing in my journal. Ten minutes until nine. Ten minutes until I had to do the damn, stupid tortuous exercises Nathaniel gave me before he left for his morning meeting.

"Fucking sadist," I murmured, finishing the page I was on.

When I agreed to this week, I'd envisioned days spent doing what we'd done last night. Lots of play followed by lots of sex. Subspace and orgasms, thank you very much.

I glanced back at the clock. With a sigh, I put my journal aside, stripped my clothes off, and set the timer on my cell phone. I walked to the center of the room and knelt down. Within thirty seconds my knees were aching. My mind wandered and I thought back to the orders he gave before he left earlier.

He spoke in the firm voice that normally liquefied my knees, but it didn't work this morning.

"Do you understand, Abigail?"

I was just a bit irritated, so I replied, "Explain one more time, Master."

"From nine to noon, you will practice kneeling. Five minutes kneeling, five minutes rest. Ten minutes kneeling, ten minutes rest. Fifteen minutes kneeling, fifteen minutes rest. Repeat three times. And while you're on your knees, perhaps you'll find it beneficial to meditate on why I have you kneel." He raised an eyebrow. *"Understand?"*

It's really quite simple. He wouldn't have believed me if I told him again it wasn't clear. "Yes, Master."

"Excellent. I want you waiting for me by the elevator at fifteen after twelve. Wear something I won't have to remove if I want to fuck." He looked as if he wanted to say more, but instead he kissed my cheek and left.

I dreaded the next three hours. Kneeling. I decided I'd rather be looking for Elizabeth's pink crayons. I'd rather be changing diapers and chasing Apollo around the house. Hell, I'd rather be working at the library cataloging new releases. Anything but kneeling in the middle of a hotel room, naked, for nearly three hours.

I made a list in my head of all the things I'd rather be doing and when I finished, I ranked them in the order I'd rather be doing them in. The timer hadn't gone off when I finished so I translated the top five into German, in case I wanted to repeat them to Nathaniel next time I was trying to withhold my orgasm.

As soon as the timer sounded, I jumped up and grabbed my journal. For the next five minutes I wrote exactly what I thought of the kneeling exercise, complete with a detailed opinion of why it wasn't good for my knees. Although I'd probably regret it later, I finished with a commentary on the questionability I now had surrounding the legitimacy of Nathaniel's birth. *Bastard.*

I settled into my kneeling position for my ten minutes and decided I'd make a list of what I needed to buy to prepare the family for summer. The kids needed new clothes, Nathaniel had already taken care of opening the pool, but Apollo needed to go to the vet. I'd made significant progress when I realized I needed to pee.

I tried to put it out of my mind, but all that did was make the need more pronounced.

Damn.

I resisted the urge to squirm, trying to keep myself in proper position. I squeezed my Kegel muscles and my lower body started to tremble. How much longer did I have? Would Nathaniel want me to break position or pee on the floor?

"You can do it. You can do it. You can do it," I chanted.

Fuck, how much time was left?

And why hadn't I positioned myself so I had a clock in view?

When the timer went off, I dashed to the bathroom and sighed in sweet relief.

I added busted bladder and the potential of wet carpets to the list in my journal on why this was a poorly designed exercise. Then, knowing I had fifteen minutes of kneeling ahead of me, I went through several stretches.

Before resuming my position, I decided the next section of kneeling time would be spent thinking up painful tortures to perform on Nathaniel's body. I dropped to my knees and started my plotting by beginning with his head and working my way down. I spent a lot of time on certain sensitive parts of his anatomy. Surprisingly, the fifteen minutes went by quickly.

I used the first few minutes after the timer went off stretching. I was walking toward the bedroom to get the paperback I was in the middle of reading when my phone beeped with an incoming text. I thought about ignoring it, but on the chance it was Linda, I decided to check.

It was Nathaniel. I bit back a groan. Probably he'd decided to add a task to the kneeling torment.

First hour is over. Thank you for doing this for me. I know it's not easy and your obedience makes us stronger.

Guilt hit me in the gut. "Damn you, you manipulative bastard."

But it had worked and for my remaining rest time, all I thought about was how I'd failed and how I could fix it. I was actually looking forward to the top of the hour.

Ten o'clock found me kneeling in the middle of the living room, head bowed, butt resting on ankles, palms on knees. For five minutes I worked on clearing my head of anything other than Nathaniel and the bond we shared. His text pained the part of me that longed to please him and wanted nothing more than his pleasure and approval.

The first five minutes passed quickly and I discovered myself looking forward to the following ten. When those were over, I spent my ten-minute rest writing in my journal again, this time reflecting on how my view of his kneeling plan had changed.

The fifteen-minute block was tough, but anytime I felt myself sliding toward complaining, I thought of him and pushed through the discomfort.

I wasn't expecting his text when it came through at ten to eleven.

Almost finished, my lovely. I'm very proud of you. For your last hour, I want you to play with yourself during your rests, but you're not allowed to come.

I groaned though I wasn't sure why. Playing with myself and not coming was more along the lines of what I'd thought he'd have me do while he was in meetings. During my five-minute kneeling time I wondered if Daniel was having Julie do anything while he was in meetings all day. But they were local and Julie worked, so he probably wasn't.

No, odds were I was the only submissive partner to someone at the conference. The thought made me feel secretive and sexy. I jotted those thoughts down in my journal during the first minute of my rest time. The remaining time, I worked my body into a frenzy thinking about the night before. Both the session before my shower and the middle of the night wake-up call I still wasn't sure had actually happened.

It took several minutes of kneeling during my last fifteen-minute period before my body calmed down.

"Deep breaths," I mumbled to myself. "You will not orgasm without his permission."

Once my nerve endings had returned as close to normal as they were going to, I reviewed everything I'd learned that morning. I didn't want to forget anything since I planned to do a blog post about my experiences. And I thought about how glad I was I didn't have much longer to keep my orgasm at bay.

I'd have to meet Nathaniel outside by the elevator shortly after my time was up. That didn't give me a lot of time to get ready. Hopefully he'd laid an outfit out for me to wear.

When my kneeling time was finally over, I went into the bedroom and climbed onto the bed. This time I didn't think about the night before. The fantasy playing in my mind when I closed my eyes involved Nathaniel taking me in front of a group of people.

I jumped when a pair of hands joined mine on my breasts.

"Now this is a sight to come home to. No, keep your eyes closed," Nathaniel said. "I might start making you wait for me like this every day."

"I might like that, Master."

"Keep your hands moving. Don't stop just because I'm here."

I moved my right hand back to my clit and teased it.

"There we go," he said. "I was sitting in that boring meeting and I decided I didn't want to miss out seeing you like this. Aroused and not able to come."

I wondered if that meant he wasn't going to let me come during his lunch break?

"And," he continued. "I decided it didn't make any sense for you to get all dressed and ready. Know why? Keep your hands moving."

I restarted teasing my clit. "You're going to fuck me," I said in answer to his question.

"No, though the suggestion is tempting. But I'm not going to fuck you during lunch." He stayed quiet for a long moment, making me wonder what his plans were before. "I'm going to watch you fuck yourself."

I loved and hated when he watched. Loved it, because I knew it aroused him, and nothing pleased me more than knowing he became turned on by something I did. Equally, though, I hated it because if he was simply watching, he wasn't touching. And the selfish part of me wanted his hands on me.

"Don't stop," he said. "Keep it up."

I let my head fall back and closed my eyes. I imagined I was on a stage with a group of people watching. Their eyes were riveted on me while I pleasured myself. I slid my fingers through my wetness and ran one lightly over my clit. As I pictured in my mind how the audience reacted to my display, I started to work my fingers faster.

Not being able to bring myself relief was borderline painful. I kept waiting for Nathaniel to undress and join me on the bed, but when I cracked an eye open to peek, he was still fully clothed. Suddenly afraid I would push myself over the line if I kept my actions up, I slowed my fingers.

"Smart," Nathaniel said. "I was starting to think you were going to come without permission."

He hadn't told me to stop, so I kept teasing myself. "It was tempting, Master."

"You can stop now." He stood up and walked to the closet, talking while he shuffled clothes. "There's been a change in plans. We're staying in for lunch. It'll be delivered shortly after our guest arrives."

My body had somewhat relaxed since he'd told me to stop, but I tensed at the word *guest*. "A guest, Master?"

"Yes, it's not a stranger. You'll recognize him." He pulled out a lightweight blue sundress and held it out. "No bra. No underwear. And you'll be serving us both."

I think my heart rate jumped to about one hundred forty beats a minute. We both agreed not to play sexually with anyone else, so any serving I did wouldn't involve anything intimate. And still the thought of interacting with another Dominant appealed to me.

"Go ahead and change," he said, with a muffled laugh that told me he picked up on exactly what I was thinking. "You don't have time to take a shower."

I climbed out of bed, took the sundress he selected, and hurried to the bathroom to get ready. I kept my hair down because I knew he preferred it that way. I applied only light makeup and, lastly, I slid into the dress. Seconds later, I found Nathaniel in the living room.

"Very nice, Abigail," he said. "I can't wait to show our guest what an excellent submissive you are. Especially when you're sober."

I could count on one hand the number of times I'd been drunk, so I didn't understand his comment until I answered the knock on the door.

"Hello, Abby," Jeff Parks said, his voice just as gruff as I remembered.

My mouth moved soundlessly for several seconds before I remembered how I was supposed to act. I pulled the door open wider, allowing him to enter the room. "Very nice to see you again, Sir. Please come in."

He nodded and walked inside to shake Nathaniel's hand. "Nathaniel."

"Welcome, Jeff. So glad you could join us."

I took my place by Nathaniel's side and slid closer to him when he placed a hand at the top of my ass.

"Would you like something to drink, Sir?" I asked.

"Not right now. I'm fine," Jeff said.

There was another knock on the door.

Nathaniel's touch on my back grew rougher. "That's lunch, Abigail. I need to discuss a few things with Jeff."

In other words, lunch setup was mine.

"Yes, Master," I said and stepped away to let the deliveryman in.

The only table in the suite was the one Nathaniel caned me on. It'd been cleaned since then and there was nowhere else to set up. We just wouldn't tell Jeff. I took the china and silver from the cabinet nearby and set the table for two, not wanting to assume I'd be invited to eat with the men.

I left the food covered and on the pushcart beside the table, thinking that would enable me to serve better. I idly glanced at the clock and then the closed bedroom door; almost ten minutes had passed. Whatever could the two guys be discussing that took that long?

I went to the middle of the living room and knelt to wait for them. After all the time I'd spent kneeling earlier in the day, it actually felt more natural to wait for him on my knees than it did to stand.

They entered the room quietly. Only the faint scuff of shoes against carpet gave them away. Neither one of them spoke to me as they walked by on their way to the table. Maybe they were going to serve themselves and I'd stay on the floor the entire time.

"Look at this," Nathaniel said to Jeff. "My Abigail has set the table up for lunch. What do you think?"

"I think she went a bit overboard, since we won't be using all that dinnerware."

I wasn't sure I heard that right. They weren't going to use the dinnerware? They would if I put the food on it.

"I believe you're right," Nathaniel said. "And we're missing something."

"I wasn't going to mention it, but since you brought it up. Yes, we are."

Missing something? What had I missed?

"Abigail, Come here, please."

I mentally went through everything I'd put on the table, but couldn't figure out what I'd missed. The plates, silver, napkin, glasses. Everything was there. What had I missed that was so huge both men picked up on it?

I rose to my feet and walked over to him. He didn't look angry; he looked calm and relaxed with just a hint of sexy promise in his eyes.

He stopped me before I could kneel. "Remain standing."

Jeff stood behind him, but I kept my eyes on Nathaniel.

"Thank you for setting lunch up," Nathaniel said. "I didn't give you any instructions and what you did would be exactly what I'd want you to do if we were sitting down for lunch. But we're not."

I looked over his shoulder to Jeff, but his expression was neutral. Like the weekend we met, he wore all black. He still looked intimidating and stern, though at the moment his arms weren't crossed.

"Take the dress off, Abigail," Nathaniel commanded.

I wanted to protest that I didn't have anything on underneath the outfit, but of course he knew that. I'd been naked in front of people before, but never with only two men present. This was very close to my fantasies. I shot a quick glance Jeff's way, but he looked completely unaffected by Nathaniel's instructions.

My fingers trembled with anticipation as I reached behind my back and unzipped the dress. Hadn't I just put it on? I should have just remained naked.

Though that would have given the deliveryman the shock of his life.

I drew the dress over my head and let it fall to a puddle on the floor. As it fell, I sank deeper into my headspace. For now, I existed only for my Master. I was his to do with as he pleased and if he wanted to show me off to his friend, I'd make him proud.

"Leave the heels on," Nathaniel said and his voice was rougher than it had been minutes earlier. He leaned close and whispered, "You look fucking hot wearing nothing but those heels and my collar."

"Thank you, Master."

"As you're aware, Master Parks is a Dominant. But what you might not know is that he has a certain fondness for bondage."

"Very interesting, Master." I was surprised at how calm my voice sounded. The fact that he was telling me Jeff was into bondage could mean only one thing.

"Yes, I thought so, too. Which is part of the reason I invited him over." He looked over to Jeff. "Can you get the chair ready?"

Jeff nodded and moved one of the chairs into the middle of the room. His eyes met mine and the corner of his mouth lifted into a half smile. He was a good guy; I felt safe and comfortable around him. But of course, I knew Nathaniel would have never staged this scene with Jeff if we couldn't trust him.

Now Jeff turned away and went through a bag I hadn't noticed before. One of the men must have brought it into the room while my head was bowed.

"Safeword if you feel the need," Nathaniel said. "Otherwise, I want you to listen and obey. Master Parks is here by my invitation as my guest and he is well aware of my rules and your limits."

"Yes, Master." My eyes were fixed on the chair Jeff was entwining with rope. Nathaniel might have informed him of rules and limits, but it was like a line in the sand. You could toe it without crossing and I had the suspicion that line was getting ready to be toed.

Jeff stood up and nodded at Nathaniel.

"Abigail, go sit in the chair. Master Parks, will you bind her?"

"It would be my pleasure," Jeff said.

I hesitated for just a moment. Though I'd figured out he would be the one to bind me based on what Nathaniel had said, my mind was still caught up on the fact that someone other than my Master was going to bind me to a chair.

"I didn't hear a safe word," Nathaniel said. "You better move faster unless you'd like to show our guest how nicely you handle a discipline session."

I hurried to the chair. Jeff stood beside it, waiting.

"How do I sit, Sir?" I asked Jeff. "Facing the back or the normal way?"

His eyes widened briefly; I guessed he didn't get questioned by submissives on their way to sit in a chair very often. But I'd been tied up enough to know not to assume anything.

"I think the normal way will be fine," he said. "Hands to your side and slightly behind you."

The chair in question had a cushion and high back. The one Nathaniel had in his playroom had a lower back and he'd tied me to it before with my arms over it. That would have been a difficult, if not impossible, position with the hotel chair.

"Should we tie her legs?" Nathaniel asked.

"If there's a question between tying and not tying, I always go for tying," Jeff answered.

Nathaniel laughed. "Good point. I think I want her blind-folded before we go any farther. Will you do the honors?"

"Of course."

My heart pounded. They were going to take my sight away? How would I know who was touching me?

"Don't look so frightened, Abby," Jeff said, blindfold in hand, and his voice was soothing and kind. "One word and you can stop everything."

Though his words didn't say it, in my mind he still saw me as a drunk submissive who'd wandered away from her Master. I lifted my chin. I'd show him. "I'm fine. Bring it on."

"Bring it on, *Sir*," he said, securing the blindfold around my head. "Or Master Parks. Either one works, but I expect that level of respect. Otherwise, I have permission to punish you, and since I'm limited with what I can do, it'll be very creative."

I decided I'd rather not experience his creative punishment. "Understood, Sir."

He silently went to work binding me to the chair. His touch differed from Nathaniel's, but both men had a firm and sure touch. I took a deep breath and focused on his fingers. It wasn't often another Dominant was given permission to touch me. Jeff's touch spoke of nothing but confidence and strength.

When he went to work on my arms, he moved behind me and began to whisper. "Your skin is so pale. I bet these ropes leave a mark."

And Nathaniel joined in. "They will. Her skin marks so beau-tifully."

"I once played with a blonde who had skin like this."

A finger traced the inner plane of my arm and I shivered.

"Mmm, she shivered like that, too."

Jeff's hands were rough as he tied my wrists and then my arms to the chair. He didn't veer from the parts of my body necessary to touch in order to do his job. Nathaniel was in front of me, and while his hands gently stroked my body, Jeff continued his whispers.

"Do you like being bound for your Master? And blindfolded so you can't tell what's going to happen next? Does it turn you on knowing I'm going to ensure your body is at his complete disposal?"

Nathaniel's finger swept along the outside of my pussy. "I can answer that one for you."

"Nice," Jeff replied. "I like knowing my efforts haven't gone unappreciated."

Nathaniel pushed his finger inside me and I shifted my hips, surprised by the sudden invasion. "Definitely not unappreciated. But I think some of it's due to the fact that you're here." He held his finger against my lips. "Clean it."

I parted my lips and tasted my arousal on his fingers. It turned me on even more when I imagined the way we looked. Me, naked and bound to a chair, one man behind me, whispering naughty tidbits in my ear, and my Master in front of me, caressing my body. It was sinfully decadent. And I wanted more.

"I've finished with your arms. Now I'm going to tie your ankles to either side of the chair." Jeff was once more whispering in my ear. "You'll be at your Master's mercy, unable to move or close your legs. So beautifully vulnerable."

He shifted to one side of me. I couldn't tell where Nathaniel had gone; he wasn't talking and I couldn't feel him near me. But I knew he'd be somewhere close by, watching me.

"I'm using a black rope," Jeff said. "It stands out so nicely against your pale skin. And once I take it off, the red marks from it will look even better."

I loved it when Nathaniel unbound me. It felt like I was emerging from a cocoon. And if I was lucky, he would trace the rope marks with his finger or, better yet, his mouth. Would he still do that if Jeff was the one who unbound me?

"Tell me what you're thinking," Jeff commanded. "I don't know your body language or your gestures, so I'm going to have you talk to me."

I licked my lips. "I was thinking about the last time Master bound me and how much I enjoyed him tracing the rope marks after."

"The way your breathing changed, I thought it was an arousing thought." He tightened the rope around my left leg and I heard him stand. "There we go. Are you ready over there?" he asked Nathaniel.

"Just about," he replied, and it sounded like something dropped onto a silver tray. Seconds later I heard the unmistakable sound of the pushcart being brought close to me. "All set."

"Nice spread," Jeff said and I couldn't tell if he was talking about me or whatever it was Nathaniel had brought over.

"It only gets better," Nathaniel said and then he addressed me. "Look at you, Abigail, naked and tied to a chair in front of two men. Your nipples are pebbled and you're wet just thinking about it. We haven't even done anything yet."

One of the things I loved about being his submissive was the mind games he'd play with me. We'd been together long enough that I could trust him utterly. I knew beyond a shadow of a doubt that he would never intentionally hurt me or violate my limits.

Knowing that allowed me the freedom to anticipate whatever it was he had planned. It was similar in some ways to watching a scary movie; I could watch it knowing he was with me and would keep me safe. I could give him uninhibited access to my body because he'd proved over and over that he'd protect it.

"I thought we'd play a little game this afternoon," Nathaniel said. "Master Parks and I are going to ask you some questions. You get them right, you get points. Answer them wrong and we'll take them away. Any questions?"

"No, Master."

"We'll start easy," Jeff said. "What's your name?"

"Abigail West."

"Very good. One point. What's my middle name?"

What? How was I supposed to know that? Then it hit me—I wasn't. The best I could do was guess. "Um, Robert?"

"Wrong. Minus one point. See how it's played?"

I saw that they could ask a bunch of questions I didn't know the answers to and I'd wind up with negative points. "Yes, Sir."

"This is a black scarf." Something gauzy passed over my breasts, pebbling my nipples even further. Nathaniel chuckled at my gasp. "What color is it?"

"Black, Master."

The scarf swept over my nipples again. "This is a red scarf. What color is it?"

I had a feeling it was the same scarf. I couldn't see how they could have switched it so quickly. Did I say it was black because I thought it was the same one or call it red because that's what he said?

"Red, Master."

"Very good." Nathaniel's lips took mine in an unexpected kiss, his lips claiming mine with an intensity that seemed to come out of nowhere. He lowered his head to my breasts and sucked a nipple, biting it lightly.

I jumped in surprise. Or I tried to jump. Jeff had done an excellent job of tying me up and I couldn't move very much. Where was Jeff? Was he watching while Nathaniel enjoyed my body?

Nathaniel pulled away. "Hand me the first item."

The first item? That didn't tell me anything. Besides, I thought they were asking me questions. An item could be anything. My thoughts were interrupted by a sharp pain on my left nipple.

"Holy fuck," I gasped. Clearly item one was a nipple clamp.

"Next one," Nathaniel said.

This time I held my breath and tensed.

"Kind of kills the surprise for the second one. What would you do?" he asked Jeff.

"She's too uptight. I'd relax her." I hadn't noticed until he spoke just how close Jeff was to me. Every word he spoke sent warm breaths of air across my neck. "Tease her. Tempt her."

While he whispered, Nathaniel nibbled his way down my body, swirling his tongue at the crook of my elbow, nipping the skin of my wrist that was not covered by rope.

"That's it," Jeff whispered. "She's getting there. I can see the tension leaving her body. You like it when he bites you, Abby? Like having his mouth on you? I bet you really want him back sucking on you, don't you?"

As he spoke, Nathaniel slowly made his way up to take my other nipple in his mouth. He ran his tongue over it, flicking it back and forth. Between what he was doing and what Jeff was saying, I felt like one big jellyfish. If I hadn't been tied to the chair, I'd probably have slid to the floor.

I was so focused on Jeff's words and Nathaniel's mouth, I didn't notice any additional movement until Nathaniel pulled back and the other clamp came down on my nipple.

"Shit," I groaned again.

"Worked like a charm," Nathaniel said.

"That's the way to distract her. However, I'm trying to decide if that was a reward or a punishment?"

"I don't know about her, but it was certainly a reward for me."

Jeff stifled a laugh at Nathaniel's remark and I smiled, enjoying the banter between the two men. Even if nipple clamps were involved.

"Think she's ready for the second question?" Jeff asked.

"I sure as hell am. Can you check the cart and make sure everything's clean?"

Clean? That was good, but why would something be dirty?

"Looks like everything's spotless."

There was a muffled shifting of the two men. Or at least that's what it sounded like. But when a pair of hands brushed the skin along my upper inner thigh, I recognized them as Nathaniel's. Jeff spoke once again from behind me, his heated whispers teasing my ear.

"I've got to warn you, this one's tough," he said. "Good luck to you."

Nathaniel's hands grew more urgent and insistent. Then, ever so slowly, he pushed two fingers inside me.

"What's inside you?" Jeff asked.

"Master's fingers, Sir," I replied.

"You like his fingers inside you or would you prefer something larger?"

I squirmed as much as possible, which, to be honest, wasn't a lot. His fingers pumped slowly in and out of me, each time teasing that one spot that drove me wild whenever he touched it.

"I like his fingers, Sir, but I wouldn't be opposed to something larger," I said.

I imagined him crossing his arms. "Very safe answer, Abby. I'll have to see if your Master and I can't shake you up a little."

"Or at least fuck it out of her," Nathaniel added.

"Agreed. Thinking along those lines, why don't you go for the second one?"

"You think she can handle that one? You don't think it's too big?"

"Only one way to find out."

Jeff dropped back behind me. "Your Master is going to slide something else inside that hot pussy. You have one chance to guess what it is. If you're wrong, we'll be fucking your ass with it."

I whimpered.

"Of course, maybe you'd like that."

"She would," Nathaniel added. "But you'd have to untie her and you wouldn't like that."

"Hell, no. All that work I'd have to redo? I wouldn't like it at all." Jeff squeezed the back of my neck. "I suggest you guess correctly the first time, understood?"

"Yes, Sir," I whispered. I didn't know Jeff all that well, but from the little I had seen and heard, I got the impression a submissive did everything she could to follow his commands to the letter.

"Here it goes," Jeff said and I felt something large and smooth rub against me. "He's going to ease it in slowly, so relax and take it."

"Oh, fuck," I said as it stretched me going in. Nathaniel pushed the object with one hand and rubbed my clit with the other.

"Not even halfway," Jeff said. "I like that he's going slow, his only goal to get more of that monster inside you. And watching your pussy split so wide around it. Fuck, it makes me so hard."

The feeling of being penetrated by something so large was sweet torture. Especially with Nathaniel working my clit the way he was. The only problem was he was moving too slow. I wanted more. I wanted it deeper.

"Oh, shit, please," I cried.

He withdrew it slightly. "What do you want, Abigail?"

"More, please, Master." He withdrew it even more. "No, not yet."

"Your call, Jeff," Nathaniel said.

I tried to get more of it inside, but I once again found he'd bound me way too securely. "Please, Sir."

"I do love it when a submissive says please," Jeff said. "But I only like begging when I ask for it."

He didn't say anything else and the silence seemed to pound like waves in the room. Nathaniel kept the object just at my entrance so it was barely inside of me. I felt so empty and it was *right there* and I needed it. I bit the inside of my cheek so I wouldn't beg and forced my hips to be still. My breaths came in short pants as I waited.

"Fuck her."

My mind hadn't registered the words before Nathaniel pushed the object inside me with one smooth move. I groaned as the fullness of whatever it was filled me completely and then he started to pump it in and out.

"Like that, Abby?" Jeff asked.

I couldn't form a coherent thought. My focus was on the sensations flowing through my body. "Ahhh . . ."

"Is that a yes?" he asked Nathaniel.

"I think so. I don't think I've ever heard that sound." Nathaniel shifted the object just slightly and it starting hitting me in a different, more sensitive spot.

I grumbled something and even I wasn't sure what it was.

"I think that means she wants it harder," Jeff said. "Is that right, Abby? You want him to fuck you harder?"

Nathaniel didn't wait for an answer, but immediately started thrusting the object faster and harder. My fists clutched at the empty air and my body rode the crest toward release. I was almost there when I realized I didn't have permission. I sucked in a breath and started reciting the German alphabet backward and since I was so close to coming, I intentionally left out every other letter.

"What's she saying?"

There was a smile in Nathaniel's reply. "She's studying German, and she recites it to keep from coming."

"Then it's time to get her mind on something other than her pleasure. What's inside you, Abby?"

Nathaniel didn't slow his movements and I took several deep breaths. "What, Sir?"

"Tell us what your Master is fucking you with. Keep in mind that if you're wrong, it's going up your ass."

Oh, no it wasn't.

All thoughts of climax left my mind as I turned my entire focus on what was inside me. Nathaniel had several dildos and vibrators, but none of them felt like what he was currently using. Whatever it was didn't feel like glass and it hadn't carried temperature like metal.

Could it have been something the deliveryman brought? I concentrated on the feel of it moving inside me. Smooth.

"We didn't give her a time frame, did we?" Nathaniel asked Jeff.

"No, that would have been a good rule though."

"Who's to say I can't change the rules? You have twenty seconds, Abigail, or else I'm bending you over the couch arm and I'll strap you before making your ass take this thing."

Smooth. Hard. Rounded at the end.

"Ten seconds."

"Cucumber!" I yelled. "It's a cucumber."

Nathaniel pulled it out and I groaned at its loss. Damn it. They weren't going to let me come. Not yet anyway. Maybe soon.

I hoped.

Why were they silent, though? Had I gotten it wrong?

"Very good, Abby," Jeff said, but he didn't sound pleased. "It was a cucumber."

I beamed from under the blindfold. Ass saved.

"There's only one problem," he continued and my smile left. "Do you know what that problem is?"

I racked my brain, trying to think. I couldn't put my finger on it. I hadn't come and I'd guessed correctly.

Jeff's voice was close to my ear. "You forgot to call me *Sir* or *Master Parks* and now I have to punish you. Shame to do it. You were doing so well. But I told you what to call me and gave you the consequences if you didn't. I have to follow through."

"Agreed," Nathaniel said. "Have to be consistent. What are you thinking you'll do?"

There was another silence as he thought. "The item in the bowl."

Nathaniel sucked in a breath. "We've never done that. I'll have to put a time limit on it."

"Of course."

Oh shit, oh shit, oh shit. What was in the bowl that made even Nathaniel hesitate. It couldn't be a hard limit. I tried to run down the last checklist we'd done, but my mind went blank.

"I usually put it in a sub's anus," Jeff said. I heard the metallic clink of the tray. "But since Abby is so beautifully bound, I think her pussy will work just fine. We can even have her guess what it is."

Nathaniel laughed. "You truly are an evil bastard. No wonder we get along so well."

Well, hell. That didn't tell me anything. Just that I was having something else put inside me. And that I'd have to guess what it was. What could be put inside me that Nathaniel and I had never used?

"There we go," Jeff said. "Nice and smooth."

I suddenly had a very bad feeling I knew what was in the bowl. I tried to stand up.

"Abigail?" Nathaniel asked.

"I just thought . . . I don't want . . . We haven't . . ."

"I didn't hear a safe word. Thank you, Jeff."

Something wet was right at my entrance. Fuck. And I was bound to the damn chair spread wide-open for whatever it was they wanted to do to me. I took a deep breath. I wasn't going to safeword over this. I could do it. I'd do it for Nathaniel.

"I think she knows," Jeff said.

"Probably," Nathaniel answered; then he addressed me. "There are a few submissives who can orgasm from the sensation. On the off chance you're one of them, remember you don't have permission."

I nodded and clenched my fists so tightly my nails dug into my palms. I would bet our house on the fact I wasn't one of those submissives. "Do it, Master."

Without saying another word, he pushed the wet object inside me. Jeff placed his hand on my shoulder and I waited for the inevitable.

It started out feeling cold, which I wasn't expecting. Maybe I had guessed wrong. But as it stayed in place, it slowly got warmer and I knew I'd been correct.

"It's ginger, Sir." Nathaniel and I had never played with ginger before, but I'd spoken with enough submissives to know it was called *figging*.

"It is, Abby. And it's going to start feeling really uncomfortable in just a few seconds."

"Thank you for the warning, Sir." It was a bit of a sassy reply, but he was silent. No doubt thinking the coming sensation would more than correct my behavior.

Gradually, just like he said, the ginger felt hotter and hotter and before too long, I was wiggling in my chair trying to get some relief. I cursed under my breath.

"What was that, Abigail?" Nathaniel asked, sounding mildly amused.

"I said, get this damn thing out of me!"

"Jeff?"

"I think she can take more."

Easy for him to say—he wasn't the one with a hunk of ginger stuck up him. "FUCK! It's hot!"

"Why did we have to use the ginger, Abigail?" Nathaniel asked.

Oh, fuck, fuck, fuck. It was too hard to think about anything other than the hot, burning sensation between my legs. "Please, just take it out, Master."

"Answer the question." He gave my pussy a hard smack and that somehow made the burn even worse.

"Okay, okay." Anything to get it out. "I neglected to treat Master Parks with the proper respect. Master."

He smacked it again.

"Owww."

"Is that the way you treat a guest I invited over?" he asked.

"No, Master. I'm sorry. Owwww. I'm sorry, Master Parks."

The burn had reached new levels of intensity. I squirmed uselessly, even trying to wiggle my arms free. I had just opened my mouth to *yellow* when Nathaniel said, "There we go," and slid the ginger out.

Relief came almost immediately and I could have wept with joy. Instead I repeated, "Thank you, thank you, thank you," over and over.

Nathaniel pressed a kiss to my lips. "You're welcome, my lovely. But that was fun. We're going to do that again in the future and I think I'll fuck you while it's inside you."

"Oh, shit," I said, but inside I wondered, how would that feel?

"Can you unbind her?" he asked Jeff.

"Will do."

He started with my ankles and as always it was accompanied by the feeling of being unwound. It was such an odd sensation, but one I enjoyed.

"You handled the ginger so well," Nathaniel said, still very close to my lips. One of his hands grazed my hip and drifted toward my belly button. "I'm going to let you come and Jeff's going to watch."

I'd thought my arousal was dead after the ginger, but hearing him and knowing Jeff was watching proved to be a turn-on. With just that one sentence he sparked a flame deep in my belly. "Oh, thank you, Master."

"Hold on," he teased. "Let me make sure I use the right hand. Wouldn't want to use the one that held the ginger."

Behind me, Jeff snorted, but continued with his unwinding. "Did that once. Had my mind on how well she'd done and wanted to please her. Needless to say, that didn't happen."

"I'm certain it was my right hand, so I promise to only use my left until I wash." His fingers inched closer, coming to rest on my inner thigh. "Show Jeff how fucking gorgeous you are when you come."

With that, his hand slipped between my legs and he teased my needy flesh. He traced my entrance before dipping a finger inside me. I choked back a moan.

"Let me hear you." Jeff was back at my ear. "I can't touch you and I can't feel you, but I can have your sounds. Let me hear your pleasure."

"Oh, God," I groaned when Nathaniel added a second finger. "So good."

"Right there?" Nathaniel asked. "You like it right there?"

I sucked in a breath as he started pumping. "Yes, Master. I like it everywhere."

His fingers went deeper, and behind me, Jeff kept whispering. "Damn, the sight of you being finger fucked with your legs spread and nipples clamped. Makes me so fucking hard. I bet you feel so hot and wet around his fingers."

My only reply was an incoherent mumble. Nathaniel knew just how to touch me to make me come and he masterfully eased my body into a frenzy of sensations. With his fingers stroking me and Jeff's wicked whispers, I was dancing on the edge of orgasm in mere seconds.

"Let me come, Master," I panted.

"Jeff?"

"Not yet. I want to watch her like this. You can see everything she's feeling. When you fuck her and hit that spot within her, her entire body responds."

Nathaniel hit the spot again and I felt my toes curl.

"Oh, fuck. Please, Sir." I steeled my body, afraid I was going to come. I couldn't let that happen. Not after the figging with ginger.

His fingers stroked again and as they hit deep inside me, Jeff said, "Now."

I came with massive gasp and at the same time, Nathaniel released the clamps. One right after the other came off, tearing a shout from my throat and triggering another orgasm.

I slumped forward into Nathaniel's arms, surprised to find I was totally unbound. Nathaniel pulled me close, gathering me into his arms, removing the blindfold, and lifting me from the chair. He carried me to the couch, where Jeff was already waiting with a thick white robe.

Once I was wrapped up, Nathaniel sat on the couch, holding me in his lap and stroking my hair. Through the haze of my foggy, postclimactic mind, I realized neither man had experienced their own release.

Jeff passed me a glass of water. It took only one sip for my body to recognize how thirsty it was. My comprehension must have been obvious because Nathaniel smiled.

"Slowly, my lovely."

I made myself take small, measured sips. With each swallow I felt more and more revived. Nathaniel kissed my forehead.

"I'm going to go wash my hands before I inadvertently touch something I shouldn't with ginger on my fingers." He looked over to Jeff, who nodded.

"I'll stay with her."

Without Nathaniel, I expected the silence with Jeff to be awkward. He was, after all, a near stranger who'd just seen me in a very intimate and private situation. I didn't have much experience making small talk in such settings.

"I have to say, Abby," Jeff said, breaking the stillness. "I misjudged you and I'm sorry. It's not the first time it's happened. You'd think I'd have learned by now."

I'd been curled up against the arm of the couch, and at his words, I straightened. "Misjudged how?"

"That night at the club, when I brought you home and saw where you lived." He shook his head. "It was damn judgmental, but I took you for a lightweight."

"That's rather insulting to Master."

"And the fact that *that* was your first response further proves how wrong I was."

"Why did you think I was a lightweight?" I pulled the edges of the robe tighter around my body and shifted closer to him.

"Wealthy, drunk, high-society wife who also happens to be the submissive of her CEO husband." He closed his eyes, deep in thought; then he looked at me. "Like I said, it was wrong of me to judge you."

"You said you did it before. Do you often run into drunk, wealthy, high-society submissives?"

He laughed, though there seemed to be a hint of sadness clouding his amusement. "Just once before. Though she wasn't drunk."

"The blonde with the skin you like to mark?"

All traces of joviality left his face, and I realized I'd guessed right on both accounts. There was a sadness in him and it was tied to the blonde.

"Yes," he said simply. "Her."

Her.

He spoke it quietly and though it was a small word, it held a lot of weight and I wondered how long he'd been carrying that particular burden. Still, I wasn't one to pry and he didn't seem to be the sort to chatter.

He turned his face to look out the window and I studied his profile. Such rugged and handsome features. What had happened between him and his blond submissive with the fair skin to put such sadness in his eyes?

I had a sudden urge to track whoever it was down. Jeff seemed like such a strong and steadfast man, plus he was a firm and commanding Dominant. But we all had our own stories and people saw only what we wanted them to see for the most part. Whatever had happened between Jeff and the blonde was between them.

"You're a lot alike," he said out of the blue. "Wealthy, sassy, strong."

"I'll admit to sassy and strong, but I married into wealth." I shrugged my shoulders. "Though I'd have married Nathaniel if he were a pauper."

"She used to say the same. That it was just money." He snorted. "I always thought it was easy to call it *just money* when you had plenty of it."

"True."

"I'm sorry." He turned back to me and gave a half smile, though I saw right through it. "I didn't mean to make the conversation about me."

I leveled my gaze at him. "Does she know?"

"Know what?"

"That you still love her."

He looked stunned, like he couldn't believe I'd correctly nailed his feelings. But he was saved from having to answer by Nathaniel's return.

"All traces of ginger gone," he said, walking into the living room. "Jeff, can I get you something to drink?"

Jeff stood up and I wasn't sure, but he looked relieved he didn't have to reply to my question. "No, I better be on my way."

I stood to walk with him to the door. Nathaniel came alongside me and put his arm around my waist. I sighed in contentment.

Jeff shook Nathaniel's hand. "It was an honor being invited this afternoon. Thank you."

"I'm glad it worked out for you to join us."

Jeff smiled at me. "Abby, it was a privilege and thank you for the lessons you taught me." He winked. "And by the way, you're no lightweight."

We said our good-byes to Jeff and Nathaniel led me to the bedroom. Apparently, when I'd been talking with Jeff, he'd been busy. Soft piano music greeted me when he opened the door. He'd pulled the shades so the room was dim and one of the trays that had been delivered earlier was in the middle of the bed.

"Looks like you did more than wash your hands, Master," I said, taking note of the pillows piled on top of the bed.

"You never got to eat," he said, pulling me forward. "And I wanted to give you time to talk with Jeff."

"You never ate *and* you didn't climax."

He turned me so we faced each other and he pressed his forehead to mine. "You worry about me too much, Abigail. You need to focus on doing what I ask and leave the rest to me."

"I love you; of course I'm going to worry." I pressed my lips to his in a soft kiss. "Besides, you need to keep up your strength."

He smiled against my lips. "Trust me. When it comes to you, I have enough strength for half a dozen men."

"Half a dozen, Master?"

"Maybe a dozen."

"That seems more likely."

He pulled away and I was struck anew by the love and desire in his eyes. "Now come with me and we'll have a little picnic in bed. And if you're really worried about my strength, you can feed me a bite or two."

I felt almost giddy climbing into bed. He propped me up on the pillows and fluffed a few around me. I felt like a princess.

"Take the robe off, Abigail."

Okay, I felt like a naked princess. But I shrugged out of the robe, just slightly peeved that he kept his clothes on. Not that I minded being naked; I just wanted him to be naked, too. I enjoyed looking at his body, imagining all the things he could do to me, remembering the way he tasted.

"Are you with me?" he asked. "You look like you're someplace else."

"I'm imagining you naked."

"I'd rather be naked, but you had an intense afternoon and you need some rest."

I raised an eyebrow. "I feel fine."

He lifted the dome off the tray and started filling a plate with almonds and blue cheese. "You don't know what I have planned for tomorrow."

That was enough to shut me up and he laughed at my shocked

expression. "Don't look so scared. You handled today—you can take tomorrow."

His mention of the next day reminded me of a question I had. "I was thinking, if you didn't have other plans for me in the morning, that I'd call Julie and see if I could interview her for the blog."

"Julie, Daniel's submissive?" He fed me an almond.

I chewed, then said, "Yes, she's new to the lifestyle and recently collared. I thought she'd make a nice contrast to my normal posts."

"You mean since you're a veteran and have been collared forever?"

I took the block of cheese he handed me. "Something like that."

"I don't have a problem with that. I can arrange what I had planned for another day." He took a sip of wine. "In fact, I think that's a great idea and will mesh nicely with what I have planned."

"I don't even want to know, do I?"

"Probably not."

I met Julie late the next morning at a café not far from the hotel. She'd obviously been at work at her flower shop; she wore a pink polo shirt with PETAL PUSHERS embroidered on the front.

"Love the name of your shop," I said, sitting down in a plush brown chair.

"Thanks. We wanted something people would remember." She took a sip of her latte and sighed. "Mmm, that is so good. We've been so busy this morning, I didn't even get a chance to make a pot. And I stayed at Daniel's last night and we got up late . . . Well, it was late when we got out of bed. We actually woke up early."

Her matter-of-fact attitude about it made me smile. "I remember those days."

"You say that like you don't have them anymore."

"We really don't. It's hard with the kids and all."

She nodded and took another sip of her latte. "How's the week going?"

"Good. Lots of new experiences. I'll have plenty to write about—that's for sure." I took out my notebook and flipped it open to a blank page. "Like I said on the phone, I want to keep this really casual. I won't use your name or anything that can identify you and if you don't want to answer a particular question, you won't hurt my feelings. You said you met Daniel when he came into your flower shop. Did you know he was a Dom then?"

"Oh, no," she said. "I had no idea, but when he left, my friend and business partner, Sasha, tried to steer me away from him."

"Didn't work, did it?" I asked with a grin.

"No." Her smile was full of the love she felt for her Dominant. "We couldn't stay away from each other. Even though it wasn't until I attended a group meeting with Sasha that I discovered he was a Dom."

"You went to a group meeting?"

"I'd always been curious and Sasha was . . . is a submissive."

"I see," I said, even though I wasn't clear on the Sasha details; was she a sub or wasn't she?

"Daniel introduced me to the lifestyle slowly and carefully. Sometimes, I think I'm ready for things, but he holds me back and makes me wait. I don't always like it, but I'd be lying if I said he wasn't almost always right."

"Pesky Doms."

She laughed. "Yes."

"If you don't mind me asking, how long have you and Daniel been together?"

"About four or five months." She ran a finger along the edge of her collar. "I've been collared for about a month."

I nodded and jotted that down. To be honest, I had no idea she was so new to the lifestyle. But her enthusiasm was like a breath of fresh air.

"You really have embraced your submissive nature," I said. "Was it easy to accept?"

"Hell, no." She laughed. "I actually turned my back on it for a while. But it felt like I was living a lie. I couldn't give it up and still be me, you know? It was almost as if I was playacting at not being submissive."

I jotted her words down. "That's an interesting way to put it. I don't think I've ever heard anyone describe it quite that way. But it's true—it would be like a part of yourself was missing."

She nodded. "I'd have lost Daniel, too. He said he'd still have dated me even if I wasn't submissive, but I couldn't have asked him to ignore that side of his nature."

"I don't have to ask what it's like having your first Dom be so much more experienced than you are. I was like that, too."

"I think it's better someone knows what they're doing," she said with a laugh. "That's one of the benefits of belonging to a group—you get to pull from everyone's experiences. The only problem with ours is like I told you—there aren't any long-term couples."

"That is a shame. Our group in New York has several."

"Including you," she said.

"We haven't been very active the last few years. Since the kids were born."

"You're still around if someone needs you though. That counts for something. And you're helping a lot of people with the blog. I hope I can help people one day."

Julie was easy to talk with; she was down-to-earth, intelligent, and lively. It didn't take much to see why she'd captured the eye of someone like Daniel.

"You're helping now," I told her. "With the interview. Who knows? Maybe there'll be a woman browsing through blogs looking for someone who's taken the leap and she'll come across the piece I write on you."

She smiled and twirled her coffee cup. "That's a good way to look at it."

The café was relatively quiet with only a few people inside with us. We'd been talking in low voices and Julie had just finished sharing about her collaring ceremony when the door opened and we both jumped.

"Julie!" a tall, willowy blond woman called, approaching our corner seats. "Sasha said I'd find you here. Sorry to interrupt. Can I speak to you for a minute?"

Julie jumped up. "Are you okay?"

Whoever the woman was, she looked beautiful in an ethereal, angelic way. Her blond hair danced around her shoulders in loose waves and her eyes were a warm blue. She spoke animatedly to Julie for several minutes while I checked messages on my phone to give them privacy. The two ladies hugged and turned to me once again.

"Hi, I'm Dena," the blonde said. "Again, I'm so sorry to crash like this, but I'm traveling the rest of the week and had to speak to Julie."

I shook her hand. "Abby, and don't worry about it. I think we were just about finished anyway."

"No, no, don't stop because of me. I'm really going. And thank you, Julie. I'll call you when I'm back in town."

"Speak soon," Julie said. "I won't mention anything to Daniel, but I still think you should tell Jeff."

My head spun to Dena at Julie's comment. *Jeff?* No way, it

couldn't be. The fact that she was blond was just a coincidence. But the look on Dena's face made me think maybe it was more. Her expression was a copy of the one Jeff had worn just the day before.

"I know I should," Dena said. "But I can't. I just . . . can't."

Julie looked just as sad. "Call me."

The atmosphere had changed when we sat down after Dena left. Julie looked a bit shaken. She picked at the remnant of her blueberry scone.

"Everything okay?" I asked. I didn't want to pry, but clearly something had upset her.

"Yeah. It goes back to what we were saying earlier. When you lie to yourself, you're just playacting and it always leads to trouble." She leaned forward with her head in her hands. "And I told her I wouldn't tell Daniel."

I thought that had *bad idea* written all over it, and even though we weren't close, I felt I still needed to say something. "It's none of my business, but I'm going to give you some advice anyway."

She looked up. "I have a feeling I know what you're going to say."

"Then let me say it. I'd be very careful about keeping things from Daniel. It's a slippery slope you don't want to start down, because you'll find you have a hard time working your way back up to the top."

"I know. You're right." She shook her head. "I wouldn't like it if Daniel kept things from me. But I also gave Dena my word."

I could almost see the emotions battling inside her as she tried to decide what to do. She sighed and I knew she wasn't going to tell him. Her decision hung in the air for several long seconds.

"Well," I finally said. "I can't leave on a down note, so let me ask one more question."

"Hit me with it," she said, and some spark of her previous joviality returned to her eyes.

"Favorite thing Daniel wears in the playroom and you can't say nothing. We all like our Doms naked."

She laughed. "How did you know I was going to say that?"

"Because I know what I'd say." I picked up the notebook and pen. "So? What's it going to be?"

She leaned back into the chair and crossed her arms. "Give me a second. I have to think. When I tell you, will you tell me what yours is?"

"Of course."

"Okay, it's a tough call, but my favorite is when he wears a white dress shirt. I don't care if it's part of a suit or if he's wearing it with jeans. Definitely a white dress shirt."

I jotted that down. "You know the next question: why?"

"When we're in the playroom and he's wearing one and he slowly unbuttons his cuffs"—her voice had a breathy quality to it as she spoke—"his eyes are on mine and he begins to roll the sleeve up. Carefully. Methodically. All the while watching me. To see him preparing for whatever it is he's going to do makes me all quivery inside. And then once he has it rolled up, you can see just a hint of muscle and you know that within minutes those muscles are going to be put to work for my pleasure?" She sighed. "White dress shirt. No question."

"Damn, girl," I said, my pen frozen in place. "That's about enough to make me want to change my answer."

"That's cheating. You have to tell me yours."

"Okay, fine. It's his belt."

"Belt?" she asked, wrinkling her nose. "Why?"

"Because when I'm bent over something and he comes up behind me and I hear the belt slowly slide from his pants, I know what's coming. Sometimes he'll have me kiss it and the smell of the leather fills my head as he steps behind me and I hear it whistle through the air." I shivered just thinking about it. "But it doesn't stop in the playroom. He'll wear it the next day to work or out with the family and seeing it around his waist brings back every slap and stroke. His eyes will catch mine and he'll give me a little smile because he knows exactly what I'm thinking."

She fell back against her seat and sighed. "Wow, that almost has me wanting to ask Daniel to use a belt on me."

We looked at each other, both with big grins on our faces, and before long we were giggling. When I left a few minutes later, it was with a light heart and quick feet.

I hurried back to the hotel. Nathaniel wasn't due for another couple of hours, but I needed to work on getting my notes on Julie's interview typed up. And I really wanted to take extra time to prepare for when he did return to the room.

The afternoon with Jeff yesterday had been more of a turn-on than I would have ever thought possible. I wanted to write down some thoughts about it as well. Being blindfolded and knowing Jeff was watching, but couldn't touch me intimately had heightened the intensity of the session.

I wanted to show Nathaniel how much I appreciated him inviting Jeff over. And part of that would be taking extra special care to prepare for his return this afternoon.

I stepped inside and frowned. The shades had been pulled and the entire suite was pitch-black. That didn't seem right; whenever we'd pulled the shades before, some light was always visible. It was almost as if housekeeping had replaced the draperies with heavy-duty ones.

I reached out to find the light switch when someone grabbed me around the waist and pushed me against the wall. I tried to scream, but a strong hand covered my mouth before I could get a sound out. Any move I made to escape was anticipated and rendered useless.

My heart pounded frantically as I struggled against the unyielding mass of muscle behind me. *Oh, God. No.*

His voice was rough. "Your safe word is *red*. Say it at any time
and this ends immediately. Otherwise"—he bit my ear—"I do
whatever I damn well want to with you."

My mind recognized it was Nathaniel, but my body was
poised to fight. He paused for a second, obviously giving me a
moment to safeword. I didn't want to safe out; I wanted to see
how far he'd go. His hold loosened slightly and I took the opportunity to wiggle my arm free and swing at him.

It was a blind swing, but his grunt confirmed I'd connected
with some body part. He cursed and pushed me harder against
the wall. He pulled my arms behind my back, even as I struggled
to resist. "You're going to pay for that."

So quickly I didn't immediately realize what he was doing, my
arms were tied behind my back. I twisted one way and then the
other, but his bonds were sound and I got nowhere.

"Go ahead. Fight. It just turns me on more."

"Bastard." I kicked a leg back toward him and hit nothing
but air.

His chuckle sent shivers down my spine. "Call me all the
names you want—we both know this will only end up one way."
He grabbed a fistful of hair and pulled my head back. "And that's
with me fucking the shit out of you."

"Sounds messy."

He pushed my head against the wall. "Enough. If you say
anything other than *red*, you'll regret it. Understand? Nod if
you do."

I nodded. For some reason his cool reminder of my safe word
seemed even scarier than if he'd said nothing about it.

He pushed a knee into my lower back and tied a blindfold over my eyes. I told myself it was okay, it was only Nathaniel, but for some reason my body still trembled.

"We're going to walk into the living room nice and quietly. And if you know what's good for you, you won't fight me."

We walked the short distance to the living room. He led me while keeping hold on my tied hands. I decided to act like I was playing along and when we came to a stop, I'd make a break for it. Just to see what he'd do.

I hid a smile. Nathaniel thought he had the upper hand and while I appreciated his willingness to act out my capture fantasy, I was beginning to relax with the thought that this was only a well-planned role play.

We stopped in what I guessed to be the middle of the room, near the couch. I tried to anticipate his next move, tried to decide the best time to make my break—when I heard a sound from the far side of the room that made my blood run cold and turned my feet into stone.

A cough.

Chapter Ten

"Gentlemen," Nathaniel said in a frightfully calm voice. "Our entertainment for the afternoon has arrived."

Faint applause came from the same direction as the cough. More than one person. Two maybe, but no more than three. Unfortunately, my surprise cost me. During my hesitation, he untied my arms and rebound them, spread above my head.

I pulled on the restraints and tried to guess what I was tied to. I couldn't remember anything in the room that could bind me in my current position. My heart started racing again. We'd played in front of people before, but nothing even close to this. Even yesterday with Jeff hadn't been like this.

Nathaniel grabbed my chin. "Are you going to be a good girl for my guests?"

I pressed my lips together, refusing to give him an answer.

"Going to be like that, are you?" He let go of my chin and I felt him move away. "Very well. Hope you aren't overly attached to this shirt."

Something sharp pressed against my back. For a second, I thought it was a knife, but I felt it open and realized it was a pair of scissors. With determined efficiency, he cut through my T-shirt and I gasped as cool air met my skin.

"A lovely bra," he said, tracing the edges of the lacy cup.

"Beautiful," an unfamiliar voice called out and I jumped at its sound.

"Anyone else want to see her tits?" Nathaniel asked.

More applause came from the side of the room along with a jumble of voices I couldn't make out.

Nathaniel stood behind me, running his hands over my shoulders, and he whispered in my ear, "You're standing in the middle of the living room, facing them. I'm going to strip you naked and they're going to see every inch of you. First I'll start with your bra."

He undid the clasp at the back. "Your breasts will be like a little teaser. Soon, I'm going to have you undress the rest of the way and show them just how wet being treated like this makes you."

He palmed my breast under the material of the bra and pinched my nipples. His hands were rough as they pulled and stroked. "Too bad you're all tied up. I'm going to have to cut this bra off so that everyone can see you."

With two snips of the scissors, my bra was gone and I was topless. There was a murmuring of voices from the men in the room, but they spoke too low and I couldn't make out what they were saying. Nathaniel was stroking me again.

"Normally, I'd put clamps on her, but she had them on yesterday so I thought I'd do something different today."

I felt his absence as he stepped away and I couldn't hear what he did, but there were whispers of approval from across the room.

"Mark her."

"Make her whimper."

Just hearing them made me throb with need even as I struggled to hear a hint of what Nathaniel was doing.

"Give me a number, S," Nathaniel said.

"Five," a voice that sounded vaguely familiar replied.

"Five on each it is."

Five what?

Something swished through the air and a sharp slap stung my
nipple. Fuck, a crop.

"Again," someone said and the crop landed a second time, but
on the opposite breast.

I couldn't hold back the, "Owww," when it landed a third
time.

"Silence." Nathaniel struck a fourth time. "Or else I gag you
and double it."

I bit the inside of my cheek to keep quiet. It fucking stung.
The men in the room started counting each strike and I focused
on that to stay quiet.

When they finally called, "Ten," Nathaniel pressed himself
against me. My breasts ached when they rubbed across his shirt.

"You handled that well," he said. "Now for a little reward."

His mouth engulfed a nipple, sucking hard and deep, running
his tongue across the tip. I swallowed a moan and pushed my
chest forward, wanting, *needing*, more. He granted my request,
moving to the opposite nipple and taking it between his teeth,
tugging sharply.

He continued his sensual assault on my breasts and it felt as if
he was feasting on me. My nipples had grown more sensitive
with each of my pregnancies. At times I thought I could come
from breast play alone. Every tug, every nip shot straight between my legs, making me crave more.

"I could do this for hours," he murmured against my skin,
"were I not so ready for the next course." His hand slid down my

side and curved around to rest on the top of my ass. "Though I warn you, if I find out you're not wearing panties, you will be punished."

He knew as well as I did that he hadn't laid out panties for me today. Just to be obstinate, I brought my legs together. He hadn't tied them apart, after all.

"You're only making this harder on yourself." The cool metal of the scissors pressed along the cleft of my ass, cutting slowly through the thin cotton of my shorts "Such a waste." The sharp tip inched around to my front. "I suggest you hold still. I'd hate for my fingers to slip."

I don't think I took a breath as he methodically cut my shorts completely away. Inch by torturous inch, the material parted and the metal drew closer and closer to my needy flesh. I whimpered as the scissors slid past my throbbing clit.

"Tsk-tsk-tsk," he scolded as the shorts fell away. "Look at this. It appears the naughty girl isn't wearing panties. You know what that means?"

"About time," a strange voice called from the back of the room.

"Such a shame," another voice said, and this one I recognized from the day before. From the way Jeff said it, I could tell it wasn't really a shame.

Nathaniel cupped my ass. "First of all, I have to do something about these legs."

I felt him move away and when he returned, he attached my ankle to what I recognized as one end of a spreader bar. Being open and exposed shouldn't have turned me on as much as it did. But knowing that Nathaniel was getting ready to do wickedly depraved things to me while others watched heightened my arousal more.

He came behind me, wrapping his arms around my chest. He

fondled my breasts and then ran his hands down my side, sliding a finger along the wetness between my legs.

"You look so hot like this, naked and spread like a sacrifice." His breath was warm against my ear and my skin broke out in gooseflesh. "They're all watching me touch you, wishing they were the one with their fingers buried in your pussy. When they're in bed tonight, I bet they'll dream about having their dicks in you, fucking you while you're tied like this. One of them already has his cock out. He's stroking it."

I moaned at the thought. Would it be Jeff? I doubted it. That left the stranger and the man with the familiar voice I couldn't place.

He slapped my ass. "I can smell you, Abigail. That makes you horny, doesn't it? Knowing he wants to fuck you? That they all want to take turns fucking you?"

It did. God help me, it did.

"They all know, though, that only one cock is allowed that privilege." He pushed his jean-clad erection against my ass. "But to help them get a feel for how it would be, I might bend you over the arm of a chair and let them watch while I fuck you senseless." He began rocking his hips. "You'll be in the perfect position for them to see my cock slowly push inside your pussy. Buried so damn deep inside you. Then I'll pull almost all the way out and plunge back inside again."

His fingers had been sliding in and out of me while he talked, but right as I neared my climax, he pulled away.

"No release yet," he said. "First you have to take the flogging I'm going to give you."

Something light and airy brushed across my thighs. *Rabbit fur.* I sighed and relaxed in my bonds. This was what I loved. Nathaniel commanding me as my unyielding Master. Allowing me to hold nothing back, but to give him my all and knowing as I did, that he would give me the same.

He spent a long time working my body with the light flogger, a sign I took to mean that he planned to use heavier ones for quite some time. I'd grown accustomed to the breezy feel of the fur when a harder thud hit my backside. Then there were two, two floggers striking me over and over as his fingers caressed me, transforming the pain into intense pleasure. I was free.

"How are you doing?" Nathaniel asked in a whisper.

"Green," I managed to get out. "Green, Master. Don't. Stop."

He chuckled. "A little more then."

"Thank you. Thank you," I replied, but wasn't sure he heard.

The flogger tails landed faster and harder and carried me along on a pleasure-filled high unlike any I could remember experiencing before. And he was with me the entire time, his strength supporting me, his adoration protecting me.

"Beautiful," an unknown voice said.

"Amazing," said another.

"Stunning," said a third.

But it was the voice I loved that I listened for and finally heard. "Mine."

I could tell the minute he started bringing me down, carrying me slowly off the mountain peak I'd been on. And though I wanted to protest, I forced myself to remember that he knew best and that I had to trust him. I doubted our afternoon was over. Something told me he wouldn't be going without his own climax today.

"Are you with me?" Nathaniel asked.

"Yes, Master." I was still highly aroused, but the floaty feeling I'd had while he flogged me was wearing off.

He bent down to unbuckle my ankles from the spreader bar, massaging my legs as he did. Then he released my arms from whatever they were attached to, but left them tied together in front of me.

"I'm going to take you to the couch," he said, gently rubbing my shoulders. "Are you able to walk?"

I stretched each leg. "Yes, Master."

I'd thought the men were sitting on the couch, but I didn't feel their presence when he led me to the plush sofa and told me to sit down. I listened, but didn't hear any movement.

"You're wondering if they're still here," Nathaniel whispered. "Or maybe you're thinking you imagined the entire thing and they were never here to begin with."

I'd long ago learned he could nearly read my mind, so it didn't surprise me like it used to when he voiced what I was thinking. But it hadn't occurred to me I might have imagined them. I hadn't done that, had I? They had been here. I'd heard them.

"Maybe they're here and they're just being quiet because they're concentrating on you. Part your lips."

I obeyed and he put a finger up to my mouth, tracing my lips but not having me suck his finger.

"Maybe they're watching and imagining this is their finger touching you. Better yet, it's their cock and you're getting ready to show them what a good cocksucker you are."

My heart pounded and he continued to oh-so-easily tease my lips. "Does it make you wet thinking about how aroused you're making them? You like it when people watch you. Don't you, you naughty girl?"

It did. Fuck. It got me off.

His hands left me briefly and there was again nothing but silence until I heard him behind me.

"Let's say the three gentlemen are, in fact, still here. Show them how wet you are thinking about them watching. Knowing they're getting hard just at the sight of you."

Still no sound from anyone other than Nathaniel.

He slapped my thigh. "Spread them. Now."

I moved my legs apart, but since my hands were still tied in front of me, I don't think they saw much.

"How forgetful of me," he said. "Let me take care of that." And with a snip of his scissors, my hands were free. "I want your hands on your knees. Keep your legs spread."

I felt wanton and wild, but I did as he asked.

"Wider."

Apparently, it felt like they were wider than they actually were. I moved my knees apart until my position felt obscene.

"That'll do. Stay still," he said. "Gentlemen, how about some drinks?"

There was a general murmur and clinking of ice in glasses. I expected Nathaniel to say something to me, but instead I was simply ignored. Or at least it felt that way. The men in the room started chatting in voices so low I couldn't make out their words.

I stayed in position and waited.

And they talked. And talked. And talked.

Eventually my arms grew tired and my legs ached. And still they ignored me. It was as if I wasn't even in the room.

Someone put more ice in their glass. I felt like pouting. What point was there in being naked and blindfolded if I was going to be ignored? I briefly considered taking a nap. After all, who would know? I had a blindfold on.

"I think someone's feeling neglected," Nathaniel said and I jerked at the surprise of being addressed.

I heard him walk toward me. Something wet was placed on my upper right thigh.

"Don't let the glass fall," he said and walked away.

"Mind if I put my glass down?" the unknown person asked.

"Go ahead," Nathaniel said. "Her other thigh looks bare. It'd be nice for it to be symmetrical."

There was a snort of laughter from another man and I felt another glass on my left thigh.

"Don't let that fall, girl," the unknown voice said. His voice was smooth and seductive. "Though it would interesting to see what your Master would do."

He didn't touch any part of me, but I shivered at his words and immediately regretted it. The glasses wobbled, but didn't fall.

"Now maybe you won't zone out while we finish our discussion," Nathaniel said.

Holy shit! They were going to keep talking? What started out as a hot scene had grown tiresome and boring. I was naked in front of a group of men and instead of doing naughty things to me, they were using me as a makeshift coffee table.

I wondered what my blog readers would think of this.

Could I safeword out of boredom?

"Well, Abigail," Nathaniel said after what felt like hours later. "I hope you enjoyed your little rest. It's time for the fun to really begin."

I snorted.

I didn't mean to snort; it just kind of came out. I blamed it on the time I'd spent on the couch doing nothing but balancing glasses on my thighs. Unfortunately, it did come out and it wasn't soft. One of the men actually stifled a laugh.

"Was that a *snort*, Abigail?" Nathaniel asked.

It was probably a rhetorical question. After all, it really didn't sound like anything other than a snort and even if I tried to pass it off as something else, there were three men other than Nathaniel in the room and they'd certainly heard it.

"Yes, Master. It was a snort."

"Would you care to explain why you snorted?"

"Well, I was sitting here on the couch, trying to be good and not let the glasses fall and after a while I just got bored. Then I tried to imagine what I'd write on the blog about the last hour. I imagined an entry I would call, *I was a coffee table*. Probably wouldn't get a lot of hits. Seriously, what's hot about a coffee table?"

"I assume you're getting to the part soon where you snorted instead of all this babbling?" he said.

"Right, the snort. It was just hearing you say it was time for the fun to begin. I thought, 'Hell, anything would be more fun than this.'"

"Is that all?"

"I may have also thought, 'About damn time.'"

"I see," he said. "So I was boring you?"

At that moment I realized I'd stepped in over my head. "You weren't boring me, Master. It was the coffee table part."

"Nice of you to finally call me 'Master.' Now let me get this straight: you snorted not because I was boring you, but because what I chose to have you do was boring?"

"And it'd make a bad blog post," I hastened to add so he'd see it wasn't all *me*.

"Right. No one wants to read about a coffee table."

In the silence that followed, the air shifted around me as he came to stand before me. He put one hand lightly around my neck. Nothing restrictive; it was just there.

His voice was cold. "Let me make one thing perfectly clear. I don't give a *fuck* what would make a good blog post. I do what I do because *I* want to, not because of what makes your readers happy. The day our relationship becomes all about your blog is the day the blog and the job stop. Understand?"

I cringed at the way it sounded coming from his point of view. My heart pounded in my throat. He probably felt it. "Yes, Master."

"As for being bored, I thought you'd already learned this lesson, but apparently you haven't." He moved his hand. "Would you gentlemen be so kind as to tell my submissive what we were discussing over drinks?"

The unknown man coughed. "I mentioned how lovely you were sitting on the couch. The light from the window crossing your body right below your breasts. Would be a gorgeous photo."

"I told your Master how impressed I was that you remained so still," Jeff said. "Then I suggested he fondle those perky tits to see if he could make you drop a glass."

That left the man Nathaniel called S. "I was a bit more explicit than these two," he said. "I told your Master he should fuck you while you struggled to keep the glasses in place. See if you can be still with a cock plundering your pussy."

"Thank you," Nathaniel said. "Were any of you bored at all watching Abigail on the couch?"

They all three replied negatively.

"So you see, Abigail," Nathaniel said. "While you may have been bored acting like our table, we were having a drink and enjoying the sight of you. It pleases me to show you off and if I decide to have you be a coffee table for everyone to enjoy, what should your mind-set be?"

"That I am here for my Master's pleasure."

"Yes, and sometimes that doesn't mean pleasure for you. Sometimes it means being a coffee table. But you do it anyway because that is what pleases me."

"I understand, Master."

"That might well be the case, but just to make sure, no release for you today."

He took his glass from my leg. "Take the other one and offer it to S."

I held up the glass, and S came over and took it. "Too damn

bad about no releasing. I was looking forward to watching you come. Maybe another time."

I no longer felt bored. I felt disappointed. Disappointed in myself for not having the right mind frame. For putting my blog first.

"On your knees in the middle of the room," Nathaniel said. "I'll direct you verbally and I want you to crawl."

Ever so slowly, I made it down off the couch and following Nathaniel's commands made it to where he wanted me. It had to be one of the most ungraceful crawls ever, but I did it because he'd asked me to. Once in place, I knelt with my head down.

I heard a zipper being unzipped in front of me. Even though I knew it wouldn't be anyone else, the thought crossed my mind it could be.

"I'm taking my cock out, Abigail."

I opened my mouth, ready to have him inside me and eager to please him.

"Not today. That mouth doesn't deserve my cock in it. Your pussy doesn't either."

I closed my mouth and blinked back tears under the blindfold.

"Straighten your spine and lace your hands behind your back. Keep your head up."

Doing so pushed my chest forward. Obviously his intention.

"What do you think, gentlemen?" he asked. "Have you ever seen anything hotter than a submissive bowing before her Master's cock?"

"Mark her tits," S said and the other men cheered.

"I'm stroking my cock, Abigail," Nathaniel said. "It's getting so hard. Just think, if you had behaved, I wouldn't have to use my hands. I'd be pumping my dick in and out of you. Fucking you nice and hard, just the way we both like." He groaned. "I'm stroking it faster. Faster."

I loved the sight of him masturbating and he wasn't even going to let me enjoy that. I listened as hard as I could, taking in his breathing as it grew shorter and shorter. I imagined his hands working his erection while listening to the sounds of flesh against flesh.

"They're all watching," he panted out. "Looking at you kneeling on the floor, ready to take my release." He groaned again. "Are you bored now? Think your readers want to hear about you with your breasts pushed out, silently begging for your Master to mark them? I marked them earlier with the crop. Now I'm going to mark them with my release."

I held as still as possible. I couldn't see anything, but I could picture it vividly in my head. I grew wet between my thighs, but I did my best to ignore it.

This isn't about me. This isn't about me. I am here for my Master and I take pleasure only if he allows.

"Fuck," he ground out. "Here it comes. All over those gorgeous tits."

I didn't move as he released on me. I only wished I wasn't blindfolded so I could see. This wasn't something he did often, but I always got a secret thrill out of it when he did. It felt so primitive. So raw. I loved the feel of his pleasure on me.

"So damn hot," he said. "On your knees. Wearing my collar. Decorated with my release."

He zipped himself back up and there was rustling around me as the other men started to chat among themselves.

Nathaniel stroked my head. "Stay where you are."

It wasn't the same as acting like a table. Instead I felt sort of like a statue. Unmoving. In place for the amusement of others. After Nathaniel's commentary on my thoughts while on the couch, I revised my thinking while I knelt on the floor.

I wasn't *just* a statue. I was Nathaniel's statue and I was an object of desire. Especially when I was marked by him the way I was. I held still while the men did whatever it was they were doing. I steered my focus away from my knees when they began to ache and focused on being and doing what Nathaniel wanted.

"I have to leave now, Pretty Abby," the unknown man with the smooth voice said. "But thanks to this afternoon, you'll be joining me in my fantasies tonight."

He didn't touch me, but his words washed over me like a sensual caress. I bet he could drive submissives wild with that seductive voice. It hit me then. I had no idea what he looked like.

"Thank you, Nathaniel," he said. "I'll confirm everything tomorrow with my admin, but it all looks good from my end."

"Thank you, DeVaan," Nathaniel replied and I heard the two walk to the door.

That left the other two men still in the room. The familiar one and Jeff.

They both walked up behind me at the same time.

"A pleasure as always," the familiar one said. "Though a bit different than last time."

It took me only a few seconds to place the voice as being Simon's. The first thought that entered my head was, "What was he doing in Delaware?" That was quickly followed by my surprise at not recognizing him immediately. I wondered what he thought about taking part in the fantasy I had talked about at lunch a few months ago.

"Why don't you go freshen up in the bathroom," Nathaniel said as soon as everyone had left.

That sounded like a wonderful idea, so I took my time with my shower and blowing my hair dry. While I'd been bathing, he'd hung a white fluffy robe on the door hook. I slipped it on, sighing at its softness.

I opened the door and gasped.

"Master."

He'd placed lit candles on every flat available surface and put on soft piano music. Since the walls were painted a simple off-white, everything looked and felt soft and inviting. In the middle of the room was a massage table covered with thick warm towels. Nathaniel stood beside it, holding out his hand.

I walked to him and he began to untie my robe. "You've given yourself to me for the last few days. You're serving me well." He ran his hands up my body, sliding the robe from my shoulders. "Now I want to serve you for a while."

A shiver ran through my body and he dropped a tiny kiss first on one shoulder and then the other.

"You're incredible," I said. "Do you know that?"

"If I am, it's because you make me that way," he whispered in my ear. "Up on the table, on your belly."

I kissed his cheek before getting into position. He followed behind, pulling more towels and a blanket over me. He started by caressing my back and shoulders over the blanket, and I sighed at how good his hands felt. Gently, he worked his way down my back, slowly increasing the intensity of his hands. After a few minutes, he eased the blanket midway down my back and swept my hair to one side. He pressed a kiss at the nape of my neck, causing my skin to pebble with gooseflesh. He laughed and kissed me again.

He slowly took his time working the knots out of my back and shoulders. After he worked his way down my arms, the entire room smelled like the citrus ginger lotion he used. My eyes grew heavy.

"You have the most amazing hands," I mumbled at one point. "You make everything feel so good."

He lifted my hand to his lips and kissed the palm. "Your hands are pretty amazing, too."

"Yeah, but you don't let me massage you."

"Nope," he agreed. "Massage after play is for me to do for you. It's my way of caring for you."

It was an argument we'd had often over the years. His insistence that the aftercare he gave me wasn't something I could perform on him. Certain things we did together. A shared bath and glass of wine was a favorite. Or holding each other in bed or on the couch. And sometimes we'd just make love, a sensual easement back into our weekday lives.

"I'd argue with you, but I'm too relaxed right now," I teased. "I'll eventually work my strength back, though, and then you better look out."

"Oh?" He lifted the blanket and started massaging my right leg.

"Yeah," I said with a yawn. "As soon as I find the energy to get off this table."

He chuckled, fully aware that by the time he finished with the massage, odds were good I'd be asleep.

"Turn over for me, baby."

Baby. I loved it when he called me baby while I wore his collar.

I flipped over to my back and met his gaze, bathing in the love and devotion I found there. I didn't say anything, but closed my eyes and allowed him to serve me.

Chapter Eleven

He woke me up the next morning with room service breakfast in bed. I slowly blinked awake, prodded along by a kiss and whispered promises of coffee. I went to roll over to get up and groaned. Every damn part of me hurt. I'd enjoyed the day before—well, most of it—but I'd forgotten how sore I'd be the morning following such play.

"Take these," Nathaniel said, holding two tablets to my mouth and passing me a glass of water. I gulped them down and then pulled myself up to a sitting position.

"Bit sore?" he asked.

"I think that's an understatement, Master." I took a sip of coffee and sighed. *And thank fucking goodness I didn't sleep on the floor.*

"I won't say I'm sorry."

"I wouldn't want you to."

He put the breakfast tray in front of me. Everything looked delicious. I reached for a fork, but he shook his head and instead lifted a piece of pineapple to my lips.

"I'm free all day."

"Really?" I said around the pineapple.

"Yes, we can spend the entire day together." He fed me a bit of scrambled eggs. "There's an art gallery I want to take you to. Then we can have lunch, maybe do some shopping."

"I'd love to visit an art gallery, Master."

His smile was mischievous. "I know."

He must have eaten while I was sleeping because he didn't take a bite of anything. Instead, he fed me. He took his time, giving me pieces of fruit, eggs, and ham. It'd been a long time since we'd enjoyed a leisurely morning in bed and having Nathaniel feed me was one of my favorite things to do, so I felt fully pampered and happy.

After I finished, I went off to shower and put on the clothes he had laid out for me. He was on the phone with Linda and the kids when I came out of the bathroom. For a few minutes, I watched. He laughed at something Elizabeth said and when she passed the phone to Henry, I heard his, "Mama. Dada," from where I stood.

He told everyone good-bye and then passed the phone to me. I talked with Elizabeth first, who bemoaned the fact that Henry's obsession with the trash can had led to him throwing away everything he could pick up. She held the phone up to him and his toddler babbles warmed my heart.

"Miss you. I love you. See you soon," I said.

Nathaniel came up behind me and put his arms around my waist, and I sighed. "It's hard being away from them," he said.

"Yes."

It was always hard to be away, even knowing Nathaniel and I had to take time for ourselves and our marriage. It was easier knowing they were with Linda. They always enjoyed spending time with her and, if Nathaniel and I thought she spoiled them, we also both knew that's what grandparents were supposed to do.

He kissed the back of my head. "Let's go see some art."

He called for a car and since the requirements he'd put in place for the cocktail party were in place today, I smiled at the driver, but didn't speak. Once we were inside the car, I sat beside Nathaniel and rested my hand on his knee.

We drove in silence to the gallery. We didn't get much silence with kids in the house. I loved their giggles and chatter, but there was something to be said for quiet, too.

I'd always thought simply being in another person's presence and enjoying the stillness with them held its own kind of intimacy. Nathaniel reached down to where my hand rested on his knee and entwined his fingers with mine. I squeezed his hand gently in acknowledgment and laid my head on his shoulder. I actually wished the gallery was farther away.

I loved art galleries, though, and I was excited about this one. I discovered my fondness of art not long after we got married. Exploring galleries must be similar to how a treasure hunter feels when he finds a chest: you never knew what treat you'd find inside.

For me, it was all about impression and the emotion a painting evoked. I never judged something on what the world said it was worth. In fact, our dining room held a painting I found in an antique store for fifteen dollars three years ago. I told Nathaniel it made me feel happy when I looked at it. Frankly, he thought it looked like any other landscape, but then again, he wasn't much into art.

When we pulled up to the gallery, he held the door open for me and whispered, "I'm looking for something to go in the playroom and I'd like your opinion."

I stopped in my tracks. "The playroom, Sir?"

Putting a hand at the small of my back, he guided me inside. "Yes. I think the walls are too bare. I'd like some inspiration."

I couldn't imagine what kind of artwork he'd put in the play-room. Certainly nothing we saw as we walked through. There were several lovely pieces, but nothing that stood out.

Nathaniel spoke to the curator and he led us to a small back room. I wasn't prepared for what I saw and I stood in awe for a long minute.

The room was filled with erotic black-and-white photographs. Or else, they might have been erotic if they showed what they hinted at. Technically speaking, they were only suggestive.

I exhaled deeply and walked up to one, a shot of a submissive's back, bound by intrinsically woven ropes. "Master, it's beautiful."

"Why don't you look around and let me know if you see something you like."

I was thrilled by the idea of exploring the pictures alone. Not that I didn't want to share my thoughts with Nathaniel, but see-ing the pictures evoked such a response from me. I supposed it was because they were all of submissives and I related in some way to every one of them.

I strolled from picture to picture, noting how carefully the photographer had worked with the light. He used the shadows and the darkness in a way that transformed the women he pho-tographed. And the emotion he captured took my breath away.

"Abigail," Nathaniel said. "Come here for a moment."

He was talking with a man and they both watched me as I ap-proached. The strange man was devilishly handsome with wavy brown hair and blue eyes that almost seemed to be laughing. As if he had a secret I wasn't in on.

"Abigail, this is the gallery's owner and the man behind the camera."

"Pleased to meet you," he said, shaking my hand in a smooth-as-silk voice I recognized immediately. He was the third guy from the previous day. I faltered, just for a second. Should I say something about yesterday? Or just act as normal as possible? Did I even have permission to speak?

I looked to Nathaniel and he nodded. "Master DeVaan," he said, giving me the gentleman's name.

"Nice to meet you, Sir," I replied, deciding to go for normal. "Your work is amazing."

"Thank you. Any photograph in particular you like?"

"Your rope work is remarkable, but I think my favorites are the profiles, especially where the submissive is kneeling." I nodded toward a picture near us. It was a close-up of a kneeling sub and only a portion of her face was visible.

"Interesting," he said. "That's one of my favorites, too."

I walked to it. "It's her expression that captured my attention. You can't see a lot of it, but from what I can tell, this was taken after the scene was over. She has that sated, blissful look about her."

"Very astute," DeVaan said. "That's exactly when it was taken."

"There's something else, though." I tilted my head. "She's a bit sad, I think, or maybe unsettled is the better word. Or yearning. She doesn't want the scene to be over. She wants to serve you more, but she's obeying you and not insisting upon it. It's that conflict in her expression that makes it hard to look away."

"Yes," he said. "Yes. That's it exactly. Incredible. Most people never see that much."

"It's only because it's a position I've been in before. I recognize a kindred spirit."

"Master West is a fortunate man to have captured the heart of such an insightful woman." He tipped his head toward me. "And submissive."

"Thank you, Sir."

"He is fortunate indeed." Nathaniel came up behind me and slipped his arms around me. "So tell me, my lovely, is this the one for the playroom?"

"You want my honest opinion, Master?"

"Always."

"The pictures are all beautiful, but I don't think they're right for us."

"No?" He seemed surprised. I wasn't sure why. Did he really think I wanted a picture of another woman in his playroom?

"If you wouldn't be opposed, Master, it would be my pleasure to pose for a photo for the playroom."

He stood in shock for several long seconds before saying, "Damn."

I turned in his arms. "Master?"

"I hadn't even thought of that. It's a brilliant idea." He looked over to DeVaan. "We'd like for you to photograph Abigail. Would it be possible to set up a time for you to come to New York?"

"Absolutely. It would be an honor."

"Excellent," Nathaniel said. "I'll call you once we get back home and we'll set something up."

As the two men continued talking, I walked back to look at the pictures. Seeing how he captured the light made DeVaan's comment about the sun on my body the day before make sense.

Nathaniel came up to me and put his hand on the small of my back. "Let's go get lunch."

DeVaan had left the room, so I didn't get the chance to say good-bye. I looked over my shoulder to glance one last time at the pictures displayed. My belly tightened with excitement over having a similar picture, but of me, in our playroom.

Our car was waiting for us outside and once we climbed in, Nathaniel turned to me.

"I'm taking the collar off for lunch."

I looked at him with my unspoken question in my eyes, but didn't say anything. I slid closer to him and bowed my head while he unclasped the collar. My neck felt unusually light after having it on for so long.

"How are you feeling?" he asked.

Typically, once he took the collar off, I would notice a slight shift in our relationship as we went from Dominant and submissive back into our everyday lives. But when I looked at him then, he still had the aura of my Master.

"Good," I said. "The week has been challenging, but I'm enjoying it so far."

"Glad to hear it." He took my hand and brought it to rest on his knee. He held it there stroking my knuckles with his thumb. "We'll talk more at lunch. Unless there's something you'd like to discuss now?"

I shook my head. "Nothing right now, but I'll admit to being insanely curious about what you want to talk about so badly that you took my collar off."

He brought my hand to his lips and placed a soft kiss to my skin. "Not just yet."

"That's what I figured," I said with a mock sigh. "But I thought I'd bring it up anyway."

He'd selected a new restaurant for lunch. Even though we were a little early, there was already a line waiting to get in. Fortunately, he'd secured reservations, so we bypassed most of the crowd and within minutes of arriving had been seated in a corner booth.

I took my time looking over the menu. The restaurant had a massive amount of fresh fish. I had a hard time settling on one thing to eat but I finally decided on a crab cake sandwich with salad.

When the waitress finished taking our order and walked off, Nathaniel spoke. "I was glad to hear you're enjoying the week."

He looked around the room, as if taking note of how many people were present. "I wanted to get your opinion about expanding it."

My wineglass froze halfway to my mouth. "What?" I asked when I could actually speak again.

"I've enjoyed it more than I thought I would." He caught my gaze and looked deeply into my eyes. "I don't think I can go back to only playing once or twice a month."

I'd had the very same thought, but I hadn't seen how we could make it work with two kids in the house. Especially with one of them being as precocious as Elizabeth.

"I'm not sure I understand," I said, wanting to know exactly what he was suggesting.

"I don't want you in my collar twenty-four hours, seven days a week." His eyes were intense as he spoke. He was serious about what he was saying. That he took my collar off at all when we'd agreed for me wear it all week spoke volumes.

"Then explain to me what you meant by expanding our play and how we can accomplish that without me wearing your collar nonstop?"

"I don't know exactly how to implement it. That's what we need to talk about."

"We've been together long enough for me to think you're not just pulling this out of the air." Hell, the man planned everything. "I know you have ideas."

"I do have ideas, but I want to hear yours. I know you need time to process and think. That's why I'm bringing this up now. I'd like to have something in place when we get home."

"That soon?"

"That's my preference."

"And if I say I'm not interested at all?"

Damn, the way his eyes could pierce my soul. Especially when I said something he knew wasn't completely true to how I felt.

"Tell me you're not interested, Abby. Tell me you're okay only playing once or twice a month. Tell me you don't melt every time I call you *Abigail* and I'll never bring it up again." He spoke in a low, deep voice that gave me gooseflesh as if he'd reached out and caressed my arm. And all the time, he was looking at me knowing with absolute certainty what my response would be.

"You know I can't say I'm not interested."

"Then why did you ask in the first place?"

I shrugged my shoulders. "Because I wanted to know."

"I'm not going to run off and leave you or ask for a divorce if you don't want to play more often."

We were interrupted by the waitress bringing our lunch. I was suddenly famished. The breakfast he'd fed me earlier was totally gone. I took a huge bite of the sandwich and glanced across the table to him.

"This sandwich is so good." I nodded toward my plate, but from glancing at his, he'd ordered the same thing. He picked up his sandwich and took a bite.

"Mmmm. Yes."

We ate quietly for a few minutes. I was glad of the time to digest what he'd said, and I could tell Nathaniel was gathering his thoughts as well.

"Okay, so you're not going to leave or get a divorce. But what would you have done if you'd felt this way years ago? Like when you were looking for a submissive?"

"I don't think I can say for sure. So much of who I am is tied up in you and what we have. It wouldn't be like that with just anyone."

"True," I said. "I'll buy that." I was comforted by his words, and ready to ask the harder questions. "Would you start off with more than just weekends?"

"Probably not. Dominance is a need for me, but I don't want a twenty-four-seven submissive."

"Okay," I said. "Let's take the rest of this week to think this through. I'll come up with some ideas."

"Thank you, Abby."

"We aren't going back to the hotel?" I asked, looking out the car window as we drove away from the restaurant. From what I could tell, we were headed in the opposite direction.

"No," Nathaniel said. He closed his eyes and leaned back into the seat. "You'll have to be patient and wait to see where we're going."

"Men," I mumbled under my breath.

He hadn't put his collar back on me after lunch. I knew he hadn't simply forgotten about it. He hadn't recollared me for a reason. He also enjoyed teasing me. There was no doubt in my mind that he was thoroughly enjoying not telling me where we were going.

"It's Delaware, right?" I asked. "It can't be *that* earth-shattering."

"Wait and see," he said, eyes still closed.

"You're incorrigible."

"Thank you."

"I should have brought a book. I would have if I'd known we were going to spend half the day in the car."

"We aren't spending half the day in the car and even if we were, you'd get carsick."

"True." But it was fun being a brat sometimes. I glanced up, checking to be sure the glass divider between the back and front seats was up and the driver couldn't hear us. "Too bad he can see us. If he couldn't, we could find a way to make the time go by quicker."

He finally cracked one eye open. "Are you bored?"

"No, just saying I might be by the time we get to wherever it is we're going and that an orgasm or two would certainly make the trip go by faster."

"You want an orgasm?" he asked in that *you really shouldn't have* tone of voice.

"Um, maybe?"

"Oh, I think you do. So let's take care of that. Right now."

Exhibitionism I was into, but I really wasn't sure I wanted our driver to see anything. "We just have to be careful. We can't distract the driver and have him crash the car," I said.

"Now you're going to be all logical?" He shifted in his seat so he could see me better. "Let me worry about the details."

I wasn't sure I wanted to know what the details were.

"Normally, I'd just fuck you here in the backseat, but since you're so worried about distracting the driver, I'll have to give you an orgasm without touching you."

"What's the fun in that?"

He lifted an eyebrow. "Now you want a fun orgasm? I thought you were only after a way to make the miles go by faster."

"I think I'll quit while I'm ahead." Sassy was fun. Digging myself a hole to get out of was another thing entirely.

"I think that would be wise."

So do I get an orgasm?

"The driver can't see below your waist," Nathaniel continued. "Lift the hem of your skirt and finger yourself."

Oh, shit.

"I think I'm okay. Seriously. Don't need an orgasm after all." I looked out the window. "Look at that guy driving the motorcycle. He looks exactly how I pictured Santa when I was little. Minus the motorcycle, of course."

"Unfortunately, you've goaded me into giving you an orgasm, so if you don't have at least one in the car, I won't let you have one the rest of the time we're here."

I gaped at him. "But that's days!"

"Yes, I can do math. Maybe next time you'll think before you speak." He sounded smug. He knew there was no way I'd risk not having an orgasm for the remainder of our trip.

I still didn't move.

"Lift the hem of your skirt and finger yourself. *Now.*"

I sighed, but raised the hem of my skirt so it came midway between my upper thighs.

"Higher," he said.

I inched it up a tiny bit.

"Pull it up so I can see your pussy."

I hiked it up so I was fully exposed. I glanced at the driver, but he was watching the road. From the way his head bobbed, I guessed he was singing along to the radio.

"There we go," Nathaniel said. "Now finger yourself."

I slid a tentative finger along my slit. Fuck, I needed some friction.

"Bet you're so wet, my cock would slide right in."

"Bet you're right."

"Close your eyes," he said and his voice was firmer.

Public play was fun and it turned me on, but I liked having my sight. One of the areas I needed to work on was trusting him more in these type of scenes. I closed my eyes, but it took some effort on my part.

"Very nice," he said. "You're getting better."

"Thank you, Sir. I want to please you."

"You do," he assured me. "Now, I want you to imagine we're in the playroom. How are you situated?"

I loved it when he had me imagine a scene. I spoke the first image that came to my mind. "I'm bent over the whipping bench."

"Interesting. Have you been naughty?"

"Yes, Sir. I called you a sadistic bastard after you wouldn't let me come for a week."

He laughed. "Then I'm going to have to be a little mean to that bare pussy."

"I was hoping you'd say that, Sir." Play and imaginary punishments were fun. Had I really been bent over the whipping bench for saying something like that, I wouldn't be nearly as relaxed or as turned on as I was at the moment.

"I tell you to spread your legs wider," he said, getting into the scene himself. "Expose yourself to me fully."

I ran my finger along myself again, dipping a fingertip inside. "What do I do to you, now that you're at my mercy?"

"First of all, you spank my ass with the leather strap." Fuck, there were times I thought I could come from just thinking about him taking the strap out.

"Yes," he said. "And I make sure it's nice and pink. I can feel the heat coming from your skin after. Then, just to prove your sadistic bastard comment, I bite each cheek and then place a kiss on it."

"Ouch, that is bastardly."

"Only because that's what you called me."

He spoke so smugly, I almost opened my eyes just to call him on it. But if I did, he might end the game and I was involved enough that I wanted to see where he took it.

"What do you do after the kisses?" I asked.

"Maybe I force you to have several orgasms."

"That's a mean one." He'd done that a few times; it wasn't my favorite. Being forced to have multiple orgasms was definitely an effective punishment tool.

"That would be the reason I used it. Or I could tell you not to come. Strap you down and use you only for my pleasure."

I liked the sound of that better. I circled my clit. "Would you fuck me?"

"Definitely. I'd come up behind you, enter you with one stroke, and ride you until you wanted to come so bad you were crying. Fuck. I can imagine the feel of it."

I could, too. His cock pounding into me tirelessly. My body spread out for his use. I circled my clit again. "Please, Sir. Let me come."

"Not yet. I'm still having fun imagining all the ways I can fuck you." There was a brief silence before he continued. "Maybe I pull my dick out, lube it up, and take your ass."

"That would be painful after the strap."

"Yes, but it'd all be for me, so I wouldn't care. You'd be the one being punished."

"Are you hard now, Sir?"

"So hard it's painful, but I'm not going to drop my pants in the backseat of this car. I'll deal with it." He lightly brushed my knee and I jumped. "How are you doing?"

"Wishing it wasn't my finger touching me."

"Maybe so, but I'm certainly enjoying the show. Make yourself come. Let me watch."

I worked my fingers faster. My interest renewed at the knowledge he watched and was turned on by it.

"Fuck yes, that's hot," he said as I pushed two fingers inside and rubbed my clit with my thumb.

"I'm pretending it's your cock," I panted.

"Right like that," he whispered. "Stroke yourself again and know I'd push inside as hard and as deep as possible. Now come for me."

His words spurred me on and with another pass of my fingers, I came with a shudder.

"Always so beautiful," he said. "Love watching as pleasure takes over your body."

"Thank you, Sir." I sighed as the postorgasmic bliss swept over me.

"Of course, we still have a while to go before we get to our next stop." There was mischief in his voice. "I could do this nonstop."

"But you won't since I'm really not being punished, right?" Being forced to make myself come was not how I wanted to spend the car ride.

"Mmm, probably not. You can open your eyes now." He wore a wicked grin when I opened my eyes. "But I reserve the right to change my mind."

Fortunately, he was only playing with my mind and he finally reached over and pulled my skirt down. With a wicked smile, he took my fingers and sucked and licked them clean. After he finished, he kept my hand in his. My body was warm and relaxed following lunch and my orgasm. My eyes began to droop and before long, I nodded off.

"We're here," Nathaniel said, shaking my shoulder gently.

I blinked awake. "We're here?"

"Yes, too bad you fell asleep," he teased, whispering in my ear. "I really wanted to make you come a few more times."

I had no doubt if he really had wanted to that badly, he would have woke me up. But I loved him playing with my head.

I stretched leisurely. "Then I'm glad you let me rest, but I'm terribly curious about where we are." I popped my head up to look around. "All I see is a parking lot. Cool, but you know, they have these in Wilmington."

"Wench," he joked, pushing me playfully. "I didn't bring you here for a parking lot."

He slipped out his side of the car and came around to open my door. He held out a hand. "Come here."

I stepped out. "Nice parking lot."

"You're tempting me to put you back in the car and go with my multiple orgasm plan." But he squeezed my hand and led me a few steps so I could see around the building we were near.

"What do you see?" he asked.

I looked around and stopped in my tracks. "Is that the ocean?"

"Yes."

I threw my arms around him. "You brought me to the beach."

"I thought you might miss it."

I loved the fact that our estate was so close to the water, but it wasn't until I saw the ocean that I realized how much missed not seeing it every day.

I stood just looking for a few minutes, until he finally said, "Come on."

Hand in hand, we walked across the street toward the public access. A wooden boardwalk curved a path through tall beach grass and led to the most inviting-looking sand.

"We should have brought our bathing suits," I said as we made our way onto the sand.

"But that would have given my plan away."

We were at a quiet end of the beach, and there were only a few people near us. We kicked off our shoes and I dug my toes into the sand, enjoying the feeling of being barefoot.

"Wait a minute," he said when I would have started walking toward the ocean. He held my collar in his hand. "You're missing something."

I bowed my head as he fastened it around my neck. He pulled back and gave me a kiss. "You look beautiful."

"Thank you, Master."

We strolled down to the water's edge and dipped our toes into the surf. I inhaled deeply. "I love the sea air."

"It's so refreshing."

A family of four—mother, father, and two little boys—jogged by us, trying desperately to get a kite airborne. The youngest boy looked to be Elizabeth's age and he brought up the end, yelling, "Go, kite. Go!"

All the yelling in the world didn't help though and the kite never made it more than a few inches off the ground.

I shook my head. "I always sucked at that. Never could get the hang of flying a kite."

His gaze followed the family and his expression grew wistful. "I remember flying a kite with my dad. He was the best, never had any trouble. Mom used to laugh at us because we'd be in the backyard weaving in and out of the trees. She always said she didn't know how he managed not to get it stuck. I told her it was magic."

My heart ached as it often did when he spoke of his parents. Even after all these years, it still hurt to think of the boy Nathaniel was and how it must have been when he lost his parents.

"I imagine it was pretty tough not to get the kite tangled up in the trees," I said.

"Yes. They weren't quite as tall as they are now, but they were tall enough." He turned back to me, his expression still somber. "I never flew a kite again after they died."

I took his hand and gave it a squeeze. Words were unnecessary and couldn't change anything or bring them back. In that moment though, I needed to touch him probably as much as he needed to be touched.

"I should get a kite for the kids," he said. His face broke into a grin. "Can't you see Elizabeth running through the yard, Henry toddling along behind her?"

"Yes, but I'll have to stand on the sidelines and cheer everyone on. It's doubtful my kite-flying abilities have improved over the years."

We started walking again, holding hands and enjoying the peacefulness of the surroundings. There were a few seagulls out and we laughed as they fought over pieces of bread. Farther down the beach, the family that had been flying the kite had stopped and the two kids were building a sand castle.

"I like Delaware," he said. "And I've been thinking we should invest in more real estate."

"Oh?" We owned our share of real estate, I thought. Though, as he'd told me once before, real estate, especially land, was always a good investment because it was a limited resource.

"Tax rate would be great here. We should definitely look into buying in Delaware."

"Seriously?"

"Yes, I think Wilmington."

"I guess." We'd been married for over seven years, but sometimes he still had the ability to shock me speechless. I thought a bit more. "Yes, I like that idea."

"Why don't you look online to see what you can find?" He pointed up the shore toward the dunes. "Let's go sit."

We made our way away from the water and shared a brief laugh at the clumsy way I sat down. I told Nathaniel it was his fault. After all, he'd been the one to pick out the skirt with no panties.

"I'd hate to flash the entire beach," I said, once I'd sat down without incident.

"True. There are children present."

Which only made me think about what we could do if there weren't children present. Though that might not be a bad thing. I bet having sand in your private parts was uncomfortable.

"What are you thinking?" he asked.

"I'm weighing the pros and cons of beach sex."

"Oh? And what do you think?"

"I'm guessing it wouldn't be fun to have sand up in your parts. Because, owww. And what a pain to have to clean."

He laughed. "Yes, that fact is overlooked when they film movies, isn't it? I'm willing to bet it's actually really uncomfortable, but everyone thinks it's so romantic because of the ocean or something."

"Reminds me of how I thought going a month before our wedding without sex was romantic."

"Yes, the only thing worse would have been to be abstinent *and* covered in wet sand."

"Good thing we went to Switzerland."

He chuckled and pulled me to him so my back was against his chest. I sighed. It was one of those precious moments where everything felt right. The beach, being with him, wearing his collar, and held in his arms.

"I don't ever want to leave this moment in time," I said.

He hugged me closer. "It is rather perfect, isn't it?"

"Makes me remember the last time it was warm enough for us to have a family picnic on the beach. Remember taking Apollo and how crazy he went?" One of his favorite things to do was chase seagulls. The last time we took him, there was one who played a game of chicken with him. Allowing him to get close, but then flying away at the last second. Apollo would look at him in disbelief and then bark at him.

I felt him nod behind me. "Poor guy, he just wanted a seagull snack. He's getting old, though. We probably shouldn't let him be so wild."

I didn't like thinking about Apollo getting old. He'd been part of our lives for so long, I just always pictured him with us. "Nah, he's a trouper; he'll be fine. Running along the beach and playing in the sand probably keep him young." I twisted in his arms. "You're serious about me looking for property, right?"

"Absolutely." The wind pushed my hair in my face when I turned, and he brushed it away. "Just think, summers here and at the estate, winters in Switzerland, and New York City when we need to meet our yearly quota of smog."

"I like the sound of the beach and the slopes, but I know I couldn't be away from the city for too long. It becomes part of you after a while." I didn't mind complaining about New York's many issues, but no matter how often I did, the truth was the city would always be an important part of my life.

"The city's a part of me, too," Nathaniel said. "But the truth is, home is wherever you are."

I cupped the side of his face with my palm, my fingers brushing the familiar contours there. "Wherever *we* are."

He leaned forward to kiss me and for the next few minutes, home was found in his lips against mine, my arms around him, and the beating of our hearts.

Chapter Twelve

I woke up alone the next morning. Surprised, I rolled over to look at the clock and found it was only a little past six. He hadn't said anything about being up and out of the room that early, though he had said he'd be in meetings most of the day. I was a bit disappointed I hadn't seen him before he left for work.

I stretched under the covers, still sore and achy from the activities of the last few days. He'd been so demanding lately. It really wasn't like him. I could still see *him* though, the essence of who he was and how he felt for me, even when he was being unmovable in his dominance.

But maybe it was like him. Maybe that was where his request to play more frequently had come from. I knew he wanted ideas by the time we left so I needed to get busy.

But I knew I couldn't start coming up with ideas until I first came to terms with how I felt about it. While it was true I loved his dominant nature, how often did I want to submit to it?

I wasn't sure.

And how often was more often? We'd always agreed that a twenty-four/seven relationship wasn't for us. But if he wanted to extend our monthly time, was that where it was headed?

Tired of thinking about it, I pushed the blankets to the side and got out of bed. Maybe a hot shower would help ease my mind as well as my body.

But there was a note waiting for me in the bathroom.

> *Abigail,*
>
> *You looked so peaceful sleeping, I didn't want to wake you up. I'll be in meetings most of the day today, so you'll be on your own until I get back to the room around six.*
>
> *I want you to spend some time thinking about what we talked about yesterday. Write in your journal what you're thinking. Jot down your ideas. We can discuss them later.*
>
> *You can order room service for lunch or go out. If you go out on your own, text me to let me know where you're going and when you get back. You're falling behind on your workouts, so you need to fit one in before I get back this evening.*
>
> *Nathaniel*

I sighed and decided I'd start on my journal and thoughts after the shower.

Hours later, I had half a dozen notebook pages filled but no clear answer. I simply didn't know how I felt. Part of me was turned on by the thought of extending my collared time, but another part of me thought maybe what we did was enough. What would be the point in doing more? How would we fit it in with all our other responsibilities?

Because it was what Nathaniel wanted.

But that alone wasn't enough to justify a fundamental change in our marriage. It had to happen because we both wanted it. And would I have ever brought up playing more often if he hadn't?

My head spun while I thought over the different scenarios and outcomes until I finally slammed the notebook shut and slapped my pen on top of it.

"Enough!" I said to nobody. "You've spent enough time on this for one morning. Let it rest."

Determined to have a peaceful lunch not thinking about how and why and if we should modify our relationship, I slipped on the outfit Nathaniel had laid out for me for the day and decided to eat lunch outside somewhere. I picked up my phone to text him, but didn't. I'd send him a text when I made it to where I was going. I slipped the phone into my pocket, picked up the paperback I had been reading, and headed to the elevators.

It was eerily quiet. Apparently, everyone had meetings or somewhere to be. It almost felt as if I was the only person in the hotel. I saw no housekeeping carts, no conference attendees, no hotel employees. I stopped in front of the elevators, almost expecting Nathaniel to grab me for another scene like the one we'd had days earlier. But I told myself that was silly. He didn't even know I'd left the room; there was no way he'd have planned a scene with that much uncertainty in it.

With fresh resolve, I held my head up and stepped into the waiting elevator. For the next hour or so, I was going to be Abby West. Maybe I'd go shopping or see if there was a park nearby. I briefly thought about calling Julie, but it was a weekday and she'd be working.

I almost missed it as I stepped out of the elevator and rounded the bar on my way to the exit. But it was a sound I normally

heard when our family was outside playing, or Elizabeth had
done something silly, or Henry giggled at Apollo's tail. Or any
of the tiny little things in a day that could make a man laugh. In
fact, the last time I heard it was the day he told me I had no idea
what he was planning to do to me the next day.

I hesitated only a minute before turning around and walking
back to the bar. I stood as hidden as possible and craned my head
to look around the cutout woodwork that marked the outline of
the bar.

Sitting on a stool, looking carefree and happy and altogether
so *free* it hit me in the pit of my stomach, was Nathaniel. And on
the stool beside him was Charlene, looking as smug as the cat
who'd just feasted on the world's largest canary.

I wanted to turn and walk away, but my feet wouldn't move.
Charlene leaned close to Nathaniel and said something I couldn't
hear. She didn't touch him, but to be honest, she didn't have to.
Her body language alone was enough to convey every thought
she had. And Nathaniel appeared to welcome it.

Jealousy is a strange character. You can never predict when
he'll show up or what it'll be over. It didn't even have to make
sense. I *knew* Nathaniel would never cheat on me. But as I watched
him with her, the idea wouldn't leave my mind: what if he only
wanted to expand our collared time so he could have more control over me and, as a result, grant himself more freedom to
spend time with women like Charlene?

You know him better, I told myself.

Maybe you only think you know him, I replied. After all, his note
said he'd be in meetings all day, not that he'd take a break and
entertain a known bitch in the hotel bar.

I whipped out my cell phone. **Heading to lunch, Master. Not
sure where I'm going. Can you get away and come with me?**

From my position hiding near the bar, I watched as he took

his phone out of his pocket and read my text. He typed something and my own phone vibrated.

Afraid not, Abigail. In too many meetings.

"In too many meetings, my ass," I mumbled under my breath.

Okay. Will let you know when I get back. I glanced up to see what he was doing, but both he and Charlene had left.

I waited for a few minutes thinking they might return, but the only person who came by was a hotel employee who wanted to know if she could bring me anything. I didn't think it'd go over too well to ask if she could track down my husband, so I asked her if there was a place she could recommend for lunch.

The café she suggested was a short walk from the hotel, and since it wasn't too hot, I took my time getting there. I tried to take in my surroundings, but my mind was too frazzled by what I'd just witnessed. Once I arrived at the café, I found a seat outside at a small wooden table and didn't even try to read my novel.

I grabbed the notebook and pen I always carried in my purse and made a list of what I knew.

1. Nathaniel had grown a lot more sexually demanding lately.
2. He wanted to extend the time I wore his collar. (Still didn't know what this meant.)
3. I liked it when he was demanding.
4. I didn't like the feeling that something was going on I knew nothing about.
5. Something (I believed) was going on.
6. He had lunch or a date or a meeting with Charlene.
7. He sometimes got snippy when I brought up the blog.

8. Before we came to the conference, he had been
   working a lot of late nights.

I tapped my pen against the table. I was missing something.
Somewhere there were dots that needed to be connected, but I
couldn't see where they were to start.

I wrote another list of things I knew.

1. Nathaniel wouldn't cheat.

That pretty much summed up everything; I didn't see a point
in writing anything else. I sat back in my chair and looked at the
two lists. Knowing that Nathaniel would never cheat meant his
date or whatever with Charlene probably didn't have anything to
do with his need for dominance. Which meant I had two issues
to deal with: his request for more play and Charlene.

The waitress came by and I placed my order for a salad with
grilled chicken and water with lemon. She left, but I didn't feel
like going back to my lists, and the paperback, filled with other
people's romantic lives, suddenly didn't look so appealing.

The vibration of my cell phone saved me from having to pick.
I jerked it off the table and answered without looking at who had
called. I was certain it was Nathaniel.

"Hello?" I said, fully expecting to hear his low and sultry
voice.

"Hey, girl!" Felicia said.

I exhaled. "Oh, hey."

"Sorry. I'm not who you're expecting. I can hang up and call
back later if you're in the middle of something."

I closed my eyes and reminded myself Felicia was my dearest
and oldest friend. She was also eight months pregnant with her
and Jackson's fourth child. At her last doctor's visit, they'd told

her that her blood pressure was too high and she would have to spend the rest of her pregnancy on bed rest. As the mother of three, including high-energy twins, she'd once shared with me how she felt torn between doing what she knew was best for her unborn child and doing what she wanted for her other children. Jackson did his best to make sure she got the amount of rest she required, but they did not have a submissive/Dom relationship.

Roll all that together and you had a tightly wound ball of pregnancy hormones, mamma guilt, and stir-crazy just ready to explode.

"I thought you were Nathaniel," I explained. "But I'm glad it's you. I've been wondering how you're doing."

"I'm as big as a whale and getting bigger by the second. Jackson only lets me up to pee. He'd buy a bedpan if he didn't think I'd beat him over the head with it."

I had no doubt she'd do just that. Never say Jackson wasn't a smart man.

"I'd say he's only doing what he should be doing," I said. "But you know that already. So instead I promise when we get back home, I'm coming to your house and we're going to watch girlie movies. I'll do your toenails and we'll talk trash about our husbands."

"I'm up for movies and trash talk, but there is no way in hell I'm letting you near my nails."

"You're never going to let me live down the fact that I mixed up top coat and base coat that one time, are you?"

"Not if I can help it." She laughed. "What have you been up to? How's Delaware?"

"Going okay. Miss you guys and the kids. But I'm meeting some nice people." I twirled the straw in my water. Felicia hadn't always been supportive of my submissive life. She wasn't someone I could talk to about Nathaniel's request.

"Nathaniel in meetings a lot?"

I hesitated, trying to decide how to reply and finally said, "He is today."

"O-kay," she said. "You don't want to talk about it. We'll change the subject. Linda's going to pick up all the kids this afternoon and keep them until tomorrow. I don't know what I'll do with a quiet house."

"Think about Linda with all five of our kids."

"She's a brave woman. Last Thanksgiving about did me in."

We both laughed, remembering. Jackson had been pretend flying one twin while the other one, along with Elizabeth, decided to "help" with dinner. Felicia had been with me in the other room and by the time anyone figured out what the kids were up to, the potatoes and stuffing, along with Linda's signature crème brûlée, had been salted and sugared and peppered.

My salad arrived and for the next twenty minutes, Felicia and I chatted and laughed about anything and everything. I couldn't remember the last time it had just been the two of us talking. Before we hung up, I promised again to come visit as soon as we got home.

I was smiling after we said good-bye. Jackson had come into the bedroom with a snack and Felicia wasted no time getting off the phone. They were so good together. I'd wondered at first if they had gotten married too quickly, but hearing and seeing them so many years later, it was obvious they'd made the right decision.

I looked down at the list I'd made and frowned. For once, writing hadn't helped me clear my head. Sighing, I waved the waitress over to take my plate away and bring the check. I had to fit in a workout before Nathaniel made it to the room, but I wanted to go for a run and I had to let my food settle first.

I sent Nathaniel a text. **Finished lunch. Going to go for walk before I run a mile or two.**

His reply was almost instant. **Be careful.**

You too, I couldn't help but say back. He didn't text anything else.

For about an hour, I walked around the neighborhood where the restaurant was and did a little bit of shopping. As it got to be two o'clock, I hailed a cab so I could get ready for my run. But more important, so I could prepare mentally for Nathaniel.

"What would you like to eat?" Nathaniel asked me five hours later, while we sat at an upscale steakhouse.

He'd changed the rules for the evening: I didn't have to sit next to him and I didn't have to keep my hand on his thigh. He had picked out my dress, though, and I still wasn't allowed to speak without permission.

Usually when he asked me that question, I'd reply with something like, "Whatever you wish, Master," or, "I don't care—you decide." But tonight I didn't want him to decide for me. He raised an eyebrow when I replied with my salad choice, entrée, and beverage, but nodded and gave my order to the waiter.

I fidgeted in my seat. The collar felt unusually heavy tonight, like a weight. I wondered why I had ever agreed to an entire week. How many days had passed and how many were left? And feeling the way I did, why would I ever agree to do something like it on a more permanent basis?

"You seem withdrawn tonight," Nathaniel said and took a sip of red wine. "Distant. And you're restless."

"I'm not allowed to speak unless you give me permission."

He sighed heavily and templed his fingers on the table. In the dim light of the restaurant, the faint lines around his eyes were noticeable. Of course those green eyes of his were just as intense and knowing as ever. I forced myself to remain still under his scrutiny.

"I'm not going to take your collar off in the middle of the restaurant, but I do wonder what's going on in that head of yours."

"Do you?" I asked. "I was under the impression you wanted me to be some sort of robotic submissive."

"What gave you that idea?" He spoke calmly with no hint of judgment or anger in his tone.

"Not even a full week into an experimental twenty-four/ seven role, you decide you want something more structured and intense than what we've always had and agreed to."

"And that equates to me wanting a robotic submissive?"

Hearing the words said out loud exposed them for being as nonsensical as they were. I lifted my chin. "It made more sense in my head, but yes, that's what I think."

"We've been together how many years and you can think that of me?" His voice was still calm, but it now held an icy edge. "I'm insulted."

"I'm being honest—isn't that what you wanted?"

"I don't know. To hear you talk, I want a robot."

"You can be so obtuse sometimes."

He opened his mouth to say something, but closed it. He leaned back in his chair and crossed his arms. The intensity of his scrutiny made me feel more exposed than when I'd been naked before him.

"Tell me what's going on," he said, once more calm and in control.

"Why do you assume something's going on?"

"Because I know you." He leaned forward. "Every inch of your body, every response it has to me, every sigh you sigh in pleasure, and every moan you give me in need. And I know you love everything about being on your knees before me. So for you to sit there and tell me otherwise leads me to believe there's something else going on."

I acted as matter-of-factly as possible and shrugged my shoulders. "Think whatever you want. I just don't believe it's a good idea to change things up."

"I'm giving you one last chance to tell me what's really going on."

Or what, I wanted to say. "There's nothing going on."

Our conversation was interrupted by the waiter bringing our food. Nathaniel kept his eyes on me while he spoke to the young man. "We've had a change in plans. Wrap these up to go and bring me the check."

He was silent on the way back to the hotel. Unlike the quiet, peaceful silence of a few days ago, this silence had an uneasy and uncomfortable undertone to it. I didn't even try to do anything to ease it. I slid all the way over to my side of the backseat and stared out the window.

We didn't touch as we got out of the car when it arrived at the hotel. Nathaniel held the door open for me and took the take-out boxes without saying a word. If I thought the night couldn't get more uncomfortable, I was wrong. Charlene was standing in the bar area as we rounded the corner to the elevators.

"Nathaniel!" she called, walking over in heels that made her legs look impossibly long. "I was hoping to run into you."

I snorted. "I'll bet."

"Charlene," Nathaniel said. "Is there any way this can wait?"

She came to a stop in front of us and swept a curl behind her ear. "Not for very long. Is it possible to get in touch with me later this evening?"

No fucking way.

"I can call you in an hour," he said, his tone flat.

Un-fucking-believable. I'm sure my jaw hit the floor. Rage boiled inside me so hot, my insides quivered.

"Looking forward to it." She waved at me. " 'Bye, Abby."

I gave her my best fake smile. *Bitch.*

Nathaniel ran his fingers through his hair once we got inside the elevator. A sure sign he was agitated.

Well, good. That makes two of us.

If I'd thought the car ride to the hotel was uncomfortable, the elevator ride to our suite was even worse. I could almost hear the *tick, tick, tick* of the coming explosion. I waited until we made it into our room and he closed the door behind me.

"I don't feel like talking," I said. "I think I'll go to bed. You go call What's-her-name."

"Not until you tell me what the fuck is wrong with you."

"Okay. Fine." I stopped and put my hands on my hips. I had his collar on, but since he'd asked, he was going to get his answer. And I probably wouldn't be respectful about it, but at the moment, I didn't care about consequences. "You want me to tell you? I know why you couldn't have lunch with me."

His expression didn't change. He made one hell of a poker player. "And why was that?"

"I saw you with her in the bar! You said you were in a meeting."

"I was in a meeting."

"In a bar?"

He took a step toward me, and his face still didn't reveal anything. "The conference is in a hotel. Where should I have met with her? In her room?"

"Right, like that would be better."

"Do you think if I had something to hide or was even contemplating doing anything remotely resembling what you're suggesting, that I would do it in a public bar?"

"Yes."

He took a deep breath and clenched his fists. "Are you saying you think I'm fucking Charlene?"

"No, I know you're not fucking her. If I thought for an instant you were, we wouldn't be having this conversation because you'd be dead and I'd be in jail. What I was saying was that if you *were* going to fuck her, you'd be sly enough to use the 'We're just meeting in the bar for business' line so people wouldn't think anything of you being seen together."

"I see. So I'm not a cheater. I just have a devious mind."

"You don't get to be CEO of a successful business by playing nice in the sandbox."

"This isn't a damn sandbox."

I put my hands on my hips. "And then you throw on me that you want to extend the time I'm collared and, oh, yeah, let's do it right now."

"Sit down and let's talk this out like calm adults." He turned and walked toward the couch, stopping on the way to pull the curtains closed.

"Why did you meet with her for lunch? What are you talking about tonight?"

He spun around to face me and his features were hard and cold. "It is business. We were talking about the nonprofit."

"You refuse to tell me."

"I just did."

"I don't believe you."

We stared at each other for several long seconds, my words hanging in the air. Each judging the other, weighing what to say next, anticipating what might be done. We were so different in

many ways, but so similar in others. Neither one of us changed
our minds easily.

"I'm not pleased at all you just said that," he said and by *not
pleased at all,* he meant *mad as fucking hell.*

I thought about what I could say to diffuse the situation, but
his phone vibrated and he reached into his pocket and pulled it
out. He frowned at the display.

"Who is it?" I asked.

"Her."

"Fuck diffusing the situation," I said. "I'm going to bed. *You*
sleep on the floor." I stomped into the bedroom and slammed the
door. I waited for a few minutes, staring at it, expecting him to
bust in or knock or do something.

Surprisingly, he didn't say or do anything. In fact, when I
crawled into bed, he still hadn't knocked. I strained my ears, listening for any sort of sound from the other room, but finally gave
up and fell into an uneasy sleep.

Rough hands woke me up at some point, shocking me out of
sleep. I flinched and struggled to get away.

"Damn it, Abigail," Nathaniel said while I twisted out of his
hands. He grabbed me again and turned me onto my stomach.
"Go ahead. Fight me."

His knee dug into the lower part of my back and I heard him
rip his shirt off. The mattress bounced as he threw it to the
ground. Fuck. He was angry. I tried to turn over, but he held me
tight to the bed. He shifted again and his body was pressed along
the length of my back.

"I should spank your ass for ever thinking I'd want anyone
other than you. How dare you say you didn't believe me. And I'll
be damned if I'm sleeping on the floor." He grabbed me by the
nape of my neck and bit my ear. "Do you understand?"

"Fuck you," I said, fully awake and remembering every word of my outburst.

He jerked the hem of my gown to my waist and slapped my ass. Hard. "I'm mad as fucking hell right now, so you better watch your language."

I tried to kick back at him, but missed. "You think I'm not mad?"

"I really don't care how you feel right now."

"Asshole."

He slapped my ass again and shoved my legs apart. His erection pressed against my anus. "Speaking of assholes, what's keeping me from fucking yours right now?"

Shit. He wouldn't, would he? He'd never treated me like that when he was angry.

But he held my upper body and arms down, showing me he could if he wanted to.

"You wouldn't dare."

His laugh was evil. "No. No, I wouldn't, but you're walking a thin line. I understand you're upset and angry, but you need to watch it."

I struggled again to break away, but he held me fast. "Fuck you," I said again.

He slapped my ass for the third time, even harder. "Only one of us is getting fucked tonight," he said and lifted my hips to enter me with a powerful thrust.

"Fuck," I said, because even though I was angry at him, it still felt good.

He shoved a hand over my mouth. "Don't you dare disturb the hotel guests. Fucking you is the only thing keeping me sane right now." He pulled his cock out and thrust inside again as if proving a point. "So you're going to damn well take it. And don't think for one minute this negates what's coming tomorrow."

I didn't want to think about tomorrow just yet. My body yielded to his control, but my mind was still pissed. His hips moved in a punishing, violent rhythm and though I fought it, I craved it. There was freedom in his control. In his use of me.

"I'm busy tomorrow," I said, like he wasn't pounding into me and we were just having an everyday conversation.

"Like hell." He lifted my hips so he could drive even deeper.

I couldn't twist away from him even if I wanted to. But his hand rested near my face, and without giving it much thought, I turned slightly and bit his palm. He jerked in surprise and slid out of me.

Everything was a blur as he flipped me over and pinned my arms above my head. "Did you just *bite* me?"

"Damn straight, asshole. You think you can just come in here and shove your cock in me? Like you own me?" He lowered his head in a way that looked as if he was going to kiss me, but I turned my head. "Damn dominant men. You guys think every woman on the planet is just waiting for an opportunity to spread her legs for you."

He whispered harshly in my ear, "I believe, Mrs. West, that the first time you came into my office, you were, in fact, waiting for an opportunity to spread your legs for me." He held both my hands in one of his and shoved the other inside my thighs, pushing two fingers inside. "And look at this, you're still wet at the thought of doing it again."

I couldn't deny the way my body reacted to him, so instead I said, "Sometimes, I don't like you very much."

His eyes were dark and cold. "Sometimes, I feel the same."

We stared at each other for long seconds. We were similar in so many ways. Stubborn and hardheaded. I felt the anger and fear and relief rolling off him and I knew he sensed the same from me. Neither one of us could attack the person we wanted to, so instead we were taking it out on each other. With our emotions running so high, there was only one way to find release.

"Use me, then," I finally said. "Make it hurt."

This time when he moved his lips to mine, I let him kiss me. But even though his mouth was rough on mine, I was just as rough on his. He let go of my hands and palmed my breasts, squeezing them. I grabbed his ass, needing him back inside me, and dug my nails into him in the process. Neither one of us would get through the night unmarked.

He bucked against me, but still didn't take me.

"Damn you," I said, trying to reach his cock, but failing. "Do it."

Breathing heavily, he sat up. Keeping his eyes locked firmly on mine, he took my upper thighs and pried them apart, his fingers so rough I'd have bruises in the morning.

"You see?" he asked, panting. "Just can't wait to spread for my cock."

"Bastard," I spat.

He took his cock in hand, chuckling. "That might be the case, but it's your pussy that's getting wet just watching me stroke myself." I opened my mouth, but he added, "Tell me I'm wrong and I'll have you watch as I jerk off and come all over your stomach."

I glared at him.

"Speechless, are you?" he asked. "Good. I hate it when chatter interrupts a nice hard fuck."

He put his hand firmly over my mouth and, with the other, placed his cock at my entrance. "I don't want you to talk or think about anything—there'll be time for that tomorrow. Right now all I want from you is what you've got between your legs." He plunged into me with one hard stroke. "And I'm going to damn well take it."

Our joining was rough and violent. He hammered into me, the entire time keeping his hand over my mouth. I grunted with each thrust of his cock, but raised my hips, desperate for more. Before long, we were both sweating and he cursed under his breath.

I wrapped my legs around his waist, pounding his ass with my heels in time with his thrusts. He felt hard and thick and long and I wanted him to stay inside me forever.

"Fuck," he said, slipping a hand down between us to circle my clit. "Get there, Abby."

Though a part of me wanted not to, just to defy him, I couldn't do it. My back arched as my orgasm swelled inside me. His thrusts became urgent and his fingers moved faster.

He spoke through clenched teeth. "Fucking get there."

I fell apart, screaming against his hand as a massive orgasm crashed over me. He grunted in relief and allowed his own release to follow, gasping as he came inside me.

The silence that followed was deafening. I'd not realized just how loud we'd been until there was nothing left but our hearts beating. I feared moving, not wanting to break the stillness.

He moved first, rolling us so he was under me and I rested on him. "Damn you, Abby," he whispered coarsely, but holding me tight. "Damn you for what you do to me. You are everything to me and part of me dies when I think you don't trust me. I'd never do anything to hurt you."

I stroked his cheek, feeling the wetness there. "I love you, too," I whispered.

He wasn't in the bedroom when I woke up the next morning. I heard him talking in the living room, though, so he hadn't left to start his meetings for the day. I wasn't quite ready to face him just yet. I wanted to wait as long as possible. I didn't know what had gotten into me the night before. I'd never spoken to him like I had while wearing his collar.

I rolled out of bed and went to take my shower before seeing him. He would be able to hear the water running, so I made my shower last as long as possible without being overly obvious. I used it partially as a delay tactic.

Nathaniel had laid my outfit on the bed while I showered. Of course, "outfit" wasn't quite the right word for the thong, bra, and robe waiting for me. They were black. His color choice for discipline sessions. Had it been a regular session, they'd have been silver. My head pounded harder. Damn my mouth for talking in the heat of the moment. I should have handled the situation better.

I finally walked into the living room. He sat at the dining room table, reading the paper and drinking a cup of coffee. At the seat next to him was a silver dome-covered plate I assumed to be my breakfast.

"Good morning, Abigail."

"Good morning, Master."

"Come sit down and eat."

I did so, but I hated the unresolved tension between us. It was as if our encounter in the middle of the night hadn't happened. Breakfast was tasteless, but I knew I had to eat something. I'd told him once how much I hated knowing I had a punishment coming and how the time before he dealt with it made me sick. He'd nodded. Another layer of chastisement, he'd said.

While I ate, he read the paper, though I imagined he kept an eye on how I progressed with breakfast. I ate slowly, dreading what was coming, but acknowledging it had to be done to get us back to where we wanted to be. The truth was, I needed his collar. I just needed to think more about what I needed with respect to what he wanted us to move to. I might as well have been eating cardboard.

Nathaniel wouldn't let me put it off forever though. I'd eaten

most of my pancakes when he stood. "Living room in ten minutes," he said and then walked into the bedroom.

I pushed the plate aside, unable to eat any more and ready to
get it over with. Deciding I'd rather spend my time mentally
preparing, I stood and walked to the middle of the living room
and knelt.

He entered a few minutes later and I stayed as still as possible
and waited for him to speak. His arms were crossed. It hit me
then that there was a reason he didn't follow me into the bedroom immediately last night. He'd been too angry and he would
never punish me in anger. He had waited until morning when
he'd calmed down. When we'd both calmed down. So he could
talk and I could listen and understand.

"As your Dominant, I made a vow that I would never have
another submissive service me. As your husband, I promised to
never be with another woman. I have not, nor do I intend to,
break either vow." He walked to the bag where he'd packed his
various toys and took out a heavy flogger. I winced. He'd used it
before. "But that's not why I'm going to punish you. This is for
your attitude, disrespect, and calling me a liar. Do you understand?"

"Yes, Master."

"I am not happy to be doing this."

I'd called him on that once before, how I didn't buy into the
whole "this hurts me more than it hurts you" thing. He'd very
calmly sat me down and explained so eloquently how he felt, I'd
never doubted him again. I knew as he motioned me toward the
window, he took no joy in what was coming.

"Face the window and hold on to the cords," he said, walking
to stand behind me. "It's going to be hard and fast."

By that time, I wanted it hard and fast. And painful. I needed
the physical pain to help me release the emotional turmoil of the

previous night. It was the only way I'd be able to forgive myself. It was so difficult to describe, even to myself, but I needed to cry. And I needed him to be the one to ensure it happened.

I took a cord in each hand, pressed my forehead against the curtains covering the window, and waited. I heard him take a deep breath and then he started. There was no warm-up, just stroke after stroke along my backside and upper thighs. The first blow made me gasp and tears filled my eyes by the fifth.

Unlike the way he normally flogged me, there was no pleasure, no blissful subspace to help me transform the pain into pleasure. As the flogger fell, it was as if he was giving me his pain. And giving me that pain allowed me to understand how I had hurt him. I took it willingly, knowing that when it was over, we'd both have found absolution.

Though the strokes were fast, the session itself was not and by the time he dropped the flogger, my backside felt like it was on fire and my face was soaked with tears. He oh so gently pried my fingers from the cords and lifted me into his arms. I buried my head in his chest. With determined steps, he carried me out of the living room and into the bedroom.

We left Delaware the next day. The tension from that one night lessened, but didn't dissolve completely. That in and of itself was strange. Always before we'd found our footing following a discipline session. On top of that, before we took our seats on the jet back to New York, he took my collar off and, for the first time, I didn't mourn its loss. I didn't quite know what to do with that knowledge. Nathaniel seemed to be just as perplexed; he held the platinum choker for a few extra seconds, just looking at it.

I simply went to my seat and buckled myself in.

He sat down beside me. "Are we going to talk about this?"

I closed my eyes. "Not right now, I'm tired."

"You can sleep if you want to, but we're going to discuss it eventually."

Maybe, I thought. But I was going to put it off for as long as possible. I wanted to think about things for myself before we discussed them as a couple.

When we arrived at home, the kids were waiting for us and there was no time for anything but hugs, kisses, and did-you-bring-me-anythings for the rest of the night. Nathaniel went into work early the next morning and I started writing blog posts.

Meagan called around ten thirty.

"Hey, girl," she said. "How'd the week go?"

"It had its ups and downs." I certainly wasn't going to be writing or blogging about the incident with Charlene and what followed. I didn't even feel like discussing it at the moment.

"Mmm," she hummed and I had the feeling she wasn't really paying attention. "Listen, I know you just got back from being out of town, but is there any way you could get here by this afternoon?"

"What?"

"There's been some restructuring of the program. Hell, we've been in meetings for a solid two days. Nothing that concerns you, but your name came up last night and I said I'd see if you could come in."

My heart pounded. Had it been a good thing when my name came up or was I being fired? Would they bring me in to fire me? Couldn't they do that over the phone?

"What's the deal with me coming in? Can't I join through video or phone?"

Meagan spoke to someone, but it sounded muffled; she must have placed her hand over the phone. "The thing is, Mr. Black is leaving this evening for a trip to LA. He wants to see you before he goes."

Mr. Black was CEO of NNN. To be honest, I was shocked he'd even heard my name. I knew him only by name and reputation. But I knew enough to realize that when he wanted a meeting with you, you didn't just blow him off.

"Just for this afternoon?" I asked, trying to decide if I should remain in the city overnight. "No chance I'll need to be there tomorrow?"

"I don't think so. We're all really keen on getting this taken care of and agreed upon by the time he leaves."

"Give me twenty minutes. I'll call you back."

I drummed my fingertips on the table. The only thing to do was to see if Linda could keep the kids. I hated asking her to watch them again so soon after she'd already done so for a week, but the truth was she wouldn't mind. Nathaniel and I had decided when the kids were born that we wouldn't hire a nanny or au pair. Perhaps it was time to rethink that decision.

I called Linda and she said she would love to come over. She admitted she missed the kids already. I knew how she felt. But she also said the CEO wanting to meet me was only a good thing. She was also excited about the potential outcomes of the meeting and made me promise to call her as soon as it was over.

I only hoped Nathaniel would be as excited. I decided not to call him, but to leave a little early and stop by his office. It didn't take long for me to shower and change. Linda had a key to the house, and by the time I'd finished getting ready, she'd let herself in and was playing with Henry. I tried to thank her again, but she waved it off, saying there was nothing she'd rather be doing.

Apollo padded over to the front door as I picked up my briefcase. He sat right under the doorknob and tilted his head as if saying, "Didn't you just get back?"

"I'll be back tonight," I promised with a quick pat on his head. "It won't be like the last time."

He let out a big doggy sigh and lay down.

The ride into the city was uneventful, leaving me plenty of time to stop by Nathaniel's office. The front desk clerk greeted me warmly and called to let Nathaniel's admin know I was on my way up.

"Sara said Mr. West is in the employees' gym," he told me. "I'll buzz you in."

He usually worked out at home and I wondered why he was working out at the office. Working off extra tension?

When I found him, he was shirtless and doing push-ups. I glanced around the room, happy to see we were alone.

"Abby," he said, standing up and wiping his face with a nearby towel. "Everything okay?"

For a split second I stood frozen, staring at his chest. *Damn. He should never wear a shirt.*

"Meagan called," I started by way of explanation. Meagan would never be one of Nathaniel's favorite people after that infamous night at the BDSM club, but he put up with her because she was my boss.

"What did she have to say?" he asked, though I was certain that wasn't the question he really wanted to ask. Or maybe it was. Nah, he probably wanted to know what I was doing in the city and where the kids were.

"Mr. Black wants to meet with me," I said, enjoying the way his eyes grew wide with surprise at my statement.

"That's great. You're going to see him now?"

"Yes, he asked to meet this afternoon because he's leaving for the West Coast later tonight." I'd already decided I wasn't going to ask permission. It was my job. My life. I wasn't wearing his collar now. "Linda's watching the kids."

"Are you staying in the penthouse tonight or going back to the estate?" he asked.

"I'll be heading back to the estate after. I've been away from home enough lately. I miss the kids."

He nodded. "I understand."

Our conversation was cordial enough, but it felt off. There was a weird lack of emotion in both of us. It made me sad how quickly things had changed between us.

"I'll let you know how it goes," I said, and then turned and walked out of the gym, hot tears filling my eyes.

Mr. Black was short, chubby, and balding. He seemed chronically short of breath, and I thought if he didn't fall over dead from a heart attack sometime in the next few years, it'd be a medical miracle. If I'd seen him in a lineup, I never would have picked him as the CEO. Looks didn't tell the complete story, however, because it became apparent as soon as I sat down across from him that his mind was sharp. He welcomed me and then proceeded to fill me in on the changes that would soon be implemented in the TV show and my relationship with it.

But as I listened to him, one thought popped into my head that I couldn't shake.

Am I looking at Nathaniel in another ten years?

I tried to imagine the man I walked in on while he was doing push-ups earlier today becoming so busy that he didn't have time to take care of himself, and he got this unhealthy. Was this what the demands of running a huge corporation meant? Would I be at risk to lose him? I couldn't bear it. To raise the kids alone and to be without my soul mate?

"Everything all right, Mrs. West?" Mr. Black asked when he caught me staring at him. "You look pale."

"I'm fine," I assured him and realized I'd held my pen in a death grip. I wiggled my fingers. "Please, don't let me interrupt."

"I was just getting to your new proposed role."

I sat up straighter in my chair and poised my pen to write.

"As you're aware, your posts and cross posts from the Submissive Wife blog have some of the highest hit rates we've seen all year. We want to capitalize on that audience. We'd like for you to do a question and answer session, just ten minutes or so, at the end of the Monday night show."

My pen froze. I blinked. "You want me to what?" I finally asked.

"We'd like for you to answer questions on the air once a week." Meagan tapped him on the shoulder and they put their heads together and whispered for a few very long seconds. Didn't really matter. I was so surprised by what he'd said, I doubted I'd have heard or understood anything they were talking about.

Me? On TV?

"I understand there may be a concern about privacy," Mr. Black said. "I assure you, we don't want you to do anything that would put you in an uncomfortable position. We can work out a way to ensure you are not identified."

"We can put you in a floppy hat and big sunglasses," Meagan suggested. "Sell you as a lady of mystery. People would eat it with a spoon."

"The questions wouldn't be live, would they?" I asked. *Holy shit, am I seriously thinking about accepting the position?* "I'd get a list of them ahead of time, so I could do some research if necessary?"

"That won't be a problem," Black assured me. "One of your strong selling points is your realism. We don't want you to answer anything without doing the necessary research." He looked at his watch. "Unfortunately, I have to be on my way to California. Meagan, can you take over?"

Meagan jumped to her feet. "Yes, sir."

I stood and shook his hand. "Nice meeting you. Safe travels."

"I'm glad you're on our team, Mrs. West," he said, looking at me with intelligent eyes. "Let's go one step higher, shall we? Think about it. Meagan will fill you in on the details."

My mind was still stuck on: *Me? On TV?* But I managed to mumble something that sounded somewhat similar to "I'll think about it."

When the door closed behind him, I dropped into my seat. "Damn."

Meagan leaned forward. "Well, what do you think?"

"I think I'm still in shock."

"It's a lot to take in. And I understand you'll need to talk it over with your husband." Her long platinum hair had been straightened today. Paired with the silver and black suit she wore, it looked like she should be the one getting in front of the camera.

"I don't know anything about television," I confessed.

"Abby, dear." She walked over to me and pulled me up out of the chair. "That's why you'll be perfect. Come here."

She led me to a picture window. We were about sixty stories high, making the people on the sidewalk look like Elizabeth's play dolls. I could almost envision reaching down, picking one up, and carrying them to a new location altogether.

"You see all those people?" Meagan asked. "Take those that you see and multiply times one hundred—heck, say a thousand. That's a hell of a lot of people. You know what most of them are looking for?"

"What?"

"Something real. They can smell the fake shit from two blocks away, but they'll always be drawn in by the real thing." She lightly punched my arm. "That's you. You're the real thing. I told you this when you started writing for the site and I'll remind you again: people are drawn to you because they know real when they see it, when they read it, when they hear it, and when they feel it."

"Live TV?" I imagined all the people below the window watching me on the air and almost hyperventilated. "Do you know how many ways I can mess that up?"

"You know we won't let you do that." She took me by the shoulders and spun me around to face her. I recognized the look in her eyes immediately and I remembered her once saying she topped women. "Focus on who you are, what you know, and who you can help. When you're in your collar and your Master asks you to do something you're not sure about, do you fret about messing it up or do you focus on him?"

"I force myself to focus on him."

"Why?"

"Because it makes me leave doubt behind."

She smiled. "Yes, and if you decide to do this, we'll have a lot of mock situations and practice questions. We'll go over the routine so many times, you'll be sleep-talking your answers. You've got this. Trust me, okay?"

I let out a shaky breath. "Okay."

"There you go," she said. "Do you want to go see the set? You want to chill out in my office or just go home and think?"

It would be fun to visit the set, but I could always do that another day. And while it was nice of her to offer her office, I really wanted to get back home, throw on some comfortable clothes and think. Nathaniel would wonder how the meeting went; I needed to call him before I talked to Linda or anyone else about it. And I wanted to swing by Felicia and Jackson's house, since I promised her I'd stop by.

"Thanks for the offers, but I think I'm going to go home. Get out of these shoes and do some thinking."

She gave me a quick hug. "Okay, call me if you have any questions."

I had just reached for the doorknob when she called, "Abby." I turned.

"How'd the week go? With Nathaniel?"

I'd told her before we left that I'd planned to wear Nathaniel's collar all week. She'd been interested, not only because of the pieces I could write when the week was over, but also as a switch. She'd told me the longest she'd ever worn a collar was a day.

I'd been so confused and hurt and angry. Now, with miles separating us, I felt only sad. I dropped my shoulders and exhaled.

"That good, huh?" Meagan asked.

I slowly turned to face her. "Parts of it were great. He pushed me more than he had before and I liked it. Not always when it was happening, but it was all good." I wiped my forehead. It suddenly felt hot in the private conference room. "But toward the end, we got into a huge fight over the stupidest things. It was like we were looking for ways to get on each other's nerves. And we succeeded." I didn't want to give her the details. It was enough to know we had fought.

She gave a low whistle and pointed to some empty chairs. "I'm so sorry to hear that. Arguing is never fun."

We sat down. "Right," I said. "And this morning, I had your call, so I'm here. He's at work. And we still haven't talked."

"When you get home take it easy." She patted my knee. "Take time for you, read or watch a movie. Then talk to your man."

"Why do you say that?"

"I'm no expert, but I have been in the lifestyle for twelve years. To me it sounds like sub drop."

"Sub drop?" The intense emotional and physical reaction a

submissive experienced after a scene when the endorphins wore off? It didn't make sense. "But he always does aftercare and I've been his submissive for years."

"True, but have you ever had a week as intense as that one before?"

"No."

She nodded, as if I'd given her the response she anticipated. "There are those who say sub drop is actually *worse* in long-term committed partners."

"Really?" I didn't think I'd had anything remotely resembling sub drop for years. But as I thought about what I'd felt last few days and compared it to what I knew from both others and my own experience, it did sound an awful lot like what I had gone through.

"Really. So do like I suggested, talk to your Master, and give me a call in the morning. Let me know how you're doing so I don't worry."

We stood up and I hugged her. "Thank you, Meagan."

"I've been there," she said, but the strong Domme look had left her eyes and in its place was a haunted expression. "I know what you're feeling. Just know you're not alone."

I called Nathaniel on the way home. He would probably just be finishing up his meetings for the day. I thought about waiting until he got home, but I had promised to let him know how it went.

"Abby?" he asked, picking up on the first ring. "Everything okay?"

Though I had been angry and upset with him earlier, my body felt more at peace hearing his voice. Something about hearing him say my name, in the soft gentle way only he could, partially erased my unease.

"Yes," I said with a smile. "Everything's very good."

I heard the relief in his voice. "I'm so glad to hear that. The meeting with Mr. Black went well?"

"I guess you could say that." I couldn't believe I was getting ready to say the next words. "They want me to be on TV."

"What?"

"I know. Exactly what I said."

"On TV doing what?"

"Just on Mondays for a question and answer session with viewers, to tie into the blog." I rushed to add, "They said they'd disguise me so I'd be unrecognizable."

"This is incredible. What a great opportunity."

Any lingering tension in my body left with his affirmative words. I didn't realize until he said them how much I'd feared he wouldn't be excited or think it was a good idea. Though I didn't need his permission, I craved his approval.

"You think it sounds good?" I asked.

"I think it's beyond good. I think it's fantastic." His voice lowered. "I'm just not sure I'm ready to share you with the rest of the world. I kind of like having you to myself."

"You'll still have me Tuesday through Sunday. You only have to share on Mondays. And only for ten minutes or so."

"I don't know. Ten will turn into twenty. Twenty into thirty. Before you know it, you'll be famous and you won't want to have anything to do with us."

He was teasing, but I wondered if there wasn't a bit of truthful worry in his tone. We hadn't left each other's company on the best of terms. That mixed with me being offered a position in television was enough outside of any plan he'd ever thought up that he was probably about ready to crawl out of his skin.

"That'll never happen," I assured him. "The world can have me for ten minutes on Monday nights, but that doesn't change the fact that I'm yours."

"I hate it when we argue," he said, out of the blue.

I swallowed the lump in my throat. "Me, too."

I made it home early in the afternoon. Linda left a note saying she'd taken the kids to see Felicia and to keep the twins company and out of trouble.

I picked the newspaper up from where I'd left it on the floor early in the morning. It'd been ages since I'd read the paper and had a cup of coffee, and at the moment it sounded like the perfect thing to do.

I was curled up on a couch in the library, coffee at my side, when I flipped to the political section. I almost missed it. If it hadn't been for the paper crinkling up at just the right spot, I never would have seen it. But the paper crinkled and as I was straightening it out, I realized my thumb was beside a picture of Nathaniel.

My hands shook as I looked closer. He wasn't the subject of the picture; that honor belonged to the council member who'd just been accused of misuse of public funds. Nathaniel simply had the misfortune of being seated nearby in the photograph of a fund-raising dinner. Nathaniel and his dinner date, that was.

Charlene. She was gorgeous in that naturally beautiful way some women were born with. I remembered from seeing her in person, but it was even more obvious from the profile picture. And while that was irritating, it was the look captured unknowingly by the photographer that made my chest tight. Nathaniel and his date were gazing into each other's eyes, completely oblivious to their surroundings.

I set the paper down. Was it taken the day I saw them in the bar or some other time? I couldn't make out exactly what Nathaniel was wearing, but I assumed it was taken in Delaware.

I didn't like the thoughts forming in my head. While I knew, *I knew,* he would never cheat on me, the fact remained he'd had dinner, or lunch, alone with a woman and he hadn't told me about it. That itself didn't sit well.

Circumstantial evidence, one part of my brain said.

Still pretty damning, said another.

I should call him. Call him up and talk about it. But the more I thought about, the less it sounded like a good idea. There wasn't any way to bring it up that didn't sound accusatory. And we'd already fought over her once. Besides, I knew it was nothing.

The sound of Linda pulling into the driveway caused Apollo to bark and I decided to think about Charlene and Nathaniel later.

I found my chance to bring it up later that night. I'd put the kids to bed and everything was quiet. Nathaniel was in his office working. I picked the newspaper up from where I'd left it on my desk and opened it to his picture.

He looked up when I entered the room. "Abby?"

I put the paper down so he could see the picture. "Was this taken while we were in Delaware?"

His eyes widened as he looked down. "Damn, I didn't see a camera."

"Really? That's how you're going to answer? You didn't see a camera?"

He picked up the paper and looked closer. "Yes, this was taken while we were in Delaware."

I crossed my arms and waited.

"I don't know what you want me to say," he continued and he sounded tired. "We've already argued about her once. I really don't feel like rehashing it again."

I sat down in the leather chair across from his desk. "Then let's not rehash it. Tell me what your business is with her."

His lips pressed together tightly and for a long moment, I thought he wouldn't say anything. But then he sighed. "I offered her a position."

I shot up. "You what?"

"Running the nonprofit."

Shit. It really was the nonprofit. I started pacing. And he'd offered her a job? She was never going to go away and I'd have to hear about her and talk with her and be sociable. "Why would you do that?"

"You know, I don't make it a habit to routinely question you on your business decisions." He narrowed his eyes. "Sit down. You're giving me a headache."

"No," I said and stood behind the chair, holding on to the back. "She's trouble. Why would you hire trouble?"

"She's exceptionally qualified and is looking to diversify her résumé. It wouldn't be for a long period of time."

"I think it's a bad decision."

"I don't think it's your concern. But if you must know, she's the best person for the job, is willing to take it on, and can make it into something I can't."

"And you know she's not going to cause anything but problems for us."

He didn't say anything, just looked at me. There was disappointment in his eyes. "What's your problem with her? I've never seen you like this before. You don't act like this around women I've played with."

"Those women are in the past. She's right here, in the flesh, and she's now."

"Are you afraid I'm going to be tempted to do something with her?" he asked.

I thought about that. "No," I said, honestly. "It's her I don't trust."

"I'm with women all the time. Every morning you say good-bye to me and I'm willing to bet you never think I'm walking out that door to fall into the clutches of the world's most evil women."

So what was it about her that rubbed me the wrong way? "There's something about her I don't like. I can't put my finger on it."

He sighed and shuffled the papers on his desk. "You're going to have to find a way to deal with it if she accepts the position."

I snorted. "Mark my words. You'll regret this."

"Thank you so much for your insight. Your warning is duly noted."

He said it with a hint of sarcasm and that just made me angry. I thought about what I could say to make him as angry as I was. "I don't want to wear your collar this weekend."

But my words didn't have the desired effect on him. He calmly looked me in the eyes. "That won't be an issue. I'm not going to allow you to wear my collar until you work through the trust issues you have with me."

"What?" I asked, certain I'd heard him wrong.

"You can't wear my collar if you don't trust me. So until you can once again believe that I'm trustworthy, you won't be wear-ing my collar."

"It's not the same."

"It is," he insisted. "You have to trust me in all things before you accept my collar. There's no room for doubt."

"You're being unreasonable."

It was like he didn't hear me. "And I was going to tell you later, but I'll go ahead and tell you now. I'll be home late tomor-row because I have a late meeting with Charlene."

"You're meeting with her?"

"I'm expecting her to accept my offer."

There was little else he could have said that would have made me angrier. "So will you be going out to dinner after to celebrate?"

"Damn it, Abby."

"I think it's a reasonable question."

"I take issue with your definition of 'reasonable.' "

"And yet you haven't answered my question."

"No," he said in a cold voice. "I'm not having dinner with her. I'll be coming home to my wife and children. Because that is what I want and this is my place." He stood up. "Why don't you go on to bed? I'll be in the guest room tonight."

"I really think that's going overboard."

"No, it's not," he said. "I'm giving you time to think, because I know you'll search for the truth and when you find it, it'll lead you back to me."

I tossed and turned all night. He'd been wrong about one thing: being away from him hadn't soothed or calmed me. It made me only more irritable. I'd think about him meeting with Charlene and I'd punch my pillow.

The first time I heard the sound, I thought I had imagined it. But it continued, softly and sweetly and when I realized what it was, my eyes filled with tears.

Nathaniel was playing the piano.

Though he played well, there were only two reasons why he'd play in the middle of the night: he was angry or he was troubled. His mood dictated his song choice, so the melancholy, hauntingly beautiful melody he picked meant it wasn't anger he was working through.

Two o'clock was late, though. Had he been unable to get to sleep, just like me? I could slip downstairs and sit with him while he played. That might help us both.

Then it hit me: maybe he wasn't up late because he couldn't

sleep. Maybe he was up late because he'd been talking with Charlene.

I pulled the covers up and buried my head under the pillow. Anything to get away from the music.

He left for work early the next morning, so by the time I got up he'd already left the house. I put on a happy face for the kids, but as soon as I dropped Elizabeth off at preschool, Henry and I drove over to Felicia and Jackson's house.

Jackson took Henry when we arrived and motioned with his head toward the bedroom. "She's in there. Be careful."

I was willing to bet I was in a bad enough mood to handle anything negative she had to say. And we'd known each other long enough for her to know my moods. Either that or Nathaniel was right when he told me I should never play poker.

As I thought, Felicia picked up on it as soon as I sat down next to her bed.

"Someone's in a bad mood," she said.

She was propped up in bed, surrounded by pillows and what appeared to be balls of yarn, tangled up in knots, somehow attached to knitting needles. I couldn't tell if she had actually knitted anything.

I ignored her question and pointed to the unidentified blob of yarn. "What is that?"

She shoved everything to the end of the bed and covered it with a blanket. "A very, very bad idea. Jackson thought if I taught myself to knit, it'd give me something to occupy my mind while I'm stuck here all day."

"Didn't work, huh?"

"No, the only thing occupying my mind is constructing new ways to torture him with yarn. Or knitting needles."

I laughed. Poor Jackson. "How many have you come up with so far?"

"Forty-two. I wrote them down; want to see?"

I had a feeling she was serious. "I'll pass."

She shrugged. "I told him this was it. I'm finished after this one. The uterus is closed."

"I told Nathaniel the same thing after Henry was born."

"Not going to go for number three?"

"I don't think the kids should outnumber the adults."

"Yes, well," she said. "It helps that Jackson never really grew up."

"You wouldn't want it any other way."

Her smile gave away her thoughts before she spoke them. "No, I wouldn't. I love the big oaf with all my heart. Only for him would I be doing this"—she pointed to her belly—"again."

Felicia didn't enjoy being pregnant. She said she could deal with it because she knew it wouldn't last forever. I, on the other hand, thoroughly enjoyed both of my pregnancies. I loved putting my hand over my belly, feeling the life growing inside me. Knowing Nathaniel and I had created something bigger than ourselves.

"So tell me what you've been up to lately," she said.

She wasn't typically one to ask how others were doing. Her request caught me slightly off guard. But as I sat beside her bed, she daintily put her hands in her lap and looked for all the world like a queen. Her head tilted to the left a tiny bit.

"I'm not going anywhere. I have all day," she said.

"I had a call from WNN. They had me come in and talk about a new position."

One of her perfectly sculpted eyebrows lifted. "Oh?"

"On TV. Well, once a week at least."

"What for?"

"A tie-in for the blog."

She gave a low whistle. "It's not enough to write about the kinky sex. You have to go on television and talk about it?"

"Felicia," I chided. "We're talking me. On TV. Some excitement would be nice."

"Yes, and now when you walk down the street or go shopping, everyone will know you as the BDSM lady."

"They're going to disguise me."

"Then you'll be the mysterious BDSM lady."

"Who won't be recognized walking down the street or shopping," I added.

"There's that." She narrowed her eyes. "Tell me what you're really doing here."

"I came by to see you." My words sounded rushed and made up to my own ears. "Why would you even question that?"

"You've been twisting your wedding band the entire time you've been here."

I looked down to see she was right. Without realizing what I was doing, I'd been rotating my wedding band between my thumb and forefinger. I turned the band one last time.

"Nathaniel and I had a fight." I shook my head, remembering. "Or it would have been a fight if he hadn't slept in a separate room."

"You want to talk about it?"

I didn't think I did. I had never been one to make idle chitchat or complain to others about Nathaniel. Not only would doing so have been an insult to him. I also thought it unfair to the people I would complain to. Why should I burden them with all the negative stuff in my marriage? Because that's mostly what the women I knew did. Then later when I'd be around the person I complained to, everything felt awkward. At least on my side.

"No," I replied. "I don't want you jaded next time you see him."

"Okay, suit yourself."

Jackson stuck his head in the doorway. "Hey, Abby, I was getting the kids a snack—can I get you something to eat or drink?"

Nathaniel's cousin was a huge block of a man, but he had a charming smile and a playful manner. In fact, I couldn't remember ever seeing him angry or with anything other than a grin or smile lighting up his face. It went without saying, he was great with kids. "No, I'm fine, thank you."

"Why don't you and Nathaniel and the kids come have dinner tonight? We haven't seen you guys for ages."

It was so tempting. I loved being around Felicia and Jackson, and their kids were a delightful source of entertainment. But it'd be awkward considering the issues Nathaniel and I were having.

"I better not," I told him. "I'm really tired and Nathaniel said he might be late tonight. He has a meeting in the city."

Of course, Felicia's ears perked up at that.

"All right, well, when you talk to your husband, have him call me. We'll work something out." He crossed the room to where Felicia still sat up and brushed his lips against her cheek. "Ready to eat?"

She whispered something to him and he just laughed.

"You wouldn't know anyone who could teach Felicia how to knit, would you?" he asked, eyeing the mass of yarn that had escaped the blanket.

"No, can't say I do. I can bring some audio books by if you'd like. Oh, I know! How about some foreign language CDs? You could learn a new language." It sounded like a great idea, until I saw how Felicia was looking at me.

"Are you serious?" she asked. "Learn a second language?"

"I think it's a great idea," Jackson said and then looked down to his wife with playful mischief in his eyes. "You should learn

Italian so next time we go to Italy I don't have egg on my pizza."
He shivered as if remembering the taste. "Nasty."

"I think that was France," Felicia replied. "And I thought it
was very tasty."

"That's because you're into strange and wacky food," he
teased. "Only chicken parts I want on my pizza is meat."

I stood up. "Henry and I better head home." I leaned over and
hugged her. "I'll come back over this weekend."

Henry went down for a nap as soon as we got home. Playing with
the twins must have worn him out. I slipped out of my shoes, let
Apollo out, and made myself a cup of decaf coffee. If Nathaniel had
been with me, he'd have made his delicious hot cocoa, but I'd never
been able to make a cup quite as good as his, so I stuck with coffee.

I turned the TV on and flipped through a few channels, but
nothing caught my eye. I wasn't in the mood for a movie. There
was an unread paperback on the coffee table, but again, it was a
romance and I just didn't have it in me to read one at the moment.

I took out my phone and brushed my thumb along Nathaniel's
contact information, trying to decide if I wanted to send him a
text. But he was at work and since I'd all but accused him of
sleeping with Charlene, I didn't want to give the impression I was
checking up on him.

I scrolled through my e-mails and noticed the blog had re-
ceived a good number of questions. I tapped my fingers against
the top of the phone. Maybe I could answer a few on the blog.
Sort of like a teaser of what my TV segment would be like.

I grabbed my laptop from my tote bag and powered it up. I'd
answer only a few and I'd keep everything short. I wasn't a ther-
apist. The first question was easy.

Dear Submissive Wife,
    Have you ever gotten angry during a scene?

Uncontrolled

I typed out a quick reply.

Dear Uncontrolled,
    Yes, I have. But most of the time I'm angry at
myself for disappointing my Master. If you find
yourself so angry you can't focus, you should safeword and discuss what's going on with your Dom.

Secret Submissive Wife

The second question made me laugh.

Hey there,
    You sound hot. Will you give me your number?

Sexy Dom Dude

I had a feeling I should ignore it, but I couldn't help typing out
my response.

Dude,
    I'm happily married and in a monogamous re-
lationship. Being a submissive has nothing to do
with being promiscuous. Quite the opposite, as
you should know if you really are a Dom.

Secret Submissive Wife

I answered a few more. One asked for nonfiction resources and I listed a few that had been helpful to me early in my journey. Another asked for my opinion about online Web sites. I named some I'd heard of that were run well and gave my standard warning of safety, more safety, and you-can-never-get-enough safety.

The next question, though, stilled my typing fingers.

Submissive Wife,
Why is it so hard to surrender to my Master?
When I do it, I feel a deep and joyful peace, but
I still find myself struggling the VERY NEXT TIME.
Am I not a real submissive?

Wondering

I stared at the question until the computer screen became fuzzy. I could have written the question myself. How could I give advice on something I struggled with too? Who was I to tell this person what they should do?

I saved the document I'd been answering the questions in and opened a new one. I pasted the question at the top of the page and then let my fingers fly.

Dear Wondering,
I am starting this off by saying I am in no position to give you advice. While I never struggled realizing I'm a sexual submissive, living as one has often been harder than I think it should be.
Like you, when I'm in the middle of a scene, THAT is when I feel most like I'm my true self. It's often the time right before one that I struggle

with allowing myself the freedom to surrender to my Master. Or, it could be days after that I question why I feel the need to give myself to him.

I won't claim to know why we have this struggle and, since I still fight this battle, I can't even give you any advice. I will say, I think it's common. We're conditioned to think, "ME, ME, ME" and for us to put that to the side is hard. Which is funny, now that I'm writing this down, because only by putting it to the side does the "ME, ME, ME" become satisfied completely.

So why do we have the same fight every time? Again, I don't know. The closest I can come to explaining it is to compare it to childbirth. When I was in the middle of labor with my firstborn, I swore I'd never, ever, EVER go through that again. Yet, less than three years later, we decided to have a second child. The mind is truly a mystery; how it forgets things, I'll never know.

For the record, and for what it's worth, I do think you're a submissive. Or at least, I don't think what you've described means you're NOT. Though I have the same questions myself, my inmost soul is only whole when I am fully surrendered and obedient to my Master.

Thank you for your insightful question!

Secret Submissive Wife

With a sigh, I closed my laptop and looked around the empty room. In the stillness and quiet that followed, I finally started to understand. And I had one more thing to write.

Master,

I know we have a lot to discuss. Unlike yesterday, I'm now looking forward to it. I know our different roles are what brought us together, but likewise, they are often what bring us the most strife.

Even when we are at our worst, I have never doubted your love and devotion to me. I hope you are able to say the same.

I am waiting for you in the bedroom.

Forever yours,
Abigail

Chapter Thirteen

I knew the moment he entered the house. From my spot in the bedroom, I closed my eyes and took a deep breath, making small changes to my position to ensure I would look perfect when he came through the door.

In my mind, I pictured him finding the note I'd left in a conspicuous location and I recited the words in my head that I'd written earlier in the day. It was later than he normally came home, but not as late as I'd thought it would be when he told me he was meeting with Charlene. It was late enough, though, for the kids to already be in bed.

He didn't like to talk and discuss things when I was wearing his collar. He might not like the fact that I was naked and waiting for him on my knees in the bedroom. After thinking about how to prepare myself for his arrival, though, I couldn't come up with any other way that made sense.

His footsteps echoed down the hall and came to a stop in the doorway. I wondered who would speak to me: my husband or my Master?

"Abigail."

Yes.

I recalled the words I'd typed this afternoon in reply to the question the blog reader sent. *In this position I will find my soul satisfied.* My body slipped deeper into my headspace.

"I wasn't expecting either the note or to find you waiting like this," he said.

"To be honest, when you told me I couldn't wear your collar, I wasn't planning to either."

He sighed deeply and walked farther inside the room. "I may as well have stayed at home today. I was completely worthless."

"I'm sorry, Sir. I didn't mean to make your day more difficult."

"You didn't make it difficult. I thought about a lot of things." When he spoke again, I heard the smile in his voice. "And had you been there, I wouldn't have done a lot of thinking."

"I agree," I said and I'm sure my smile matched his. "I did a lot of thinking as well."

"I had a chance to read your blog before I left to come home."

Earlier in the day, I'd posted the questions I'd answered. Meagan had called shortly after to say the office was getting flooded with questions for me and I would have my pick of what I decided to answer on the show. We had a meeting scheduled for early next week to go over the finer details.

"I hope you enjoyed my posting, Sir."

"I did." He chuckled and the sound made me smile. "I especially enjoyed how you turned down the gentleman who came on to you."

I laughed. "I will never stop being surprised at how people act, Sir."

"I agree. Humans are entertaining."

Silence followed his statement and the brief frivolity that had been present left the room. The bed rustled as he stood.

"In Delaware, when it hit me that for even the tiniest of seconds, you thought I might cheat on you, it shook me like I haven't been shaken in years. That you would think me capable of that."

"I'm sorry." His words felt like a punch to my gut.

"I shouldn't have come into the room that night. I should have never taken you when I was so angry, but I had to prove to myself you were still mine." He framed my face with his hands and pressed his forehead to mine. His breath was warm against my skin. "It made me feel like an ass and part of me didn't want to tell you that because I *know* you and I know hearing me say it will hurt you. And it pains me when you hurt."

"I'm glad you told me, though." But he was right: hearing how my words and actions negatively affected him wasn't easy, but he was right to tell me. I needed to know, just as I had to tell him when he hurt me.

"Your feelings are never wrong. You are entitled to them and I would never tell you otherwise. But you need to know how I feel, too, and when you say and do things that make it sound like you don't trust me? That hurts me, too."

"I trust you with Charlene," I said. "I know you would never do anything to hurt our marriage or compromise your integrity."

"It's good to hear you say that, because she accepted the position when I met with her after work."

I had expected as much, so hearing him say it didn't surprise me. What surprised me was how it didn't affect me the way I thought it would. Realizing that my struggle with my submissive nature was normal, and something other submissives experienced too, had helped me realize that just because I felt jealous didn't mean I didn't trust Nathaniel. That woman's question had helped me remember it's only human to experience contradictory emotions. But I had always trusted Nathaniel and that was the most important thing. Whether Charlene could be trusted or not was another story, but I realized too that it didn't matter because I could trust him to handle her.

"I know you made the right decision. You've run the business for a long time and you've been overseeing the nonprofit for just as long. If you didn't know what you were doing, neither one would be as well-off as they are today."

"Thank you for saying that, but I do on occasion make a mistake. I'm confident, however, that hiring Charlene isn't one of them."

"I no longer doubt it, Sir."

"Thank you."

He moved and stood behind me. His fingertips brushed the nape of my neck and I shivered at his touch.

"Another thing." His fingers tangled in my hair. "I have a question for you, my lovely. Are we going to do this your way, or my way?"

My heart thumped in my throat and my need for him and what he was doing grew. I barely managed to get out, "Your way, Sir."

The fingers in my hair fisted and he pulled so I met his eyes. "Be sure, Abigail."

They say the eyes are windows to the soul and in that moment, it was true. In his eyes I found the answers I'd been searching for. "I've never been more sure, Sir."

He didn't answer immediately, but took his time, appearing to search my expression for verification of my words. Whatever he was looking for, his own features relaxed and he whispered, "Stand for me now."

He kept his hand in my hair as I stood, pulling me into his arms when I came to my feet. Lowering his head to mine, he murmured against my lips, "I missed you."

I wrapped my arms around him. It felt so good to be sheltered in his embrace. I sighed, content once more. "Life is lonely without you."

His lips slowly moved over mine, seeking, looking for answers to questions he couldn't voice. There was a gentle softness in his kiss that felt like a caress. And when he started a tender nibbling with only his mouth, I groaned in pleasure and tried to deepen the kiss.

He pulled back and whispered against my skin, "My way."

I ran my nails over the fabric on his back. "I want you." It was a need, urging me to drive closer and have him.

"My way," he said again and reinforced his words by taking my hands and bringing them behind my back. "Keep them here."

I wanted to protest, but his softly spoken, "Abigail," made me stop.

"I'm not going to take you now," he said. "But if I were, it wouldn't be strength that I would claim you with. I would take you with a gentle whisper and control you with the faintest touch. Do you know why?"

"Because you're a sadist?" I replied and I meant it a little.

"Because I don't command you by force."

I knew that, of course. My submission was given to him because he didn't demand it. I still wanted to whine.

"Submission that is coerced. Obedience given in fear. Supplication offered because it feels it has no other option. These are not things that have a place in our world. They don't belong in any relationship and I *will not* have them in ours."

"You're afraid I'm going to say I want to extend the time I'm collared because I feel I have to in order to make you happy?" I narrowed my eyes at him. "Don't you know me better than that?"

"I used to think so."

That one hurt. Was he implying he felt like he didn't know me anymore?

He sighed. "The thing is, I need to know that extending our time is something you really want to do."

"I do, Sir."

"You'll have to forgive me if I'm not one hundred percent convinced of that. You've said it before, but it's not how you've behaved."

I started to panic. What if he never wanted to collar me again? How would we live like that? We couldn't. "What can I do to convince you?"

"I want you to give serious thought to what you want our relationship to look like. Think it through well. We'll discuss it next Friday night."

There was hope then if he wanted to discuss on Friday night since that was the night he typically collared me. If everything went well, maybe he'd offer me his collar. I tried not to let it show how impatient I would be to have to wait over a week.

"Thank you, Sir."

He only nodded. I had my work cut out for me.

I met him in the library the following Friday night after the kids were in bed. Henry was on a new antibiotic and had slept well the last few nights and we were hopeful it would continue. I would be lying if I said I wasn't a little nervous about how the coming discussion was going to go. Like he'd asked, I'd spent the week thinking about what I wanted, trying not to let what I thought he wanted influence my ideas.

That in and of itself was tough. As a submissive, his wants had always been one of the main things I took into consideration be-

fore making any decision. But I'd put that thinking aside and re-
searched and talked to Christine. After all that, I'd sat down and
wrote out a list of what I wanted, what I could live with, and
what I wanted no part of.

Taking my list, I came up with a plan for what I thought our
new schedule should look like. On Friday morning, I went
through it one last time and wrote it out in my journal.

He waited for me on one of the couches. He was dressed ca-
sually in jeans and a T-shirt, and sat with a leg crossed over his
knee. It really wasn't fair he looked so relaxed with me feeling
like a ball of nerves.

"Abby," he said, greeting me by the name he used during the
week to let me know we weren't going to be formal or in our
roles for the discussion. "Have a seat. I see you've brought your
journal. Have you given my request some thought?"

"Yes," I said, sitting down beside him. "But there's one thing
I have to know before we start."

It was a question that had danced through my mind at odd times
throughout the last week. One that on the surface didn't seem important, but as the week went on, it bothered me more and more.

"What would that be?" he asked.

"Why the sudden change?" I asked. "I mean, I don't ask to be
difficult or anything. I'm just wanting to understand why the increased need for dominance now?"

"I'll let you follow my thinking," he said. "When was it you
first noticed a change in my behavior or saw an increase in my
demands?"

Good question. When had it been? I thought back. "It was
right before I was offered the position at WNN." I squinted, trying to nail it down. "Matter of fact, the big change came after I
accepted. And picked up when I became successful." It wasn't
until my post became so popular, following that dreadful night

at the BDSM club, that he suggested we play for a week. Were the two linked?

"Right," he said. "What does that tell you?"

"That you became more demanding after I became successful? On the surface it makes you sound like an ass, but I know that wasn't your intent."

"I thank you for being truthful," he said with a smile. "That tells me you're serious about this and gave it a lot of thought. If you didn't say it made me sound like an ass, I'd be worried."

"But since you didn't do it because you're an ass, you must have had another reason."

"I did. Can you remember how you felt those first few weeks after the job offer when you weren't wearing my collar? How you functioned and your mental well-being?"

I remembered precisely how I felt. "I was frazzled and stressed and didn't function well at all."

"Right," he said with what looked like a half smile. "And when you wore my collar?"

I saw his thinking almost immediately. "With the exception of the issues I had with Charlene, I felt peaceful and at ease and everything felt more manageable."

"There you go."

I looked at him in shock. "You became more demanding because I took a job?"

"In part. As you became more successful and your responsibilities increased, your need to be dominated increased."

I'd have to think about that a little. "Because I'm a submissive?"

"It's the way you're made. You need the dominance, especially in the bedroom. Your increase in position in the professional world only made that need grow."

"Which is why you pushed me so hard while we were in Delaware."

"Yes, you needed your limits tested. Pushed."

I tucked my legs underneath me and curled up on the couch. "That's quite a statement. I'll have to think about it a bit more."

"Of course," he said. "You should always look into what I think and form your own opinions."

Silence followed for a few seconds. Whether or not I believed his assessment of my need for dominance, I still wanted to discuss my journal.

"I jotted down my thoughts on how to increase our playtime."

"Is that something you still want to pursue? Even before you make up your mind on my beliefs about your need for dominance?"

I picked up my journal and opened it to the spot I'd been working on. "Yes, I still want to increase our time. I'd decided I wanted it before you gave me your reasons. Nothing you said changed my mind."

"You make me proud, Abby."

Hearing those words, the despair over the angst of the last few weeks began to ease. We weren't back to where we were, but perhaps we were on our way to a better place.

"Thank you," I said.

"Come here." He pulled me close and draped his arm around my shoulder. "Tell me what you have in mind."

"I still don't want to wear your collar twenty-four/seven."

"Agreed."

"But I would like to go back to wearing it every weekend. It'll be somewhat of a challenge with the kids, but we can work it out."

"I'm not opposed to that, but we'll have to do something about Henry and Elizabeth. I don't want you to call me 'Master' where they can hear."

"I agree. I thought about that a lot. We need to manage their sleeping time more carefully. We can get a baby monitor for our room, and then lock the door. If they wake up, we'll hear them and can stop our play so we can go to them if need be."

Nathaniel nodded. "I think that's a great idea."

"And I've also been thinking. Henry is getting so active already, we might want to start him in preschool earlier than we did Elizabeth. I found a half-day school for two-year-olds nearby. That might be perfect for him. And if you can arrange to have some mornings at home, it would give us a lot more time soon."

"Yes, I think I could arrange that. Especially now that I have Charlene taking over the nonprofit."

I met his gaze, and had to smile.

He smiled too.

Encouraged, I went on. "I also think it'd be a good idea if we had some sort of signal we could give each other if we wanted to play during the week."

He grinned at that one. "Been talking to Christine?"

Paul's wife had been invaluable. "Yes, I thought it'd be a good idea to get the input of someone who's been in the same situation I'm in."

"I would expect nothing less and it's a great idea. What do Paul and Christine use as a signal?"

"If he wants to play, he'll put her collar on her nightstand. If she accepts, and he expects her to unless she has a good reason not to, she'll bring the collar to him so he can put it on her."

"And if she decides she wants to play?"

"She'll approach him, kneel and ask to wear his collar. She said most of the time he'd agree, but sometimes she thinks he says no just because he can."

He laughed. "I'm sure he does; that sounds like Paul."

"Do you think those things will work for us?"

"The collar and kneeling?" At my nod, he consented. "Yes, I think we can go ahead and incorporate those into our weekday lives."

We spoke a bit more about the finer details, agreed that we'd discuss how we each thought things were going on a regular basis, and decided that we should each redo our checklists about our preferences and hard limits.

When we were talked out, I took his hand and stroked his palm. "I'm looking forward to our new schedule."

"Me, too," he said. "But I want you to know that if for any reason you want to scale back, it'll be okay with me."

"I appreciate you saying that, but based on what you believe, I have a feeling I'm going to want more, not less."

He cupped my chin. "Everything I do—*everything*—I do with you in mind. I may mess up on the execution, but please don't doubt my intent."

"Even when it feels like you're being an ass," I teased.

"Especially when it feels like I'm being an ass."

"Let me write that down." I started to make a note in my journal and yelped when he took the pen out of my hand.

"Write it down later." He placed my journal and pen on the table. "Meet me in the playroom, naked, in ten minutes. I feel like being an ass. Or more to the point, I feel like spanking yours."

Chapter Fourteen

"Are you ready, Abigail?"

His question was sincere, but in all honesty, he didn't need to ask it. I'd been looking forward to this day ever since we visited the gallery in Delaware. DeVaan stood in the corner of the playroom with his camera and lights. Nathaniel blindfolded me as soon as we entered the playroom, probably as a way to ensure my entire attention was on him.

"Yes, Master," I replied in answer to his question.

"As far as you're concerned, who is the only person in the room other than yourself?"

"You, Master."

I had no idea what he had planned for our play/photography session. Behind the blindfold my eyes were closed and I closed off my mind to everything but the sound of Nathaniel's voice.

"Very good, Abigail. For this moment, you and I are the only people on Earth. This time is ours and I intend to ensure you enjoy it to its fullest."

"You always do, Master."

It'd been four weeks since we agreed to the new terms of our relationship. I didn't believe him at first, that submitting to him more frequently in the bedroom would improve my overall ability outside of it. It didn't make sense to me. Hell, I'd thought they weren't even related.

But he'd been right. Setting up a schedule of playtime, wearing his collar all weekend, and kneeling at his feet every morning and night somehow made things seem less hectic. I had more patience when I was with the kids, and when problems came up at work, I had the mental focus to work through them.

"Come up to your knees," Nathaniel said. "And put your hands behind your back."

He would bind me next. I sucked in a breath. He hadn't bound me since Delaware, though why that was, I wasn't sure. Nathaniel had decided on a rope bondage session because I'd told him that had been my favorite picture in the gallery.

He started at my shoulders and took his time, weaving the rope under and around my arms, tying them together in a way I imagined had to look fabulous.

"You look fucking gorgeous," he said. "Hands tied behind your back, your chest pushed forward. You're passively begging me to do something to those sweet breasts."

He walked toward the cabinets, and I imagined he was looking for nipple clamps. Instead, I jumped when the first strands of a flogger bruised against my exposed skin.

"I'm going to flog your breasts," he said. "Make them red, because it makes me so hard to see my marks on you."

He started with slow, easy strokes. It wasn't one of his heavy floggers, so at first, the strokes felt like a sensual caress.

"What are your safe words, Abigail?"

"Green, yellow, and red."

"What color are you now?"

"Green, Master."

The sound of shuffling came from by my side. "Good, but I'm going to use a heavier flogger now. Let me know if it's too much."

I braced myself for the first stroke of the new instrument and sucked in a breath when the tails landed sharply against my skin.

"No harder than that," he said.

I nodded, giving myself over to him, and placing my entire being in his capable hands. He didn't continue for a long period of time, only a few minutes. My breasts were sensitive and couldn't take too much stimulus. But he drove me right to my limit, taking me to where I knew I could go and then taking me a little further. Showing me as he did so that I was capable of so much more than I thought I was.

"Beautiful, Abigail," he said, and though I couldn't hear anything, I was fairly certain DeVaan was taking pictures of my reddened skin.

Nathaniel gently helped me stand and together we walked to the padded table. It would have been easy for him to remove my blindfold. But he didn't. He was teaching me another lesson in trust. That he would lead and I could follow even when I couldn't see with my eyes that it was safe to take the next step.

"Who's holding on to you, my lovely?" he whispered.

"My Master," I said.

"Will he ever lead you somewhere dangerous or unsafe?"

"No, Master."

"Why is that?"

"Because he loves me," I whispered back.

"He does," he said, pushing me over so my cheek rested on the high table. "Spread your legs for balance."

I thought for a moment I heard the soft clicking of a camera, but I wasn't sure. I pushed the sound from my mind and turned my attention back toward Nathaniel.

Since our discussion and agreement weeks ago, our relationship was even stronger. Making time for us to explore our roles, giving those roles importance, had somehow strengthened every part of our lives together. We were more connected, not just physically, but mentally and emotionally. Somehow in making our schedule more structured, we'd found what had been missing all along.

Balance. Just as I was giving my body balance by widening my stance, by submitting to him and accepting his dominance over me, I was able to balance out all sides of myself. My submission, my family, my job—everything was grounded and held in place by the collar around my neck and the rings on my finger.

"Interesting thing happened yesterday," Nathaniel said. "I realized it had been months since I read your journal. I've just been reading on your blog."

Oh, shit. There was no telling what he had read in the journal. I suddenly remembered ninety percent of what I'd written in the journal over the last few months.

"There was quite the commentary on your thoughts about kneeling from when we were in Delaware."

I gulped and forced the words out. "Yes, Master, I remember."

"I briefly wished I'd never told you that nothing you wrote would be held against you." He laughed softly.

I took that as a good sign.

"The end of that commentary was very different from the beginning."

"Yes."

From behind me came the crinkling of paper and I frowned.

"But even more interesting was this: Things I Know About Nathaniel," he said with a smile evident in his voice.

He'd found the list I'd written the day I first met Charlene. "You weren't supposed to see that, Master. I meant to take it out."

"Ah, but you didn't and I read all three pages."

I groaned.

"I don't know why you wouldn't want me to read it," he said. "I enjoyed the one about the artwork. I happen to like that painting, too, by the way."

"It's just embarrassing," I mumbled.

"I thought it was very sweet and it inspired me to write my own list." He kissed the back of my neck. "Things I Know About Abigail . . ."

As he recited his list, he ran his hands over the slope of my ass and down my legs. Then slowly, he began to tie my legs to either side of the table with sure fingers. I shivered while he worked. The normal intensity of a bondage scene was heightened by his softly spoken words of adoration.

He stepped back once I was secured. "What do you think of my list, Abigail?"

His words and touch had lulled me into an almost hypnotic state of blissed-out arousal. My body craved his hands on me again and my mind wanted to hear more.

"I'm not sorry at all now that I left that list in my journal," I said with a sigh. "But I'll admit, your list was better than mine, Master."

"You wrote yours off the top of your head. I had a lot more time to think about mine."

He stepped back and I wondered idly if DeVaan was taking pictures of me bound to the table. From the back corner of the room came a gentle humming sound. He was doing something. But even though it was relatively quiet in the playroom, I'd yet to hear the camera shutter.

Another sound filled the quiet spaces of the room. This time it was the unzipping of pants and the rustle as they came off. I jumped when a cool trickle of lube fell along my backside.

Nathaniel eased a prepared finger into me and at the same time whispered, "He's also taping this. Remember your fantasy from when Simon and Lynne came over?"

"Yes, Master." I did and I'm not sure why I was surprised he remembered as well.

"I'm going to fuck your ass and he's going to tape it. But first, you're going to ask for it like a good girl."

My body tensed at his words. It'd been so long since we had anal sex. Sure, I used a plug occasionally, but there was a big difference between that and his cock.

"None of that now," he said and his free hand worked itself between my legs and played with my clit. "It's been a while, but you know how good I'll make it. And I can't wait to feel your tight ass take my cock."

Slowly, his touch worked my body back into a state of arousal where I didn't care what he did. I just wanted him inside me. However he chose that to be.

He pressed the head of his cock against my anus and slipped in just the tip. "Fuck, you're tight." He pushed in a bit more. "Been too long."

His hand was still between my legs, ensuring I stayed on the edge, with his knowledgeable fingers stroking me just so. His hips worked slowly, inching in and pulling out. Never going completely in, but teasing me by making me think the next thrust forward would be the one he entered me fully.

But it never was and with each passing stroke and slide, the need to have him inside grew and intensified. But I couldn't figure out what he was waiting for. My entire body pulsed with the desire to be filled. His grunt of self-restraint proved he felt the same. So why was he waiting?

His words echoed in my head, *"You're going to ask for it like a good girl."*

"Take me, Master," I begged.

With a satisfied sigh and "Yes" he pulled out and thrust in me completely. He was right—it had been too long and I gasped at how full he made me.

"Fucking love this tight ass," he said, smacking it sharply. "Makes my cock feel so good." He pushed two fingers inside me, pressing that spot that made me squeal. "I think someday soon we'll have a week where I only take your ass."

His deep strokes and wicked fingers were making my internal throb worse and I skirted the edge of my release, knowing I wouldn't be able to hold out much longer.

"Please let me come, Master."

He thrust into me with a grunt. "Whenever you want."

I didn't even try to hold out, but simply let my body relax as my orgasm rippled through. He didn't stop.

"My turn," he said in a half growl and started fucking me harder. The burn of his possession drove me toward another climax. As he pushed in and held himself deep inside, his release triggered my second.

Normally, he'd stay pressed against me while we recovered, so I was surprised when he almost immediately pulled back. I nearly balked at the emptiness. Nathaniel moved to stand near my head and gently removed the blindfold.

I was faintly aware of DeVaan stepping closer, but I focused my attention on Nathaniel. He looked at me with a combination of love, lust, and something else I couldn't place. Then the corner of his mouth quirked up. "I forgot one thing on my list."

High on the aftereffects of my orgasms, it took me a few seconds to remember what he meant. "Oh."

"You never stop taking my breath away," he whispered and leaned down to kiss me.

It was only then, with his lips on mine, that I finally heard the faint sound of the camera. I allowed myself a few seconds to wonder how I must look: tied on a table, kissing my Master. But I somehow knew that when I looked at the pictures taken that day, I would see more than the way I was physically tied. I would see that I was bound not only by rope, but with bonds of love and trust and a promise that would last forever.

Epilogue

D aniel brought the beers over to the table where he and Jeff were watching the football game. He set one down in front of his friend. It was halftime and no one was watching the sportscaster's commentary.

"I meant to tell you about a conversation I had with Julie not too long ago," Daniel said, sliding into the booth.

Jeff looked up. He'd been texting someone, and Daniel wasn't sure, but he thought it might have been Dena. But then Jeff took the phone and shoved it in his pocket. Had he been discussing anything with Dena, he wouldn't have done that. Maybe it was a family member. He'd mentioned earlier that his father had called.

"What kind of conversation?" Jeff asked, reaching for a beer and taking a swig.

"At the conference I went to recently, she met the couple you knew from New York. Nathaniel and Abby?"

Jeff nodded and his lips curved up just a bit. Not enough to count as an actual smile, but possibly it could be called a grin. Maybe.

"Yeah," Jeff said. "I remember them."

"Julie said something to Abby; she brought it up to me later that night. It's bugged me ever since."

"Oh." Jeff seemed genuinely surprised. "What was it about?"

"She said one of the reasons she liked Abby's blog is that it shows the experiences of a long-term Dominant and submissive couple. And then she said our group didn't have one."

The grin left Jeff's face at that, and for a minute, Daniel kicked himself. If Dena and Jeff hadn't broken up so many years ago, they would have been the couple in the group who'd been together the longest.

"She's right," Jeff finally said. "We don't have any long-term couples." He took another swallow of beer. "Damn shame. A long-term couple would bring a sense of stability to the group."

Daniel glanced up at the TV. The commentators were still chatting. "You spent some time with Nathaniel and Abby when they were in town, didn't you?"

"Yes, and you know I can't discuss details."

"I'd never ask you to do that. I just wondered about their interaction with each other. How they work together as Dominant and submissive."

Jeff picked at the label on his bottle. "He's stern, but loving. She's playful without being bratty. Good dynamic." He took a long drink. "I actually talked with Nathaniel a few days ago. He mentioned they were discussing buying some property in Delaware."

"Really?" Daniel steepled his fingers. "I wonder . . ."

Jeff grinned. "I know that look. What are you thinking?"

"Why don't we ask them to come to a meeting? Maybe do a

demo or something. Then, if they move here and they seem like a good fit"—Daniel shrugged—"problem solved."

Jeff leaned back in his seat, thinking. "Nathaniel said they had done a bit of mentoring before they had kids. They're a nice, down-to-earth couple. I think they'd fit in well with our group."

"Even better. You know them more than I do; would you mind calling Nathaniel to see if he's interested?"

"I'll call him as soon as the game's over."

Visit the

SUBMISSIVE WIFE BLOG AT

http://secretlifeofasubmissivewife.blogspot.com.

Here's a sneak peek at the next book

in the Submissive Series,

The Collar

Coming in trade paperback from

New American Library in July 2015.

Prologue

—ABBY—

New York City

    I stood in front of the large picture windows in our New York City penthouse bedroom, and gazed outside. It was almost eleven at night and I'd turned off the lights to allow those outside to illuminate the room. From behind the glass, everything appeared so peaceful and calm.

Footsteps echoed in the hallway and I turned to watch Nathaniel enter the room. He'd been on the phone when I left the living room earlier. *Probably that Charlene woman again.*

I was trying to trust my husband with his choice of employee, but it was hard when that employee clearly wanted a different sort of relationship. My fingers drifted to my neck and I traced the platinum collar I wore. I smirked. Charlene could never even begin to imagine the type of relationship Nathaniel needed.

Nathaniel cleared his throat and inclined his head slightly toward the center of the room.

Shit. I scurried to the middle of the floor and knelt.

"You left the room," he said. His voice held no judgment and he wasn't angry, but there may have been a trace of disappointment.

"I wanted to give you privacy, Master."

"And the call concerned you, so I would have preferred for you to remain. Next time, you will wait for my dismissal before leaving."

The call concerned me? That meant it probably wasn't Charlene. "I'm sorry, Master."

"Nothing to apologize for. I didn't give you any instruction regarding your behavior while I was on the phone."

I waited for him to tell me how the call concerned me. He surprised me by walking to me and holding out his hand. Curious, I let him help me to my feet and we went to sit on the bench at the foot of the bed.

"It was Jeff on the phone," he said.

"Jeff Parks?" I asked. From Delaware? Why would he be calling?

"When we were in Delaware, you had a talk with Daniel's submissive, Julie."

"Yes." We'd actually talked twice: the night I met her at the cocktail party and days later when I interviewed her for my blog and National News Web site. I'd revisited the interview notes a few days ago. I couldn't imagine anything we chatted about being interesting enough for her Dom to ask Jeff to call mine.

"Julie told Daniel that she wished their BDSM group had long-term couples like us."

"Ah." Yes, I remembered that. I stroked his cheek, the skin scruffy under my fingertips. "She told me we gave her hope that she and Daniel could make it."

His eyes grew dark with longing and he leaned in close. "I would like nothing more than for us to be an example of a committed, long-term Dominant and submissive couple. Beating the odds. Staying together."

I tried to bring his head down so I could kiss him, but he didn't budge.

"Wait," he whispered.

I swallowed my sigh, trying not to show how impatient I was for him, but he saw right through me anyway.

"In a minute," he said. "Jeff wanted to invite us to their next group meeting and play party. He thought we could lead a discussion and do a demo scene."

We had just started meeting again with our own group, but that didn't preclude us from meeting with another.

He ran his fingers through my hair and his lips brushed against my cheek, sparking my arousal. "Is that something you're interested in?"

"Yes," I said, not even needing to think about it. "I really liked Julie and Daniel and Jeff. And you know I like doing demos."

He starting working on my shirt buttons, undoing them one at a time until my shirt hung off my shoulders. "I'll call him back and tell him we'll be there." He pushed the material of my bra aside, exposing a nipple, and I groaned as he gave it a slight pinch. "Later, though. Much, much later."

Chapter One

Jeff Parks knew it was taking all of Dena's willpower not to look his way. And since he had once had that willpower bend to his command, he was well aware of the strength involved. On any other given night, he'd be using his own willpower not to stare, but in light of his recent decision—

"Have you been listening to anything I've said in the last five minutes?" his friend and fellow Dom, Daniel, asked.

Jeff looked back to the man at his side. It was late on a Thursday night and their local BDSM group meeting had just ended. No one was in a hurry to leave though; everyone wanted to stay around and talk with Nathaniel and Abby. At the moment, Nathaniel stood beside Daniel, grinning. The guest Dominant had led a discussion about keeping D/s relationships from getting stale. Considering the two scenes Jeff had participated in a few months ago with the married couple, staleness wasn't an issue between Nathaniel and Abby.

"Sorry. What?" Jeff asked Daniel.

"Nothing important; just going over plans for the play party tomorrow night."

"Your house at ten."

"At least you remember that part," Daniel said in his not quite teasing voice.

"I've got a lot on my mind." He might as well go ahead and tell Daniel everything. He'd find out soon enough and the two of them had been friends for long enough that he deserved to hear the news from Jeff himself. "I'm moving."

"You're what?" Daniel asked in shock.

"Why?" Nathaniel asked at the same time.

Jeff's gaze automatically found Dena again. She was talking with Abby and Julie. Daniel's submissive must have said something funny, because Dena snorted in laughter, shaking her head. Her long blond hair swayed with the movement.

"Ah," Daniel said.

"It's not what you think."

Daniel pushed back from the table, drumming his fingers on its surface. "Julie told me about watching you two play."

Jeff had imagined as much; in fact, he would have been more surprised if Julie had not told Daniel. That night, months ago, he and Dena had played for Julie while she was trying to decide if she could accept her submissive nature. Though that night had helped Daniel and Julie, it'd only served as a catalyst for Jeff's decision to move. He gave a nod in reply.

Daniel watched the two women. "It slips my mind sometimes. Your history with her."

"Nothing slips your mind."

Daniel tipped his head. "There just isn't any intensity between the two of you like there once was. Don't worry—no one would ever guess she's the cause of you moving away. Does her work within the group bother you?"

Dena was the most experienced submissive within their local group. As such, she was often called upon to participate in demonstrations. She also worked with Daniel and other senior Dominants when they had mentees.

Once he uncollared her, Jeff knew he no longer had the right or authority to dictate what she did and did not do with other Doms. The truth was, though, it didn't bother him. What *did* bother him was that Daniel thought there was no intensity between the two of them.

But that was what he wanted, wasn't it? Wasn't that why he'd worked so hard to keep distance between them?

"No," he said in answer to Daniel's question. "That's not it. Her work here doesn't bother me."

Jeff didn't really want to talk about it. Months later and he still couldn't shake that night off. Having Dena kneel before him again, for her to offer herself for their mutual pleasure. To have her back in his house and arms. He wasn't sure he wanted to shake it off.

Dena finally looked his way, saw him watching, and dropped her eyes. It hadn't done her any good either; odds were she was still dealing with her own memories of the night.

Daniel, of course, noticed the slight response Dena had at catching Jeff's gaze. "How many times have you played since you two broke up?" Daniel asked.

"Once. That time Julie watched."

"I see."

"It really doesn't have anything to do with Dena." He wondered if the lie sounded as wooden to Daniel as it did to him.

"Of course it doesn't."

Daniel didn't say anything further, but instead kept his gaze on Jeff as if expecting him to confess everything. Had Jeff not used the same tactic himself numerous times before, it might have worked.

"It doesn't," Jeff stated again. "We split up years ago. We weren't right for each other then and nothing's changed. She's high society and I'm a high school dropout."

"Bullshit," Daniel said. "You're my friend."

"And mine," Nathaniel echoed. "In fact, if you tried to tell me we couldn't be friends because of something you did when you were sixteen, I'd kick your ass."

"It's different with a woman," Jeff said. "Besides, I'm moving to Colorado, at least for a while. Going to help Dad with the business. He needs to retire and he's been asking me to help get everything in order."

Daniel's laughter drew the attention of several group members. "Insurance? You?"

Jeff's father ran an insurance company he'd taken over from his own father. That Jeff wanted nothing to do with it had always been the bane of his dad's existence. Jeff had opened his own business, a security service, eight years ago. It was a two-man operation, small, but profitable enough.

"It won't be forever, just a few months. Tom said he could handle the business here." His partner had actually been less than thrilled, but realized he didn't have a choice.

"Hell, you're serious," Nathaniel said.

Jeff couldn't find a response for that. He answered with his own silence.

"Have you told Dena?" Daniel finally asked.

He resisted the urge to look at her. "No."

"I heard her father's on the short list for vice president."

Dena's father was a senator with career aspirations that

reached to the White House. That paired with Jeff's past had been part of what made him decide to break things off with Dena three years ago. He forced himself not to think of the other reasons.

"From what I know of Senator Jenkins, he'll get it." Jeff wasn't surprised at the bitterness in his voice.

The two men looked at him sharply, but seemed to sense his unwillingness to discuss the man in question. Jeff had come to terms with the senator a long time ago, but that didn't mean he liked him or wanted to talk about him.

"You're still on to be Dungeon Monitor tomorrow night?" Daniel asked, changing the subject.

"Yes. I'll be there." His last play party with the group. He wondered if Dena would be attending with anyone. Would his last sight of her be watching as she offered her submission to another? Maybe it would be better that way. If he knew she had someone to look after her, perhaps then he could somehow find the strength to leave her once and for all.

Tara Sue Me wrote her first novel at the age of twelve. It would be twenty years before she picked up her pen to write the second.

After completing several traditional romances, she decided to try her hand at something spicier and started work on *The Submissive*. What began as a writing exercise quickly took on a life of its own, and sequels *The Dominant* and *The Training* soon followed. Originally published online, the trilogy was a huge hit with readers around the world. Each of the books has now been read and reread more than a million times.

Tara kept her identity and her writing life secret, not even telling her husband what she was working on. To this day, only a handful of people know the truth (though she has told her husband). They live together in the southeastern United States with their two children.

Also available from
New York Times bestselling author

TARA SUE ME

Abby King yearns to experience a world of pleasure beyond
her simple life as a librarian—and the brilliant and handsome
CEO Nathaniel West is the key to making her dark desires a
reality. But as Abby falls deep into Nathaniel's tantalizing
world of power and passion, she fears his heart may be
beyond her reach—and that her own might
be beyond saving...

ON SALE WHEREVER BOOKS ARE SOLD

tarasueme.com

penguin.com

Also available from
New York Times bestselling author

TARA SUE ME

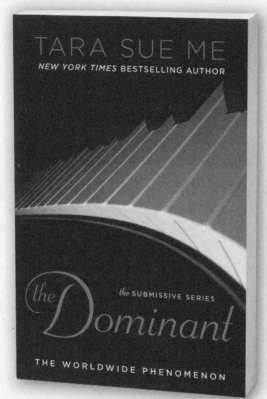

Nathaniel West doesn't lose control. But then he meets Abby King. Her innocence and willingness is intoxicating, and he's determined to make Abby his. But when Nathaniel begins falling for Abby on a deeper level, he realizes that trust must go both ways—and he has secrets which could bring the foundations of their relationship crashing down...

ON SALE WHEREVER BOOKS ARE SOLD

tarasueme.com

penguin.com

Also available from
New York Times bestselling author

TARA SUE ME

It started with desire. Now a weekend arrangement of
pleasure has become a passionate romance. Still, there
remains a wall between Nathaniel West and Abby King.
Abby knows the only way to lead Nathaniel on a path to
greater intimacy is to let him deeper into her world
than anyone has ever gone before...

ON SALE WHEREVER BOOKS ARE SOLD

tarasueme.com

penguin.com

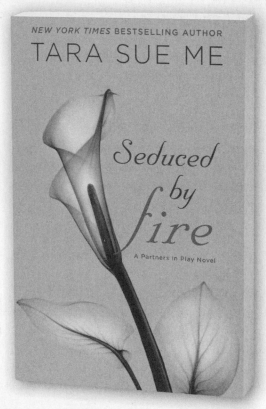
NAL